THE BLACK ROOM

She shoved her backside out as she bent, trying not to think of the vulnerable position she was placing herself in.

Mr Smith stepped calmly behind her. He placed a hand on her rear and stroked her arse through the fabric of her short skirt. There was nothing particularly sexual about his touch. His hands simply traversed the contours of her rear. He did not try to tease the crease of her sex with his fingers or touch the sensitive valley that led to her anus.

Jo felt the heat of her arousal increasing.

'Feel this.' His voice was almost conversational, hardly the tone she would have expected from a man brandishing a cruel birch came.

A NEXUS CLASSIC

THE BLACK ROOM

Lisette Ashton

This book is a work of fiction.
In real life, make sure you practise safe, sane and
consensual sex.

First published in 1998 by
Nexus
Thames Wharf Studios
Rainville Road
London W6 9HA

This Nexus Classic edition 2004

www.nexus-books.co.uk

Typeset by TW Typesetting, Plymouth, Devon

Printed and bound in Great Britain by Clays Ltd, St Ives PLC

ISBN 0 352 33914 4

The Random House Group Limited supports The Forest Stewardship
Council (FSC®), the leading international forest certification organisation.
Our books carrying the FSC label are printed on FSC® certified paper.
FSC is the only forest certification scheme endorsed by the leading
environmental organisations, including Greenpeace. Our
paper procurement policy can be found at
www.randomhouse.co.uk/environment

One

Kelly sat nervously in the waiting room, trying not to think about what she had done.

It was a clean, pleasant room with sunlight glinting through the louvre blinds at the windows. The walls were plastered with a wide array of posters, warning against the dangers of smoking and unprotected sex, in cheerful, primary colours. Dozens of the eye-catching images covered the room's entire wall space but Kelly, lost in her own solemn reverie, could not be bothered to look at them. She ignored her surroundings just as she ignored the untidy pile of glossy magazines on the seat next to her. Her fingers played nervously with the clasp of her bag and her head was tilted downward, as though she was totally absorbed by this fascinating spectacle.

Sitting alone in a discreet corner of the room, she looked like a woman trying to hide from the world.

Her thoughts were fully occupied by the big step she had taken and the greater ones that stretched ahead of her. In spite of her fiery mane of red hair and enigmatic good looks, Kelly was not a confident woman. Every decision she made was invariably dogged by grave doubt and deep misgivings. This latest one was no exception. Admittedly she had been left with no other choice but Kelly still fretted at the boldness of her own actions. This was not simply a giant step she had taken: it was a desperate leap into the unknown.

The waiting-room door crashed open. The sound was

1

so sudden and unexpected it jolted Kelly abruptly from her thoughts. She glanced up to see a young woman burst into the waiting room.

Long golden curls bounced over the girl's narrow shoulders as she ran. The hair hid her face from view as she glanced back at her pursuer. The blonde was closely followed by a brunette, taller and blessed with a muscular, athletic build. Both women were breathing heavily, as though the chase had been an arduous one.

Before the blonde could reach the room's only other door, the darker woman grabbed her by the shoulder. She pushed her heavily to the wall, pinning her there.

'One more stunt like that, Helen, and I'll see you in the black room,' the brunette said breathlessly.

Kelly considered the pair uneasily.

Helen, the woman being pressed against the wall, was a good-looking Nordic blonde. She had a haughty expression and a severe, arrogant line to her jaw. Under other circumstances, Kelly guessed the woman would have looked intimidating or austere. She had the innate self-possession of a Valkyrie warrior-maiden. Now, as the blonde stared timidly at her captor, she did not look remotely imposing. Her terrified expression hovered somewhere between desperate defiance and outright fear.

'I ... I ... didn't ... didn't do anything, Mistress Stacey,' she stammered hurriedly. Her eyes were wide with trepidation. 'I ...' She got no further.

'Don't give me that crap,' Stacey growled fiercely. She pulled Helen forward then shoved her roughly against the wall again. Swiftly, she raised a hand and slapped the blonde hard across the face. The sound echoed around the waiting room like a pistol shot.

Kelly muttered a small cry of surprise. She was briefly thankful that her own shocked whimper was drowned out by the blonde's startled gasp.

Mistress Stacey was a formidable figure, taller and

broader than the younger woman. Her powerful athletic body was clad in a loose blouse and skirt but this did not detract from her obvious physical capability. She moved her hand away from Helen's cheek, revealing the angry red blush her blow had caused. 'You're this far away from spending a day in the black room,' she whispered furiously, holding her index finger and thumb slightly apart. Her teeth were clenched together as she spoke, reinforcing her barely concealed fury. 'Why don't you just come clean and make it easier on yourself?' She paused for a moment, studiously watching Helen's face for a response. When Helen made no reply, Stacey acted swiftly. She released the girl's shoulder and made to grab at the front of her blouse.

'No!' Helen gasped. She half-heartedly put her hands in front of herself for protection.

The commanding brunette slapped Helen's hands away then brought her knuckles across the blonde's strong Nordic jaw. Helen moaned, a low, guttural sound, and raised a hand to the side of her face where she had been struck. She began to sob as Stacey placed both hands on her blouse and effortlessly ripped the garment open.

From her unnoticed seat Kelly tried fervently not to look at Helen's breasts. She had been brought up to believe in the virtues of modesty and chastity. Even though she was a reluctant witness, the scene being played out before her made Kelly feel like a depraved Peeping Tom. She employed a huge effort of willpower trying not to look at Helen's body. However, the sight drew her gaze like a magnet.

Helen's full, round orbs were barely concealed in a white lacy bra. The dark circles of her areolas were clearly visible through the skimpy fabric of her underwear. There was also a noticeable rise and fall of her chest, as though she was very excited. The hard nubs of her nipples strained urgently against their confines.

3

Her laboured breathing had deepened into low gasps of obvious pleasure. The sultry pout of her lips, and the shine of excitement in her eyes, made it clear that Helen was not Mistress Stacey's unwilling victim.

Stacey fondled Helen's breasts with a careless disregard that bordered on brutality. Her fingers roughly massaged the girl's pliant flesh through the fabric of her underwear, pressing mercilessly into the soft, sensitive skin. She paid particular attention to the taut buds of Helen's nipples, extracting a series of responses from her victim that sounded simultaneously pained and pleasured.

'We could have sorted this out a lot quicker in my chamber,' Stacey said dourly. 'Don't tell me you didn't enjoy my little game with the tawse last week?' she whispered.

Helen groaned softly, as though she were enduring the special delights of a half-forgotten memory. She closed her eyes and pressed her head back against the wall. Her bottom lip pushed forward unconsciously and she sighed happily beneath Stacey's rough manhandling.

'Tell me where it is, Helen, and we can overlook this little matter,' Stacey growled softly. She squeezed one of the blonde's nipples between her thumb and forefinger. Her grin widened as Helen tried unsuccessfully to stifle a gasp of pain. 'Speak up,' Stacey hissed in a threatening tone. 'You don't want me to play rough, do you?'

Before Helen could reply, Stacey was already acting. Continuing to hold Helen's erect nipple, she kept the blonde pressed securely against the wall. With her other hand she reached downwards and traced her fingers up one of Helen's stocking-clad legs.

'No, mistress!' Helen whispered. She breathed the words in a dark, husky murmur that sounded more like encouragement than refusal.

Stacey stared menacingly into the blonde's face while her hand continued its slow journey upward. Helen

4

wore a short, flared skirt and the hem was raised by Stacey's wrist as her hand went higher. The skirt lifted to reveal the dark tops of Helen's stockings, beneath the creamy expanse of her milky-white thighs. The hem continued to rise until the white triangle of Helen's knickers was on full view.

Stacey's fingers paused at the gusset of Helen's panties. She traced the outline of Helen's pouting labia through the thin cotton fabric. Then she drew her fingertips along the warm skin next to the elasticated band of her knickers. Each movement was slow, yet decisive, designed to arouse Helen without letting her forget who was in charge.

Helen moaned softly, the sound coming from some dark, delightful place situated between agony and ecstasy. With her eyes still closed, she licked her lips avariciously, savouring the pleasure of the moment.

Stacey continued to study Helen's face. A tight, twisted smile curled her lips, as though she was enjoying the blonde's discomfort and unhappiness. She used her fingers adeptly and shifted the gusset of Helen's panties to one side revealing the tender pink lips of the blonde's shaved pussy. With the tip of her index finger she traced a slow line back and forth along the length of Helen's crease.

Helen sighed softly. Lost in the elation of the moment she seemed to have forgotten the danger that threatened her. Unconsciously, she rubbed the tops of her exposed thighs with the palms of her hands. Her fingers were splayed wide apart as though she were in the throes of unprecedented ecstasy. Her soft sighs slowly became deeper as Stacey continued to tease the sensitive pink flesh of Helen's hole.

Stacey's cruel smile tightened as she watched Helen. She continued to squeeze one nipple, rolling it carefully between her tightly pressed fingers. Her other hand was occupied in the warm cleft between the blonde's legs, rubbing the tactile lips of her pussy with slow deliberation. Deftly, she used her index and ring fingers to part the blonde's labia, then slowly slid her middle finger deep into the heated wetness of Helen's sex.

The blonde cried out in shocked surprise, her eyes opening wide.

Kelly watched as the middle finger slid deeper and deeper into the depths of Helen's moist hole. She had never seen two women sharing such intimacy before and as her initial feelings of revulsion dissipated, they were replaced by an unbidden thrill of excitement.

She had been holding her breath from the moment the two women burst into the room. Initially she had been wary of disturbing the pair and suffering their retribution. Now she was fearful of alerting them to her presence and interrupting the erotic scene. Watching Stacey fondle Helen with such brutal disregard had been intensely stimulating, as had the sight of the brunette fingering the blonde's vagina. The heat of Kelly's excitement had brought with it a delightful moistness she had not anticipated. She was determined to see how the spectacle progressed.

Along with the middle finger, Stacey thrust her index finger upward, deep into the welcoming warmth of Helen's pussy lips. The blonde released a long sultry moan of ecstasy. Stacey twisted her hand slightly to one side, then pushed both fingers deep inside Helen's cleft as far as they would go.

'Nuh ... No, Mistress Stacey, I ...' Helen's cheeks were furiously red with the warm glow of her mounting excitement. Her refusals and denials were half-hearted in the extreme. The enjoyment she was receiving from the mistress's unorthodox body search clearly exceeded her embarrassment and discomfort. One nipple pressed fiercely against the confines of her bra, the other stood rigidly between the tips of Stacey's merciless fingers. Each breath was a short, ragged exclamation of her arousal.

6

Stacey squeezed cruelly hard on Helen's nipple, inspiring a sharp cry of surprised pain. At the same time she tugged her fingers swiftly from Helen's pussy, making the movement viciously harsh and lacking in intimacy.

Helen gasped as though she had been slapped.

The fingers slid easily from Helen's warmth, bringing with them a small plastic-wrapped package that she had secreted in the most intimate of hiding places. Both fingers, and the package, were glistening slickly with the creamy moisture of Helen's excitement. Stacey held the bag between her index finger and thumb, then swayed it hypnotically to and fro in front of Helen's face.

'Money, Helen?' she enquired knowingly. A pantomime frown of maternal disapproval stretched her lips. The charade did not mask her true feelings at making this discovery, nor did her austere tone. The fact she was delighted with this result was blatantly obvious. 'Quite a lot of money, it would seem. You know the rules about having so much cash in the hostel, don't you, Helen?' Stacey sneered. 'Have you been stealing again?'

Helen stifled a sob, closed her eyes and turned away from Mistress Stacey. A pained expression strained her features. She had placed a hand to her groin, and was rubbing her fingers purposefully against the swell of her exposed lips. Her manicured nails deftly stroked the dark-pink flesh. Spreading the folds wide open she eased a finger inside herself, moistening the pad with the creamy juice of her arousal. Suitably lubricated, she began to draw impatient circles over the hood of her clitoris. The bead of erectile tissue was slowly teased to the brink of climax with a wicked combination of skill and urgency. Oblivious to her audience, Helen furiously caressed herself to the pinnacle of pleasure. Her colour darkened and a broad smile of elated satisfaction crossed the blonde's face. She groaned happily with a climactic shiver of pleasure that coursed through her entire body.

As the waves of happiness receded she stood quietly for a moment in a state of delighted rapture. When she opened her eyes, they were shining with excitement. The expression was only a fleeting one, disappearing the instant she found her gaze focusing on Kelly. A shocked expression replaced the look of satisfaction she had been wearing. Modestly, she tugged her skirt down and coughed back a surprised exclamation.

Aware of the sudden change in Helen's mood, Stacey turned and saw Kelly for the first time. She sucked in her breath angrily, treating Kelly to a glare of the darkest venom. Acting with the instinctive alacrity of a wild animal, Mistress Stacey walked over to Kelly and pointed a menacing finger in her face. 'You didn't see anything, do you understand?' she hissed threateningly.

In her hurry to agree, Kelly found herself on the point of stammering just as Helen had done. She swallowed nervously and closed her eyes, trying to compose her thoughts before replying.

'You didn't see anything,' Mistress Stacey repeated.

Her finger was so close to Kelly's nose she could sense the fragrance of Helen's musky pussy juices that still lingered there. It was a sweet scent that filled her nostrils and unwittingly triggered the memory of her earlier arousal. Wilfully dismissing this notion, Kelly nodded her head in furious agreement. 'I didn't see anything,' she repeated. 'Nothing at all. I'm sorry,' she added unnecessarily.

Stacey appeared not to have heard anything else. She turned her attention back to Helen and graced her with a look of the darkest fury. 'We'll finish this in your dormitory,' she said in a tone of barely tempered rage. 'Wait for me there, you little thief.'

Dismissed, Helen fled from the room casting a meaningful glare at Kelly. The defiant expression only flickered in her eyes for a moment. It was not there long enough for Mistress Stacey to notice but it was sufficient for Kelly to know she had just made an enemy. A very dangerous enemy.

As the waiting-room door closed on Helen, Kelly realised she was alone with Stacey. It was an unsettling realisation and Kelly swallowed nervously, aware that her heart was beating an alarmed tattoo in her chest. She stared up at the woman uncertainly, wishing she did not feel so intimidated. 'I didn't see anything,' she repeated earnestly. 'Honestly I . . .'

Mistress Stacey reached out and stroked a finger across Kelly's lips, silencing her panicked babble. It was a gesture that should have felt unpleasant or threatening. Instead, Kelly found the careful caress was curiously stimulating. The delicate touch rekindled the deep warmth of her earlier arousal. Her finger traced its way gently along the length of Kelly's pouting lower lip, provoking a shiver of excitement that travelled from the base of her neck to the tip of her spine.

She was startled by an unexpected pang of urgency that seemed to emanate from her nipples. With an inward sigh of disdain she realised she was suffering the unexpected symptoms of pure sexual arousal. It had been so long since she had experienced such feelings, Kelly wondered if her memory was playing tricks on her. However, when the inner walls of her pussy began to throb with their own hungry desire, Kelly knew she had not been mistaken. She stared into the mysterious depths of the mistress's ebony eyes, wondering if she too had sensed that electric tingle of sexual attraction.

'Is this your first day at the hostel?' Stacey asked softly, stroking her finger along Kelly's cheek.

Kelly swallowed nervously again and nodded, not trusting herself to speak. She felt torn between conflicting emotions, not knowing whether to trust her desires or her fear. Stacey had been brutal and domineering in her treatment of Helen, and Kelly considered the woman to be utterly terrifying. However, she had never before felt stimulated or aroused by the presence of another woman and the sensation was so unfamiliar it piqued her curiosity. Struggling valiantly with her inner turmoil, Kelly suppressed a shiver and stared helplessly into Stacey's face.

The mistress's smile was not an unkind one. 'If it's your first day at the hostel, then I'm sure you won't be making waves, will you?'

Kelly shook her head, amazed that she felt so eager to please this callous, antagonistic woman. Her treatment of Helen had been cold and barbaric yet, without knowing why, Kelly felt anxious to meet with Stacey's approval. Worse than that, Kelly thought unhappily, she felt a strong desire for Stacey to touch her as she had been touching Helen.

'I guess I'll be seeing you around,' Mistress Stacey said quietly. She allowed her fingers to caress Kelly's cheek one final time, and moved her mouth close to Kelly's. The two women were on the point of kissing. Their faces were so close, Kelly knew she would only have to move forward slightly and her mouth would be pressed against Stacey's. The warmth of the brunette's breath tickled her top lip and Kelly wondered bewilderedly if she should be making that first move.

'I guess I'll be seeing you around,' Mistress Stacey said again, moving her head away from Kelly before she could make up her mind. She dropped one eyelid in a solemn wink and then left the waiting room without another word.

Kelly shivered and released the pent-up sigh of relief that had been welling inside her.

Simultaneously she felt hot and cold and more than a little confused by her reaction to Mistress Stacey. Before she had a chance to analyse her thoughts and feelings, the door to the examination room opened. Wasting no time on pleasantries, a petite, dark-haired girl curtly summoned Kelly into the doctor's office.

'I'm running a little behind schedule today,' the doctor declared, as Kelly entered the small room.

Her accusatory tone made Kelly feel guilty, as though she was in some way responsible for the doctor's problems.

'It will speed things along if you strip and answer questions at the same time.'

Kelly looked uncertainly at the doctor, wondering if she had heard the woman correctly. She was sitting behind a meticulously tidy desk, with Dr A. McMahon written in gold on the wooden desk-plaque. She had a proud head of long raven locks spilling over her shoulders and Kelly guessed she was in her early thirties. The doctor did not look as formidable as Mistress Stacey but the crispness of her voice made it clear she was not the sort of person who tolerated fools.

'You want me to undress?' Kelly asked nervously.

Doctor McMahon glanced up from the papers she was studying and graced Kelly with a despondent frown. Her eyes were the same ultra-black jet as her hair, contrasting starkly with her sallow complexion. The only thing that stopped her from looking incredibly attractive was the contemptuous curl of her upper lip. 'I haven't yet perfected the art of doing clothed examinations,' she said with icy sarcasm. 'So, I'm afraid you'll have to tolerate my lack of skill and just undress as I asked.' This said, the doctor turned her attention back to the notes on her desk.

Kelly cast a nervous glance around the small examination room. There was an examination trolley resting by the wall behind her and a chair facing the doctor's desk. Aside from these pieces of furniture, the room was bare, save for one full-length mirror and a rack of bookshelves filled with important-looking leather-bound volumes. The petite nurse who had escorted Kelly into the room was bent over a clinically sterile sink busying herself by washing her hands.

Directing her question at the doctor, Kelly asked uncertainly, 'Do I just undress here?'

Doctor McMahon drew a sharp intake of breath. She raised her head from the papers and glared impatiently at Kelly. 'Undress here if you want,' she said, speaking tightly. 'If you like, you can leave the building now and undress on the front fucking step. Just take your clothes off so I can begin the examination.'

Left with no doubt as to what was expected of her, Kelly began to undress.

'Your name is Kelly Rogers?'

Unfastening her blouse, Kelly nodded. Then, realising the doctor was not looking at her, she quickly answered, 'Yes. That's right.'

'Twenty-four years old?'

'Yes.'

'And you've been with the Pentagon Temp Agency for a month now?'

'That's right,' Kelly said quickly. 'Mr Peterson at the Agency said I'd been doing really well and suggested I should do this course and consider becoming a professional temp.'

'A simple yes would have been sufficient,' Doctor McMahon said dryly.

Blushing furiously at the other woman's cold disregard, Kelly shrugged herself out of her blouse. She folded it neatly and placed it next to her handbag, on the chair facing the doctor.

'You're qualified as a medical and legal secretary,' Doctor McMahon continued briskly. 'And you have a degree in business management.'

'Yes,' Kelly said simply, knowing that no other response was required.

She responded with one-word answers to a string of questions the doctor fired at her. They concerned a wide range of topics including the medical history of herself and her family and her ability to answer them concisely helped Kelly to feel a little more relaxed. As the questions went on, she was almost beginning to feel comfortable about the examination, in spite of the doctor's brusqueness and the distinct lack of privacy.

Doctor McMahon paused in her questioning and glanced up from the notes she was looking at. 'It says here that you're married.'

Kelly paused in the act of stepping out of her skirt. 'Separated,' she said quietly. She realised the doctor was staring at her and continued to step out of the skirt with a contrived air of feigned nonchalance.

'How long have you been separated?'

'Is that important?' Kelly replied.

Doctor McMahon shrugged, studying Kelly's half-naked body with a wry smile on her lips. 'I suppose not,' she replied. 'I was just interested, that's all.'

'It's not something I care to talk about,' Kelly said with soft defiance.

Standing in front of the doctor, clad only in her bra, pants, stockings and suspender belt, she did not feel defiant. Being totally honest with herself, Kelly felt distinctly vulnerable standing half-naked before this antagonistic stranger. Her marriage, and subsequent separation, were topics she still felt uncomfortable with. However, the thorny subject of her failed marriage was not something she wanted to discuss and she was determined not to be pushed on the issue.

From the corner of her eye she glimpsed her reflection in the full-length mirror and was surprised by the image of an attractive woman she saw there. Blazing red hair cascaded over her shoulders and down her back in a torrent of fiery, warm, orange and scarlet shades. The glossy satin sheen of the emerald-green underwear she wore complemented her whey-coloured complexion perfectly. The frilly green suspender belt went down into a V at her waist, accentuating the pronounced slenderness of her smooth, flat stomach. Her seamed stockings were still in place, and the heels she wore emphasised the length and firmness of her long, coltish legs. She wished she felt as glamorous and confident as the woman in the mirror looked but she knew such an ambition went far beyond her dreams.

'Are you practising sex with a partner at the moment?' Doctor McMahon asked briskly.

Kelly's blush deepened. 'Do I have to answer that one?' she asked.

'I'd prefer it if you answered all my questions,' the doctor replied crisply. Glancing disdainfully up at Kelly she seemed to notice the woman's underwear for the first time. 'According to my reference books, undressed usually means taking all your clothes off. Now, are you currently practising sex with a partner?'

'No,' Kelly said, reaching awkwardly behind herself for the clasp of her bra. She unfastened it and slid the garment off, placing it carefully on the pile of neatly folded clothes she had created on the chair. She could feel her blush darkening to a furious degree as she displayed her bared breasts to the doctor. Her cheeks felt as though they were smouldering with the heat of her embarrassment. Not daring to disobey the doctor's instruction, Kelly unfastened the clasp of her suspender belt and, after stepping out of her shoes, began to unroll the stockings from her legs.

'When you've finished undressing, lie down on the trolley,' Doctor McMahon said simply. Without taking a breath she asked, 'Have you ever been involved in a sub–dom or sadomasochistic relationship?'

Kelly stopped unrolling her stockings and stared at the doctor with an expression of genuine bewilderment. 'I don't know what that means,' she replied innocently.

The doctor rolled her eyes. 'During your marriage, did you ever punish your husband physically, or mentally, for sexual gratification?'

'Of course not!' Kelly declared, shocked by the suggestion.

'Did your husband ever do that to you?' Doctor McMahon persisted.

'I told you, I don't want to talk about my marriage,' Kelly said, turning her gaze away from the doctor's. She busied herself with one stocking, unwilling to meet the other woman's angry expression.

The doctor's sigh of exasperation was clearly audible in the quiet confines of the room. 'All right,' she said stiffly, making obvious attempts to control her dissipating patience. 'Have you ever been involved with anyone in a relationship like the one I've just described?'

'No!' Kelly said firmly.

'You don't know what you're missing!' a small voice whispered behind her.

Kelly had almost forgotten about the nurse until she added her wry contribution to the question-and-answer session.

'I thought you'd already learnt not to speak until spoken to,' the doctor snapped.

Placing a horrified hand over her mouth, the girl whispered her heartfelt apology. 'Please, Doctor McMahon. I'm sorry. I spoke without thinking, I . . .'

Doctor McMahon waved a dismissive hand, silencing the apologetic girl. Fixing her attention on Kelly she glanced unhappily at the skimpy pair of green satin panties she wore. 'When you eventually get around to taking your knickers off, you can lie on the couch and I can start my examination.'

Mortified by her own feeling of vulnerability, Kelly stepped quickly out of the pants and placed them with the rest of her clothes. She had never felt comfortable with her own nudity. This sensation was heightened by the close proximity of the doctor and her nurse. Staring meekly at the floor, she walked swiftly to the trolley and eased herself on to the uncomfortable, paper-covered mattress. There was no pillow or raised end and she found herself staring miserably at the ceiling, her hands folded demurely over her stomach. She could not see Doctor McMahon or the nurse from her position and, in that moment, Kelly grasped a brief moment of relief, imagining herself alone. It was only a small reprieve, the illusion of solitude being broken by the sound of a chair moving and the doctor's whispered command to her aide.

Then Doctor McMahon was standing beside her. She had removed the white three-quarter-length physician's coat she sported earlier and Kelly now saw her as a young attractive woman in a plain white T-shirt. 'Relax a little,' the doctor said, placing a reassuring hand on Kelly's shoulder. It was the first time she had spoken to Kelly without a note of vicious contempt inflecting her words. 'This won't be so bad if you ease up a little.'

Kelly tried to return the doctor's comforting smile but found her gaze was drawn to the tight white T-shirt the doctor was wearing. She noticed the woman was not wearing a bra beneath the garment and from Kelly's prone position she was close enough to see the hard nubs of the doctor's erect nipples. The sight made her swallow nervously and she was about to say something when she felt the doctor's hand gently caress her breast.

The sensation was electric. She had never had a woman touch her so intimately and the feeling was exhilarating. Remembering her responsiveness in the waiting room, when Stacey had stroked a finger along her lip, Kelly wondered if she was developing some sort of mental illness. She had never been sexually attracted to women before, yet within the last ten minutes she had come close to kissing one woman and was now allowing another to nonchalantly stroke her breasts. The fact that she was enjoying these encounters added fuel to her fear of insanity. Her heart began to race and she could not tell if it was hurried by apprehension or excitement.

The doctor's fingers traced slow circles on the soft flesh of Kelly's orbs, gently stimulating the tactile skin with her subtle caress. Her smile, although not unkind, was predatory enough to make Kelly feel acutely vulnerable. 'Relax a little,' the doctor encouraged once again. 'You're going to enjoy this. Trust me.'

Laid on the trolley, having witnessed Mistress Stacey's punishment of Helen and then endured the doctor's harsh, invasive questioning, Kelly did not feel relaxed enough to enjoy anything. All she wanted was to get the physical aspect of the examination over and done with, regardless of what it entailed. Afterwards she could shut herself in the confines of her own room and try to analyse the bizarre attraction she was feeling for other women. She glanced downwards, trying to convince herself that the doctor's touch had only been accidental. Seeing the woman's fingers casually caressing her right breast, tracing circles around the darkening areola, Kelly realised the touch had been no accident. She took a sharp intake of breath. 'You're tou ... touching me,' she said awkwardly.

The doctor smiled easily. 'Yes,' she admitted, not moving her hand away. 'You do like it, don't you?'

Totally unsure of her opinions and her body's mutinous responses, Kelly did not trust herself to respond to the question. 'Is this part of the examination?' she asked, struggling to sound indignant and failing miserably.

'Sort of,' Doctor McMahon said. She placed a finger on either side of Kelly's nipple and tweaked it playfully.

Unwittingly, Kelly found herself enjoying a thrill of pleasure she had not anticipated. The sensation was so intense a shiver coursed through her entire body. She stared at the doctor, unsure of how to respond. Without knowing when it had started, Kelly realised her breathing had deepened.

'The best part of the examination is still to come,' Doctor McMahon said softly, rolling the nipple playfully between her fingers. Her hand cupped Kelly's

17

breast and caressed the sensitive flesh with a measured degree of care. Her fingers were cool against Kelly's warm skin but the silky touch of the doctor's palms created a friction that was intense enough to generate its own heat.

Kelly heard herself moan softly in appreciation. Whatever the reason for her sudden loss of inhibitions, she knew that now was not the time to contemplate it. The pleasure she was receiving from the doctor's touch was something so exciting and new she was prepared to enjoy it now and think about it later. She glanced nervously at the doctor and was surprised to see the petite nurse peering lecherously over her shoulder.

Noticing Kelly's attention was distracted, the doctor moved her hand away and turned to the nurse. 'Is that what you found?' she asked crisply.

'Yes, doctor,' the nurse replied timidly.

Kelly could not see what they were talking about but she felt an unsettling thrill of trepidation at the doctor's curt tone. A tiny butterfly fluttered nervously in the pit of her stomach, enhancing the darkly erotic flavour of her arousal. She tried to surreptitiously shift her position and see what the pair were discussing.

'You've done well,' the doctor told the nurse stiffly. Turning to Kelly, she said, 'This was found in your handbag. Would you mind telling me why you have it?'

Kelly felt her face darken with embarrassment as she stared at the small phallus in the doctor's hand. She did not need an explanation to know that it was the same one she kept in her handbag. At the back of her mind she knew she should have been outraged by the unauthorised search. However, her inner confusion and a wave of mortified shame seemed to cloud all other thoughts. 'I didn't know I wasn't allowed to have one,' she said quietly. 'I . . .'

'That doesn't answer my question,' Doctor McMahon snapped. She reached across Kelly's prone, naked body and carelessly teased her left nipple. Her touch was deft and Kelly's response was an instantaneous sigh of delight. 'Why do you have it?' Doctor McMahon repeated.

'I use it sometimes,' Kelly replied meekly, unable to meet the doctor's gaze as she spoke.

'You use it,' the doctor repeated. She stroked her hand over the flat, smooth expanse of Kelly's stomach. The tactile stimulation was incredibly erotic and Kelly felt herself trembling with anticipation. 'Show me how you use it,' the doctor said, whispering the words softly into Kelly's ear. 'Show me.' She placed the dildo in Kelly's hand and tried to wrap her fingers around it.

'What if I refuse?' Kelly asked.

'You won't,' the doctor replied confidently. She placed her fingers under Kelly's chin and tilted her head so the two women were able to enjoy eye contact. 'During your induction Mr Smith will have told you that disobedient and recalcitrant behaviour is not tolerated here at the hostel.'

Staring into the unfathomable depths of the doctor's jet-black eyes, Kelly remembered Mr Smith's austere introduction to the hostel, earlier that morning. She suddenly felt cold as she realised how gravely she had misunderstood his words about the hostel's strict regime and its disciplined environment.

'I don't know if you've already heard of the black room,' the doctor continued easily. 'But it's the sort of last resort that I don't think you want to experience just yet.'

Kelly remembered Stacey's whispered threat to Helen in the waiting room. The woman had only mentioned the black room to her and Helen had trembled with fear. Whatever the black room was, Kelly had already decided she did not want to encounter it. Reluctantly, she allowed her fingers to accept the dildo.

'That's better,' Doctor McMahon enthused cheerfully, allowing her hand to work casually down to the neatly trimmed triangle of wiry orange hairs around Kelly's pubic mound. 'Now, I'm sure you know what to do with it,' she encouraged.

Feeling her face burn crimson with shame, Kelly closed her eyes and took the dildo in both hands. She felt the familiar modest length and girth with her fingers, trying not to think of what she was doing. Deftly, she twisted the hard plastic base all the way around. The dildo buzzed wickedly. The sound reverberated deafeningly in the quiet confines of the doctor's room. Feeling more exposed than she had ever felt before, Kelly directed the vibrator between her legs. Normally, before pressing the instrument into herself she would have spread the lips of her vagina apart. This time, before she had a chance to open herself, she felt a pair of fingers doing that task for her. The feeling was so sudden and unexpected she opened her eyes and stared down between her legs.

Doctor McMahon graced Kelly with a knowing smile, then turned her concentration back to the hand she had in Kelly's lap.

The feeling of the woman's fingers pressed against her vulva was an unprecedented stimulation. Whilst Kelly still felt embarrassed to be performing such an intimate act in front of a complete stranger, the doctor's gentle touch was disturbingly arousing. As she slid the merrily buzzing dildo into the open folds of her labia Kelly was poignantly aware of her heightened arousal. The plastic tingled on her exposed flesh in a wave of stimulation that felt delicious. She paused before pushing it any further inside, enjoying the myriad delightful prickles of pleasure to their fullest. She found herself staring into the doctor's face as the first wave of pleasure rolled through her. It seemed unreal to be focusing on the face of another woman whilst she was masturbating but Kelly realised she had not just come to terms with the situation: she was actually loving it.

The first orgasm coursed through her body as she plunged the buzzing dildo deep within the warm folds of her moist pussy lips. She had enjoyed stronger orgasms in the past but because of the bizarre circumstances surrounding this one she did not think she would ever have one as memorable. Gasping breathlessly at the ease of her own climax, she stared into the doctor's smiling face.

'Please, continue, Kelly,' Doctor McMahon insisted. She allowed her fingers to playfully stroke around Kelly's hole before moving her hand beneath the vibrator. Kelly was startled to feel one of the doctor's fingers slide rudely between the cheeks of her buttocks and into the forbidden warmth of her anus.

'Relax,' Doctor McMahon whispered coolly, allowing her tongue to tickle the sensitive flesh of Kelly's neck. 'You'll enjoy it so much more if you relax.'

Wordlessly, Kelly tried to follow the doctor's instruction as she slid the length of plastic slowly in and out of herself. The whirring sound in the room intensified and then muted as the dildo was pulled out and then pushed into the tight depths of her hole. Kelly felt the tingling increase as the vibrator filled her, sparking a wealth of dizzying pleasure. On its own, she knew the dildo would have been enough to make her climax again. Coupled with the delightfully taboo sensation of the doctor's finger playing in her anus, Kelly felt herself rushing towards another orgasm with unnerving alacrity.

As the rush of pleasure filled every pore of her body, Kelly's back arched upward. She pushed the dildo so deep into her pussy she could feel the tip tingling perfectly on the neck of her womb. The doctor slid her finger slowly in and out of Kelly's anus, creating a frisson of unimagined delight. She was perversely aware of feeling fuller than she had ever felt before and as the doctor slid a second finger alongside the first, Kelly groaned blissfully.

With her other hand, the doctor was attending to Kelly's breasts, alternating between careful caresses and punishingly playful pinches. The contrary sensations were infuriatingly well timed, hastening Kelly's ascent to the brink of orgasm.

When the orgasm struck, she shrieked ecstatically. Her pelvis bucked forward, as though her crevice was greedily trying to accept even more of the dildo. She felt the inner muscles of her pussy squeezing on the phallus with a familiar, furious tightening. A hazy red mist of joy clouded her vision and with a groan of agonised pleasure, Kelly collapsed limply on the trolley.

Several moments passed before she dared to open her eyes. When she did, Kelly found herself staring into the knowing smile of Doctor McMahon. She wondered briefly if she had passed out with the intensity of her climax. The doctor was now wearing her lab coat once again and Kelly could not recall feeling the woman remove the two fingers she had been employing so skilfully.

Hesitantly, she raised her eyes to meet the doctor's, warily anticipating a look of staunch disapproval. She was surprised to see the woman smiling indulgently down at her. Her surprise increased when the doctor reached between Kelly's legs and slowly withdrew the dildo. It was still buzzing and she quickly unscrewed the switch with well-practised ease. Kelly felt her embarrassment return as she realised the vibrator was slick with the remnants of her glistening love juice. It did not temper her unease when she watched the doctor slowly lick pussy juice from the implement.

The broad grin she graced Kelly with was wanton and avaricious. Her dark eyes sparkled merrily. 'Welcome to the Pentagon Agency, Kelly.' Doctor McMahon smiled easily. 'I do believe you're just the sort of woman we're looking for.'

Kelly closed her eyes and sighed, hoping fervently that she was doing the right thing.

Two

Jo Valentine flicked the double-headed sovereign high in the air. She watched it catch the occasional golden ray of sunlight on its upward spiral, then caught it halfway through its descent. Her reactions were lightning fast and she smacked the coin swiftly on to the careworn surface of her desk. Surreptitiously, she raised her hand and risked a supposedly nervous glance at the result.

'Is it tails?' Stephanie asked eagerly. She stared at Jo with a beseeching, hopeful gaze.

Jo smiled sadly. 'Heads, I'm afraid.' She shook her head, trying to look unhappy about the result. 'Could you take your blouse off?'

Stephanie sighed unhappily. She cast a glance towards the frosted glass on the office door and then looked hesitantly at Jo. 'What if someone comes in?'

Jo laughed humourlessly. 'I suppose there's a first time for everything,' she said cynically. 'If a customer actually came through the door I'd want to shoot it, mount it and stick its head on the wall. The only thing stopping me would be the fact that they're an endangered species.'

'It has been quiet lately, hasn't it?' Stephanie ventured.

Jo glanced slyly at her. 'Stop changing the subject and take your blouse off,' she said pointedly. 'Are you calling tails again?'

Stephanie shook her head as she began to unfasten

her blouse with an obvious lack of enthusiasm. 'Let's try cutting the deck of cards again,' she suggested. 'I seem to have more luck with that.'

Jo barely heard Stephanie's last words, mesmerised as always by the vision of her undressing. Stephanie was a petite blonde with an infrequent smile and large, expressive brown eyes. She always managed to look so frail and vulnerable that Jo felt torn between an urge to protect her, and a longing to corrupt her. Invariably, Jo found herself cautiously attempting the latter, her eagerness to possess Stephanie tempered by a strong fear of rejection.

As always, Stephanie wore jet-black underwear, a colour that contrasted starkly with her delicate wan complexion. She eased the blouse off slowly, revealing her modest orbs in their black-satin confines.

Jo stifled a breath of delight, unwilling to show her arousal to Stephanie. In Jo's opinion, her business partner had to be the most desirable creature she had ever encountered. Stephanie was not just pretty and blessed with a gorgeous body. She also had a pleasant, pragmatic personality that Jo found truly stimulating. At the back of her mind she wondered if she was in love with Stephanie or simply suffering from the effects of unrequited lust. Not given to great bouts of introspection, Jo had never troubled herself too greatly with the matter. Instead she had contented herself with various games and ploys to undress Stephanie. Her most cherished hope was that one day Stephanie would read the obvious signs and confess feeling the same about Jo.

She wondered idly if she should have changed the rules to the stripping game. Rather than the loser taking her own clothes off, Jo wondered if the winner should be allowed the privilege. It was a tempting idea and she did not know which aspect of it appealed to her the most. The thought of slowly removing garment after garment from Stephanie's pliant waiflike body was truly intoxicating. However, the idea of being undressed by Stephanie was even more enthralling. In her mind's eye Jo had summoned a mental picture of Stephanie's small, elegant hands teasing buttons from their holes. So vivid was the mental image, she could almost feel the tender, innocent brush of Stephanie's fingers against her bare flesh. Lost in her own heady reverie, Jo was unaware that Stephanie was speaking to her.

'Well?' Stephanie asked patiently.

Jo shook her head and tried to pull her gaze from Stephanie's body. 'Sorry, Steph,' she said, a wry smile twisting her lips. 'I was just thinking how nice it would be to have boobs like yours.'

Stephanie frowned. 'Don't you like your own?'

'I don't mind mine,' Jo replied. 'I'd just love to have a pair of boobs like yours,' she added wistfully. 'God, would I love that.'

'Cut the cards,' Stephanie said tiredly, pushing the deck towards Jo.

'You go first,' Jo insisted. 'Aces low, high wins.' She watched as Stephanie leant over the deck and cut herself a ten. Jo ran her thumb carefully along the edge of the cards, allowing it to stop on the slightly bent queen of diamonds.

'You have the luck of the devil,' Stephanie said incredulously.

'Don't I just,' Jo agreed, unable to stop herself from smiling. 'But I can't decide what I want you to take off next,' she sighed.

'You don't have a choice,' Stephanie said, standing up and reaching for the button at the side of her miniskirt. 'You know the rules as well as I do: all outer garments have to come off before we start on underwear.'

Jo tried to frown sullenly, but the prospect of seeing Stephanie dressed only in her bra and panties was too exciting for her to maintain the charade. She watched as the skirt spilled to the floor revealing Stephanie's gloriously slender figure clad in a pair of black stockings and high-line panties. She was a beautiful vision, in spite of her sullen expression, and Jo felt an irresistible urge to confess her desires there and then. She had managed to resist the temptation of telling Stephanie how she felt for fear of damaging their friendship and spoiling their business partnership. Stephanie had never made an open declaration of her sexuality and Jo knew an unwelcome approach would ruin their good working relationship. While she had never heard her partner talk about previous or current boyfriends, Jo was sensible enough to realise Stephanie had never spoken of girlfriends either.

Seeing her standing in the centre of the office, clad only in her underwear, Jo felt the familiar wave of desire wash over her again. Her urgent longing was so ferocious all rational thought paled to insignificance. She suddenly knew that, regardless of the consequences, she had to make her true feelings known. She had to tell Stephanie how desperately she wanted her.

'You're beautiful,' she began in a soft, husky whisper. Jo paused, trying to decide on the best way of voicing her desires. 'I want you' seemed too trite. 'Let me take you to bed' would be too overpowering. In a blinding flash of inspiration she realised the perfect words would be: 'Stephanie, let's make love.' Her heart skipped a beat as Jo realised she had hit on the perfect line. The moment was right and the words were so apt they were almost magical. The realisation that she was only a sentence away from attaining her heart's desire caused Jo to swallow nervously. 'Stephanie, let's make love.' The words were almost formed on Jo's lips when their game was interrupted by a sharp knock on the frosted glass of the office door.

Instinctively, Stephanie wrapped her hands over her breasts and glanced anxiously at the door. She snatched her skirt from the floor and stared beseechingly at Jo.

Jo pointed at the storeroom and shooed Stephanie towards it. Because her partner had forgotten her blouse, Jo picked the garment up and threw it after her.

She took a last, lingering look at Stephanie's half-naked body and tried not to think how the day might have progressed. Angrily, Jo made a mental vow that if the caller was a salesman or a Jehovah's Witness she was going to kill them.

When the storeroom door closed on Stephanie, Jo steadied her voice and settled herself back behind her desk. With a wary eye she studied the shadow behind the frosted pane in the door, wondering if this would be the month's first customer. Calmly she called, 'It's open. Come on in.'

Tall and balding, he had the nervous look of a man with a problem.

She gauged him to be in his late thirties or early forties; he wore the scars of deep frown lines that came from too much stress. Usually she found clothes were a good indicator of the sort of person she was meeting but the inclement weather had delivered this man to her door in a sodden trench coat, making such judgements impossible. The furled umbrella he carried was dripping pools on the worn Axminster of Jo's office floor, as was the aluminium briefcase in his other hand.

'I'm looking for Mr Joe Valentine,' he said crisply. 'Is he here?'

'I'm Jo Valentine,' she explained, trying not to succumb to the feeling of irritation this mistake usually incited. 'But I'm a Miss, not a Mr.'

She could see the frown of disappointment cross his face before he had a chance to mask it. 'You're Jo Valentine the private investigator?' he asked warily.

There was a note of incredulity in his voice that Jo found particularly offensive but she bit back a sharp retort. 'Yes,' Jo said tersely. 'I'm *Miss* Jo Valentine, the private investigator. Can I help you?' she asked with forced politeness.

He paused for a moment and Jo could see he was reassessing the situation in his own mind, not having anticipated he would be dealing with a woman. She tried to quell the notions of feminist rebellion that smouldered in the pit of her stomach, reminding herself that this man was a potential customer.

'May I sit down?' he asked awkwardly.

'Please,' she said, waving a hand at the chair before her desk. 'How may I help you, Mr . . .?'

'Rogers,' he supplied quickly. 'And I want you to find a missing person for me.'

Jo studied him calmly. 'I hate to push business away,' she began slowly. 'But you might find the police have better resources for that sort of work.'

'The police are a bunch of useless wankers,' Mr Rogers said in an icy tone. 'As far as they are concerned a person has to be missing for forty-eight hours before they will even deign to take their name. After that they don't do anything about it unless they find a corpse.'

Although she thought the man was viewing the situation with a modicum of jaded cynicism, Jo knew there was some truth in what Mr Rogers said. 'So who's gone missing? When? Where were they last seen? Have you got a description or photo?'

Slightly taken aback by the sudden barrage of questions, Mr Rogers shifted uncomfortably in his chair and fumbled with the clasps on his briefcase. 'My wife's gone missing,' he explained as he rifled through some papers inside. 'She was last seen, by myself, five days ago, on Monday morning. Inside this folder I've written her name, description and all her other personal details. I have also enclosed a copy of the most recent photograph I possess of her. Is that sufficient?'

Jo reached for the folder and studied it swiftly before responding. 'Can I have contact numbers for you, in case I do turn anything up?' she asked absently as she flicked through the pages.

'My business card is stapled to the back page,' he said tersely. Having closed his briefcase and placed it carefully on the floor, he reached inside his trench coat and produced a tightly packed Manila envelope. 'I would be very grateful if you could help me locate my wife,' he said with unconscious stiffness. 'This is five thousand pounds of my gratitude. If you can get a result within the next two weeks I'll happily provide you with another two identical envelopes.'

Jo studied the tightly packed envelope nonchalantly, trying not to show the customer how eager she was to accept the case. There was something suspicious about Mr Rogers that she did not trust. Part of it, she knew, was his obvious sexism, but Jo sensed there was more to her feelings of doubt. The man seemed inordinately uncomfortable in her office and so eager to get away that he shifted restlessly in his chair. It also occurred to Jo that, whilst he was asking her to find his missing wife, he had not mentioned her first name once. 'Could I just ask a couple more questions before I decide to commence with the investigation?' she asked coolly.

He shrugged, a wary frown creasing his forehead. 'If you think it will help, please do.'

'Did you and your wife argue in the week before she left?'

'No,' he said quickly.

'Is it possible she may have gone off with a lover?'

He laughed darkly. 'I think alien abduction would be more likely than that,' he told Jo, relishing his own black mirth. 'Her social circle was very limited and I've checked that meticulously. She was working for the Pentagon Temp Agency in the week before she left but they've been no help. That's why I've come to you.'

Jo made a note of the temping agency's name on her desk pad, trying to recall where she had heard the name before. It had an inordinately familiar ring. 'You've contacted them? What do you mean when you say "they've been no help"?'

Rogers snorted in disgust. 'They said they'd never heard of her,' he said sharply. 'They said she'd never worked for them and they had no one on their records with a name or details that came close to resembling my wife's.'

'How curious,' she said quietly, making another note next to the first. Jo tried to relax in her chair but found it impossible. Part of her unease was her instinctive doubt and dislike of the client. She had only known the man for a matter of minutes but already she knew that she did not trust him or his motivations. Normally she preferred working for clients in an honest, open relationship but she strongly doubted such a thing would be possible with this man.

Another part of Jo's discomfort was due to the small fortune that Mr Rogers had dropped on her desk. Work had been so sparse over the past few months that a case this lucrative would solve a lot of her mounting financial problems. She usually enjoyed the luxury of considering a case's suitability before accepting it. However, her current state of penury and Mr Rogers's generosity were forcing her into a corner.

Determined to maintain as much of her own professional integrity as she could, Jo pushed aside her reservations and pressed on. 'A lot of missing people go missing and want to stay missing,' she said carefully. Already, on her short acquaintance with Mr Rogers, Jo could empathise with any woman who wanted to leave his company. 'What would you like me to do if that's the situation in this case?'

He considered her quietly for a moment, his sullen expression making it obvious that he was unhappy with this idea. 'If that is the situation,' he began scornfully. 'I'd be grateful if you just brought my wife to this office and then summoned me. I'll take care of everything after that.' His gaze was challenging, as though he defied her to take issue with this plan.

'Fine,' Jo said simply, unintimidated by his hostile expression. 'I'll call you at the end of the week with a progress report, sooner if I have something you can use.'

He nodded curtly, aware that the investigator had enough information from him. 'If you require anything else from me, you have my number,' he said, rising stiffly from his chair.

Jo nodded. 'Thank you, Mr Rogers,' she said curtly, still trying not to look at his money as she spoke to him. 'I'll be in touch.' She waited until he had closed the door on his egress before she snatched the envelope from the table.

'Is he gone?' Stephanie peered out of the storeroom door warily. When Jo nodded she stepped out, still holding her skirt, with her unfastened blouse draped over her shoulders.

'This is how she would look after we'd just made love,' Jo thought suddenly. It was a warming thought and ordinarily she would have devoted more time to enjoying it. With the distraction of the money in her hand, Jo quickly dismissed the notion and went back to counting the crisp bundle of notes.

'We're not really taking this case, are we?' Stephanie asked, standing provocatively in front of Jo as she dressed. 'He sounded like such a bastard.'

Jo shrugged. 'It's company policy to only work for bastards with large wads of money,' she explained, still fingering her way through the notes. 'If he'd been a poor bastard I'd have kicked his arse straight out of here.'

Stephanie sniffed dismissively. 'You're a mercenary,' she said coldly, fastening the last button on her blouse.

Jo grinned and glanced up from the wad of notes. 'Yes, I'm a mercenary,' she agreed happily. 'And, right now, I'm a solvent mercenary. Care to join me for dinner?'

'Shouldn't we start working on this man's case?' Stephanie asked.

31

Jo considered this for a moment. 'You're right. You start working on the computer and see what you can turn up. I'll go out for dinner.' She jumped from her chair and rushed towards the coat stand by the office door. 'What do we know about the Pentagon Temping Agency?' she asked suddenly.

Stephanie cocked her head to one side for a moment as she thought about the question. When recollection hit her, she snapped her fingers and grinned broadly. 'Vanessa Byrne,' she said. 'Wasn't she involved with them?'

Jo nodded, knowing Stephanie was correct. She shrugged her coat on and walked back to the desk. Reaching past Stephanie she picked up the telephone and strained her memory for the appropriate telephone number. After punching the numbers into the keypad, she settled herself on a corner of the desk and listened. Her call was answered on the second ring.

'Vanessa,' Jo began quickly. 'This is Jo Valentine. It's been a long time.' She paused, listening to Vanessa for a moment, a frown of consternation creasing her brow. 'Sure. You must have a lot of things to do. Could I call you back later this evening?' she asked sweetly. 'I need to know a couple of things about the temping agency you used to work with.' There was another pause and Jo smiled for an instant. 'That's right. Pentagon.' Her smile disappeared to be replaced with a dark, unhappy frown. 'You're no longer involved with them,' Jo repeated. 'Can you give me a contact name for someone there who could help me?' She listened to Vanessa for a moment. 'I'm just thinking of employing a temp for the next couple of weeks, to help with the workload. OK. Thanks for trying to help, Vanessa. I'm sorry it's been so long since we spoke. I'll call you some time next week so we can chat about old times. Ciao!'

Stephanie stared at Jo's dark frown as the PI replaced the handset in its cradle. 'What was all that about?' she asked curiously. 'We need a temp helping out in here as much as we need a fountain in the foyer.'

'Tell me I'm gorgeous,' Jo said suddenly.

Stephanie shrugged and smiled knowingly at Jo. 'You're gorgeous,' she said with honesty. 'Why did I have to tell you that?'

'Because,' Jo said darkly, 'I have had people lying to me all day and it's nice to hear the truth once in a while. I don't know how or why, but Rogers was lying about something when he was in here, and just now, on the phone, I felt sure Vanessa was telling porkies.'

'She couldn't help?' Stephanie asked, surprised.

'She didn't want to help,' Jo said carefully. She smiled widely and clapped Stephanie good-naturedly on the shoulder. 'This is turning into quite a case. Lucrative and intriguing.' She moved to the door, tying the belt on her overcoat as she walked. 'Do you want me to bring back a doggy bag for you?'

Stephanie shook her head wearily and picked up the folder Rogers had left on the desk. 'If you get a chance, could you ask around and see if there are any real jobs available in the outside world?'

Jo smiled, fondly admiring Stephanie's legs in the short skirt. 'Would you really want to give up the glamour and excitement of being a PI?' she asked dryly.

'Try me,' Stephanie replied dourly.

Jo grinned. 'See you in a couple of hours,' she told her, sliding quickly from the room. 'And, Stephanie . . .' she called, popping her head around the door before leaving.

Stephanie glanced up from the folder she was studying, a questioning expression on her face.

'Do you really think I'm gorgeous?' Jo asked.

Vanessa Byrne replaced the telephone handset, an unhappy frown furrowing her forehead. Remembering she had other business to attend to, she shook the worries of the phone call from her head and smiled indulgently at the young man in front of her.

'You've been working here for a week now, Russel,' Vanessa said softly. 'Tell me, how do you think you're settling into the office?'

Russel felt his stomach turn over uneasily. It had been a long and arduous first week in the office and from past experience he knew this was the beginning of the end. Before she had finished, Vanessa Byrne would be saying how sorry she was that he did not fit in with the rest of the staff and how happy she would be to provide him with a glowing reference. The timing was all right. It was Friday evening, they were the only ones in the building and he had been paid for all the hours he had worked. The only things missing so far were his P45 and the envelope containing his reference. It had occurred to Russel previously that his career was not adequately described by the word 'chequered'. He was a hopeless employee with an honours degree in application forms and a PhD in apologetic goodbye letters. Wilfully quelling his own pessimistic thoughts, Russel fixed a plastic smile to his lips and said, 'I'm enjoying myself immensely.'

'You like it here?' Vanessa sounded mildly surprised.

Russel nodded. 'The work's challenging but not too demanding,' he explained, hoping his enthusiasm would win him a reprieve from the inevitable result of this conversation. 'I'm really enjoying it.'

'And tell me, Russel,' Vanessa said, slowly rising from her seat, 'do you think you will like this?' She walked around the desk to reveal she was not wearing a skirt. The loose blouse she wore would have almost covered her modesty but Vanessa held the hem in one hand so he could see the dark curls that covered her pubic mound. With her other hand she teased her long manicured fingernails through the hairs. All the time, she watched Russel, a curious unfathomable light

34

glinting in her eyes. 'Well, Russel, do you think you'll like it?'

Russel could think of nothing to say. He stared uneasily at Vanessa, wondering if this was some sort of practical joke. Vanessa Byrne had to be one of the sexiest women he had ever worked for. She was a strikingly tall woman with long golden hair that she kept tied in an austere bun. Throughout his week's employment, Russel had watched her slyly. He admired the stylish wardrobe of business suits she wore and the way they enhanced her desirable figure. At the back of his mind he had harboured a passionate desire for her and dreamt of knowing her sexually. The rational part of his mind had told him this would never be more than a wet daydream or a masturbatory fantasy. Now, she stood before him, naked from the waist down. She was displaying the enticing vision of her pubic bush, and asking him if he thought he might enjoy it. The phrase 'dream come true' did not even begin to convey the euphoria that welled inside Russel's chest. 'I think I'd really enjoy that,' he said, trying to sound calm and failing miserably.

Vanessa smiled, a cruel inflection distorting her lips slightly. 'Then get down on your knees and kiss it,' she whispered sternly. 'Now!' she added in a louder voice.

Russel needed no more encouragement. He knelt before Vanessa and caressed her inner thighs tenderly, relishing the silky-soft feel of her flesh beneath his fingertips. His nose was close enough to her sex to sense the delicate musk of her natural scent. He could feel the forceful hardening of the stiff cock in his pants.

Russel showered a series of kisses on Vanessa's inner thighs, alternating between the two and slowly moving his mouth upward as he went from leg to leg. By the time his tongue was actually stroking the delicate hairs that lined the lips of Vanessa's labia, he could taste the excited heat of her arousal. The subtle taste of her juices filled his mouth, making his cock twitch harder. Spurred on by his own excitement, Russel flicked his tongue over the tiny hood of skin that covered her clitoris. The nub of erectile tissue beneath bristled excitedly. Vanessa sighed softly in response.

Russel ran his tongue over the clit, pressing forcefully, then easing the pressure. Occasionally he would lick the delicate folds of her labia, savouring the taste of her pussy juice, but his efforts were concentrated on Vanessa's hooded pearl of pleasure. He teased it wickedly, easing it from beneath the hood of skin, then pressing it lightly between his lips. The glistening moisture on Vanessa's inner lips, accompanied by her distant sighs of enjoyment, was encouragement enough for Russel to continue. He probed his tongue skilfully under the hood of flesh and pressed her clit between his tongue and top lip. His longing for her increased as he enjoyed the faint yet urgent throb of her desire in his mouth. Unwilling to rush things for her, he moved his mouth downwards and began to properly tongue her pussy.

Vanessa's arousal was obvious from the wetness of her sex. His tongue slid easily inside her. Her pretty pink lips opened softly to accommodate him. The scent and taste of her desire was a heady musk that stiffened his erection furiously. With careful diligence, he lapped at Vanessa's honey-scented secretions like a kitten sipping milk. He could have happily drunk from her all evening if she had not stopped him with soft words of encouragement and a condescending pat on the head.

'Good boy,' Vanessa told him, not bothering to mask the obvious enjoyment in her tone. 'Now kiss my arsehole.' She moved her pussy away from him and turned around, bending over so that he had unrestricted access.

Russel had marvelled at the beauty of Vanessa's arse, which was normally encased in tight skirts, for the past week. Now, having the two perfect round orbs inches from his face, he felt incredulous at his own good fortune. He stroked the flesh lovingly with his hands before daring to nuzzle provocatively against the tightly puckered hole.

'I said "kiss it",' Vanessa said, a note of impatience colouring her words. 'Kiss it now, Russel, just as I asked you.'

Obediently, he complied. His tongue probed her anus boldly, just as it had licked inside her pussy. He heard Vanessa gasp breathlessly and, gratified by her enjoyment, continued to use his tongue. The fragrance of her scent still filled Russel's nostrils and he inhaled deeply, enjoying the intoxicating aroma. His tongue was enjoying the subtle, sour-sweet taste of her anus. The muscles of her sphincter clenched tightly on him, as he slid his tongue deep inside her dark hole. Within minutes of beginning, he heard her gasping for him to stop.

Vanessa helped him from his knees. She guided Russel back to the chair he had been sitting in at the beginning of the interview. 'There's something I'd like to try with you that I think we might both get a lot of pleasure from,' she whispered huskily, caressing the side of his face as she spoke.

'That sounds all right to me,' Russel said, so excited he would have happily committed himself to anything. 'What do you want me to do?' he asked eagerly.

Vanessa smiled quietly to herself. Her expression was that of a woman who thinks something is just too easy. She straddled the chair he sat on, resting her vagina against the hard bulge in Russel's pants. Roughly, she pushed her hand inside his shirt and scratched her fingernails playfully over his nipples. Her nails produced a shiver of excitement from the youth beneath her. After taking her hand from his shirt she grabbed both his arms firmly and pushed them behind the chair.

37

She moved her mouth close to Russel's ear and whispered, 'I want to tie your hands behind your back.'

Russel drew a heavy sigh. Before he had the chance to consider the implications of Vanessa's words, he realised he was nodding his eager agreement.

'I want to tie your hands behind your back, then use you as though you were my slave,' she told him softly. 'You like the sound of that, don't you? I could tell by the way your cock twitched against my crotch when I suggested it.'

'Yes!' Russel gasped, almost delirious with anticipation. 'Of course we can do that, if it's what you want.'

Vanessa moved back a little, rubbing her cleft purposefully over his rock hard bulge as she spoke. 'It's what I want,' she agreed. Continuing to ride herself along his confined cock, she added, 'And I'm sure it's what you want too.'

Not trusting himself to speak, Russel nodded his head eagerly in reply. He kept his arms behind him and allowed Vanessa to tie him with a pair of her stockings. She did this swiftly but with a skill that left him virtually immobile.

Standing in front of him, Vanessa smiled at her own handiwork and began to unfasten her blouse. She did not wear a bra and as soon as the blouse fell free from her body she stood naked before him. 'Do you like what you see, Russel?' she asked quietly.

He nodded quickly. She did not have the ultra-thin figure of a supermodel but he had always found those women to be androgynous and uninspiring. Vanessa was blessed with a slender figure, complemented by ample breasts and well-rounded hips. As she stood in front of him, allowing him to admire her nudity, Russel felt dizzy with anticipation.

She studied him thoughtfully for a moment, her gaze lingering on the bulge in his trousers. 'Should we find out how much you like what you see?' she asked calmly.

Not waiting for his response, Vanessa put a hand on the waistband of his trousers and slowly unfastened Russel's leather belt. She removed it from the hoops and placed it neatly on the floor, before returning to his trousers.

Russel could feel his cock stiffening as Vanessa's fingers popped the button on his waistband. His rigid member was straining against his boxer shorts as she slowly pulled the zip downwards. Before she had finished unzipping him, he saw the fabric of his underwear bursting determinedly out through his trousers. Because of his excitement, he saw his dick had already started to leak pre-come and a small dark circle of moisture soiled the otherwise brilliant white of his shorts. The circle rested immediately above the swollen purple head of his cock and he could see the organ glistening hungrily beneath the material.

Vanessa circled her fingers around his prick whilst it was still encased in the thin cotton fabric of his boxers. She smiled indulgently up at Russel as she squeezed his erection firmly in her palm. 'You really do like what you see, don't you?' she said kindly. She rubbed her finger over the damp spot on the boxers, caressing the huge purple end with the deft care of an adept tease. 'You seem so excited too.' She rubbed the tip of his erection with one finger as she spoke. 'Do you think that's because your hands are tied, and you're enjoying it?'

Russel did not know what to say. He had never been in a situation like this before and his excitement went beyond anything he had ever encountered. At least, he realised, with his hands tied he did not have to trouble himself with the worry of touching the wrong place, or ignoring a part of Vanessa's delightful body. In this situation he saw that the onus was on her to extract what pleasure she could from his securely bound body.

'Well?' Vanessa prompted, still stroking his cock playfully through the material of his shorts. 'Do you think it's nice, having your hands tied?'

'Fantastic,' he said breathlessly.

She smiled and shifted position. 'In that case, you'll love what I have planned for you next,' Vanessa told him. She tugged his trousers from underneath him and pulled them firmly down so that they pooled at the top of his boots. With an uncharacteristic show of strength, she lifted his chair and neatly dropped the legs into the legs of his pants. She grinned happily at her handiwork as she stood back to admire him. 'There you go, Russel,' she said cheerfully. 'Now you're bound hand and foot to the chair. Mine to do with as I please. How does that sound?'

Russel warily tested his feet against their restraints and realised Vanessa was correct. He was securely bound and the realisation of this fact thrilled him more than he would have believed. His shaft twitched furiously inside his shorts.

'Should we set that darling cock of yours free?' Vanessa asked tenderly. She reached into the tidy on her desk and produced a pair of office scissors.

Russel felt a moment's disquiet as she approached him, poignantly aware of his own vulnerability. He tried to shrink away from her as she approached but Vanessa was proficient at bondage and he had no real chance of escaping. Annoyingly, he realised his dick was showing further signs of arousal as the scissors neared him. 'Wait,' he gasped uncertainly. 'I don't . . . What are you doing?'

'Freeing your cock,' Vanessa whispered sweetly. She placed one end of the scissors under the hem of his boxers and quickly cut the garment from one leg, right up to the waistband.

His penis burst from its restraints and stood proudly above his flat stomach. Russel sighed heavily, not daring to contemplate what Vanessa could have done to him.

Vanessa placed the scissors down on the floor next to Russel's belt and moved gracefully above him. She stood with a leg either side of the chair, her pussy poised inches from his face. 'Kiss me,' she commanded sternly.

Russel obeyed wordlessly. His tongue worked furiously on her lips, relishing the sweetness of her heated wetness. He could taste her excitement and realised triumphantly she was enjoying this game as much as he was. Her fragrant juices began to pour over his lips and into his mouth as her delight manifested itself in a shuddering orgasm.

'Now tongue my arse again,' she gasped tersely. 'You do that so well,' she added, bucking her pelvis forward so Russel could do as she bade. She squealed with excitement as his tongue entered her behind, and then began to writhe her lower half on his face as he probed ever deeper into the darkness of her hole.

Almost smothered by the labia pressing into his nose, Russel continued to force his tongue into Vanessa's bumhole, aware that his stiff member was standing to attention with an eager rigidity that bordered on climax.

Vanessa enjoyed a second orgasm, shrieking noisily as the waves of pleasure cascaded throughout her body. A splash of pussy juice squirted from Vanessa's excited hole as she came. The spray filled Russel's mouth and covered his face with its honey-like texture. Greedily, he licked himself clean as though he were drinking nectar.

She moved lithely away from his reach and turned her attention to his dick. 'You're quite a big boy, aren't you?' she observed lasciviously.

Russel shrugged, an unaccountable feeling of embarrassment tempering his response.

'And it looks like you're enjoying this little game,' Vanessa added.

Russel nodded. 'Yes,' he panted excitedly, 'Yes I am.' The word 'enjoyment' did not begin to hint at the euphoric pleasure he was experiencing at Vanessa's hands but he supposed it was sufficient for the moment. He watched as she unfastened the buttons on his shirt and wondered exactly what she had planned for him.

Wordlessly, Vanessa pulled his shirt open and casually teased his nipples with her fingers. When both nubs were standing proudly on his smooth chest, she reached for her handbag and produced a small lipstick. As Russel watched, she applied a smear of scarlet to her lips. The sight of the phallus shaped make-up being drawn slowly around her mouth was intrinsically erotic and Russel felt himself bordering on climax just watching her.

Aware of the effect she was having on him, Vanessa smiled happily at Russel. She leant over him and placed her lips around one nipple, pressing down firmly. Her tongue deftly teased the erectile tissue until Russel felt his arousal increasing to a point that was beyond his control. As though she had sensed his excitement, Vanessa chose that moment to move away. She gracefully moved to his other side and did the same thing on his right nipple, pressing her mouth firmly over him and teasing the gland until his enjoyment was almost too much. 'There,' she said, standing back to admire him. Both his nipples were now circled with the lipstick imprints of her lips. 'Now you're beginning to look like a slave,' she told him. She leant forward and, before Russel could raise a word of protest, she had painted his lips scarlet with the stick.

Russel shuddered with excitement. The scent of Vanessa's sex was still on his face, filling his nostrils, but now the heady aroma of her lipstick was there, increasing his urgent longing. He tensed every muscle in his body, struggling to overcome the imminent climax that threatened to explode from him.

Vanessa stepped back, watching him struggle. A tight smile crossed her face as she found herself enjoying his dilemma. She reached over his body and wrote the word 'slave' across his chest with the bright-red lipstick. The word stood out garishly against his pale flesh and she smiled at the result. Without a word to Russel she went to her desk and produced a small camera.

The flashbulb had exploded three times before he dizzily realised what was happening. Even then, he could not quite believe Vanessa was photographing him. 'No!' he exclaimed hastily, struggling against the restraints that held him to the chair. 'We didn't agree to that! No!'

The flashbulb exploded again, blinding him for half a second.

'Take it easy,' Vanessa urged him. 'You're my slave. I just want a few pictures for my private collection.'

Russel tried to take solace from this news but he sincerely doubted Vanessa was telling the truth. Infuriatingly, he noticed his cock was still standing rigid in spite of his heightened feelings of vulnerability and unease.

Vanessa put the camera down and turned her attention back to Russel. She smiled fondly at him, stroking her own nipples as she spoke. 'I enjoy having slaves, Russel,' she told him earnestly. 'And you're one of the best I've had in a long time. I bet you didn't know how much you could enjoy being submissive, did you?'

'I don't suppose I did,' Russel said tersely.

'There's a certain type of person who enjoys the dominance of others,' Vanessa said knowledgeably. 'And I'd say you were one of those people, wouldn't you?'

'I suppose so,' Russel said uneasily, wary of where the conversation might be leading. He wanted to say something more but his stiff dick was burning with the desire to come and this urgency seemed to override every other thought in his mind.

Vanessa reached to the floor and grabbed the discarded belt she had placed there earlier. She held the buckle in her hand and tied a length of the leather strap around her fist, leaving a two-foot strip of leather free. 'In that case,' Vanessa said, positioning herself carefully in front of him, 'I think you ought to be thanking me for helping you to discover that fact, don't you, Russel?'

Russel stared at her nervously, a look of horror etching his features. Before he could say a word, the belt had whistled through the air and he felt the tip bite sharply at his nipple. He gasped shortly, bewildered by the sudden, excruciating pain. She had achieved her target with incredible accuracy and the agonised sting it left behind was nothing short of debilitating. It felt as though his nipple were on fire and he panted back exclamations of rebuke. Bizarrely, he realised that the blow had made his erection stiffen and Vanessa's words echoed through his head with new meaning: 'There's a certain type of person who enjoys the dominance of others,' she had said. Realising he was closer to the point of climax than he had been all evening, Russel guessed she was right. He was dragged rudely from his musings as the leather strap bit accurately against his other nipple. He bit back a squeal of pain and stared helplessly up at her.

'You haven't thanked me yet,' Vanessa pointed out coolly.

'Thank you,' Russel gasped quickly.

'You really are enjoying this,' Vanessa remarked, seeming not to have heard him. She had her gaze fixed on his cock and was watching the trickle of pre-come glistening at the head. Moving with a swiftness Russel would not have believed, she brought the belt down sharply on his inner thigh. The pain was not as severe as it had been on his chest but the belt cut the air close enough to his balls to thoroughly unsettle him.

'Thank me again,' Vanessa snapped.

'Thank you,' Russel cried desperately. He could feel his climax nearing and found himself watching his cock as though it were not a part of his body. It certainly did not seem to be responding the way he believed it should. 'Thank you,' he cried again as another blow from the belt struck his inner thigh.

'Call me by my name,' Vanessa instructed curtly, aiming a blow at his stomach.

The tip of the strap was a whisper away from the head of his cock and Russel found himself struggling to avoid climax once again. 'Thank you, Vanessa,' he hissed between clenched teeth. 'Thank –'

She cut his words off with two short blows: one for each nipple. Speaking above Russel's howl of pain she told him, 'You will refer to me as Miss Byrne from now on, do you understand?'

'Thank you, Miss Byrne,' Russel whispered quickly. 'Thank you, Miss Byrne.'

She knelt down and pressed her mouth tenderly against his. Moving her mouth away from his face, she began to deliver soft kisses to his neck, then his chest. As she moved down his body with her lips, she deliberately rubbed her bare breasts lightly over his cock. It was a carefully calculated move and Vanessa was not surprised by the rhythmic pulse of Russel's ejaculation. His seed shot forcefully from the tip of his cock, spraying her tits and chest with a creamy white shower.

Russel heard himself groan, unsure whether it was a sound caused by pleasure or shame. His eyes had squeezed tightly closed when he climaxed and when he opened them he found himself staring at Vanessa's tits.

White rivulets of his jism daubed her breasts and even covered one nipple. In spite of having just climaxed, Russel still felt excited by the image.

'Lick me clean,' she instructed him sharply.

He obeyed instantly, moving his mouth and tongue adroitly over one glistening orb, then the other. The taste of his own fluid was not as satisfying as Vanessa's sex juice had been but he was enjoying the contact with her body and he swallowed the semen greedily.

'Good boy,' Vanessa said slowly. 'Good slave,' she added, with a wry smile. She reached behind Russel and unfastened his hands. 'I suppose this will come as a bit of a blow after that little experience,' she said softly.

'But, as of five o'clock today, you no longer work for this company.'

Russel stared at her, uncomprehending. 'I'm fired?' he asked in disbelief.

Vanessa smiled and shook her head. 'Consider this as a career move,' she said carefully. She went to her desk and, as she retrieved a handful of clothes, she picked up a business card and passed it to Russel.

'The Pentagon Agency?' he said, curiously, reading the company's name from the card. 'Who are they? How do they fit in with things?'

Vanessa smiled at him as she began to fasten her blouse. 'Give them a call on Monday morning and say I recommended you. They recruit temps,' she added blithely, 'and you're just the sort of person they can make best use of.'

'What if I don't call them?' Russel asked, releasing his trousers from beneath the chair.

She leant over him and traced a finger down his chest, towards his groin. 'If you don't call them,' she explained, 'then you'll never again know the pleasure of being my slave.' She smiled at his frown of disapproval. 'If you do call them,' she continued, 'then, once they've trained you properly, I will happily re-employ you.'

'Like we just did?' he asked eagerly.

Vanessa laughed delightedly at his enthusiasm. 'Like we just did, and a whole lot more,' she said. 'A whole lot more.'

Three

'NO! I've already told you. I won't do it,' Kelly said adamantly. She stared defiantly at Helen and found her resolution matched in the blonde's fierce expression.

Helen's angry glare was intimidating to say the least. 'You'll hide it,' she hissed passionately. 'You'll hide it, or I'll make you sorry you ever met me.'

'I'm already sorry about that,' Kelly retorted.

Five minutes earlier she had been lying quietly on her bed. The hostel had provided her with a clean single room that was just large enough to house a single bed, a small hand basin and a few other items of necessary bedroom furniture. As a welcoming present to the hostel, Kelly had been given a bottle of wine. It stood alone and unwanted on the dressing table.

Her thoughts were filled with the contrast between this new lifestyle and her former life as a housewife. She still felt unable to decide whether fate had granted her a kind hand or a cruel one. There were pros and cons for both sides and she was in the process of mentally evaluating these when Helen barged rudely into the room. She entered so quickly Kelly thought she was being pursued by the resident security staff.

During her first few days at the agency, Kelly had spent her time doing two things. Primarily she had been learning the rules that governed the hostel. There were so many restrictions and regulations Kelly had felt her head begin to spin as she tried to digest them all.

Breakfast was at 7.00 a.m., lunch at noon and dinner at 6.00 p.m. All meals were in the main dining hall and tardiness was considered a punishable misdemeanour. Senior staff had the authority to discipline trainees whenever, and however, they saw fit. Tuition was compulsory and accompanied by frequent, rigorous testing. Poor results and lack of subject comprehension, were both regarded as punishable offences. So far, Kelly had managed to conform to the rules of the hostel without suffering the embarrassment of a chastisement. She had witnessed several punishments and made a personal vow that she would avoid such humiliation at all costs.

The other thing Kelly had been doing in her first few days had more to do with self-preservation. She had made a point of avoiding Helen. After their first encounter, Kelly realised Helen was simply trouble waiting to happen. She still remembered the venom in the blonde's ferocious stare as she had fled the waiting room on that very first day. Whilst she was not certain what offence she had committed, Kelly did not doubt that the blonde would seek retribution if the opportunity occurred.

Now, with Helen standing angrily before her, Kelly wondered if the woman was plotting revenge.

Helen reached out swiftly and caught Kelly's wrist. Before Kelly knew what was happening she felt something small and cold being pushed into her hand.

Helen pressed her face close to Kelly's and smiled darkly. 'Mistress Stacey is looking for me right now. She knows I've got this,' she told Kelly quickly. 'Hide it for me, or I'll tell her that you took it.'

Kelly stared in disbelief. 'You bitch!' she gasped breathlessly.

Helen's grin was unperturbed by the insult. She glanced at Kelly's hand and noticed the wedding ring that she wore. 'Have you got a husband? Why aren't you with him, instead of being in this place?'

48

Kelly glared at her. 'I don't have a husband,' she said stiffly. 'And I don't want to talk about him.'

'Did he beat you?' Helen asked eagerly. 'Do you think he'll come here looking for you?'

He didn't beat me, Kelly thought miserably. In the last years of our marriage he didn't even touch me. It seemed, she thought wistfully, as though her husband had put her high on a pedestal. After their marriage, Kelly believed he had forgotten she was up there. By the time she left him, it had been a marriage in name only. She stared sullenly at Helen, knowing that she could never confide any of this to the blonde.

'Do you think he'll come looking for you?' Helen asked curiously.

Kelly frowned. It was a thought that had not occurred to her before. Her husband had never been aggressive towards her but she knew he was blessed with a ruthless nature. He had forged his own business empire single-handedly and such achievements did not come lightly. They particularly did not come to the type of man who just allowed his wife to walk out on him.

'Well?' Helen persisted. 'Do you think he'll come looking for you?'

'I've told you,' Kelly snapped. 'I don't have a husband and I don't want to talk about him.'

Helen smiled cruelly. 'Good. That means you're here and you're all on your own. I could hurt you in a lot of ways if I wanted to,' she said coldly. 'I have dozens of friends in this place and if I told them what a pervert you were they could make your life hell.'

'Pervert?' Kelly frowned. 'What the hell are you talking about? I'm not a pervert.'

Helen's face twisted into a doubting expression. 'Really? I saw the way you were watching when that bitch Stacey body-searched me.'

Kelly began to blush as the memory of that scene returned. She could remember the deep arousal she had

49

experienced and the longing it had inspired. 'I didn't want to watch,' she said, aware that her cheeks were burning furiously. 'It just happened in front of me. I didn't have an option.'

'You got off on it though, didn't you?' Helen observed, a wicked light glimmering in her eyes. 'It turned you on, didn't it?'

Shrugging, and trying to look nonchalant in spite of her bright-red face, Kelly said quietly, 'Perhaps I did get off on it. Perhaps it did turn me on. So what?'

'Pervert!' Helen exclaimed, laughing nastily. She still held Kelly's hand with both of hers. One hand held Kelly's wrist, the other tried to squeeze her fingers closed around the metal object in her palm. Moving closer, Helen rubbed her breast suggestively against Kelly's arm. Her mood seemed to change in an instant. The taunting expression vanished from her eyes. It was replaced with a look of amorous guile. The tone of her voice altered from being harsh and threatening to a sultry sweet whisper of concern. 'Then again, perhaps you're not a pervert. Perhaps you wanted to do more than just watch?' she suggested in a soft, husky breath. 'Perhaps you wanted to make love with me?'

Kelly felt dizzy with the heat of this unwanted excitement. On her first day she had thought Helen was uncommonly attractive and she knew that her arousal had not just been caused by the highly charged eroticism of the moment. Aside from her beauty, there was something appealing about the combination of arrogance and vulnerability she embodied. Despite the unpleasant side of Helen's personality, Kelly felt a reluctant wave of desire for her.

Helen continued to rub her breast against Kelly's arm, causing a friction that was so exciting it was almost unbearable. 'It's not perverted to want to make love with another woman,' Helen whispered softly in Kelly's ear. The breath from her words tickled the sensitive flesh of Kelly's earlobe. 'I mean, I think that you are a very attractive woman. Very desirable,' she went on, keeping her voice in the same low, sultry tone. 'I could want to make love with you,' she confessed.

Kelly turned to face Helen, surprised by this unexpected admission. She saw a faint smile twisting the corners of the blonde's mouth. Her lips were broad and sensual, painted with a dark-pink lipstick that increased Kelly's arousal. As she looked at those lips, she realised they were close enough to kiss. She gazed into the cerulean depths of Helen's eyes. Cynically, she wondered if this was another aspect of the blonde's scheme to get her to hide the stolen property. She was a breath away from kissing Helen's lips, overwhelmed by the impulsive desire to find out exactly how they tasted.

'Hide that brooch for me,' Helen whispered sweetly. 'Then you and I can become better acquainted.' She smiled into Kelly's sudden frown of despair. 'I meant what I said before. I'll say you got me to steal it if you don't hide it.'

Kelly glanced at the small golden brooch in her hand. She was confused by the whirlpool of emotions that swirled inside her. It was hard to believe Helen could be so base and manipulative. Kelly had never encountered anyone so calculating before and she felt unsure of how to respond. She did not doubt the brooch was stolen and she knew there would be repercussions if she was caught with it. Similarly she knew there would be repercussions if she did not do as Helen asked. Angrily, she stuffed the jewellery into the top drawer of her dressing table, placing a couple of pairs of knickers over the top to hide it. She slammed the drawer closed when she had finished.

'It's not stolen,' Helen said, placing a friendly arm on Kelly's shoulder. 'I found it in the hall. That's all. I just know what people will think if they find it on me.'

She stroked her hand coaxingly down Kelly's arm, a winning smile on her lips.

Kelly moved abruptly away, making no attempt to conceal her annoyance. 'I don't care what it is,' she said sharply. 'But can we agree that we're quits after this? I don't owe you and you don't owe me?'

Helen smiled uncertainly. She seemed genuinely amazed by Kelly's anger and unable to reconcile it with her own manipulative actions. 'There's no need to take that attitude,' she snapped haughtily. 'I thought you and I were going to . . .'

'You thought wrong,' Kelly declared. 'Your stuff is hidden and when you want it back you can have it but, I promise you now, I won't be helping you like this again.'

Leaning close to her, Helen pushed her mouth near to Kelly's. 'What about our making love?'

'Never,' Kelly said tersely.

Helen smiled. 'Never say never,' she said knowingly. With a sudden lunge, she leant forward and placed a kiss on Kelly's mouth.

The action was so sudden and unexpected Kelly could do nothing but allow it to happen. Helen's tongue began to explore her mouth and she was thrilled by the touch of her hands as they carefully stroked her arms, shoulders and neck. The intimacy was more intense than anything she had ever experienced before and, when the kiss broke, Kelly was left feeling short of breath and bewildered.

'Still say never?' Helen asked coolly.

Kelly felt her lower lip tremble as she struggled to get her chaotic thoughts in order. 'Never,' she replied. There was a note of determination in her voice that sounded far more convincing than it felt. She saw a hesitant frown in Helen's eyes and found it comforting to think she had unsettled the blonde a little. 'Never,' she repeated.

'What the hell is going on in here?'

Helen and Kelly turned to face the open doorway, staring into the thunderous expression on Mistress Stacey's face. She stormed into the room, slamming the door heavily behind her.

'I asked a question,' she growled, bearing down on the two trainees. 'And I expect an answer. What the hell is going on in here?'

'Nothing,' Helen said quickly. Her voice was little more than a meek murmur. She glanced nervously at the dressing-table drawer, then warily back at the mistress.

Mistress Stacey appeared not to notice. She turned her questioning glare on to Kelly. 'Nothing?' she asked sharply.

Kelly nodded, hating herself for lying and hating Helen for having put her in this situation. 'That's right, Mistress Stacey,' she said calmly. 'There's nothing going on.'

Mistress Stacey nodded, not bothering to hide the expression of disbelief that distorted her features. 'Nothing going on,' she repeated slowly. 'So why are you two here, together, if there's nothing going on?'

'If you must know,' Helen said with a heavy sigh, 'Kelly and I are lovers.'

Kelly graced Helen with a shocked expression that was hidden from Mistress Stacey.

'Lovers?' Stacey repeated. She glanced doubtfully at Helen, then Kelly. A sceptical smile began to twist her lips.

As if to prove she was telling the truth, Helen put her arm protectively around Kelly's shoulder and snuggled against her intimately. 'Yes,' she said with renewed force. 'Kelly and I are lovers.'

Kelly allowed Helen's arm to stay where it was, fearful of the punishment she would receive if Mistress Stacey discovered she had been lying. She could feel herself stiffening beneath Helen's touch. It was difficult but she tried to relax and appear comfortable with her lover.

'Is that true?' Stacey asked Kelly. She stared directly at her as she spoke.

It was a forceful stare that was intimidating in the extreme. Mistress Stacey had a way of studying the trainees with a knowing look in her eyes. It gave the impression that she knew exactly what they were thinking.

Lost in the impenetrable dark depths of Stacey's brown eyes, Kelly resisted the urge to confess everything to the woman. She had already lied by saying that nothing untoward was going on in the room. In her own mind, Kelly knew that Mistress Stacey would eagerly punish her for such a lie. Unhappily, Kelly realised her only hope of escaping punishment was to support the tale Helen was telling.

'Yes,' she said softly. 'It's true.'

Stacey nodded solemnly. She did not look as though she believed the pair but for the moment she was prepared to continue with the charade. 'Do you know the hostel's policy on cohabitation between trainees, Helen?' she asked quietly.

'Relationships between male and female trainees will not be tolerated,' Helen replied quickly.

Stacey's smile was a cruel one. 'You learnt that little lesson well, didn't you?' she noted wryly.

Helen blushed, recalling a previous incident that had incurred the wrath of Mistress Stacey. Her lower lip trembled as she searched for a suitable response.

Stacey continued before the blonde could think of a reply. 'Well done for remembering that,' she told her. 'But as I can see neither you nor Kelly are male, I wonder if you'd remind me of the hostel's policy on the cohabitation of female trainees.'

Kelly frowned, sensing a tension in the room that

almost crackled with the electric charge of sexual anticipation. She did not know where the conversation was leading but she felt sure she was not going to like the end result. A flutter of butterflies erupted in the pit of her stomach.

'Female cohabitation is not condoned,' Helen said mechanically. 'But it is tolerated, subject to the discretion and approval of a senior member of staff.'

Stacey smiled confidently. 'Exactly,' she said, with meaning.

Kelly glanced warily at Helen, then at Stacey. 'I don't understand. What are you saying?'

Stacey's cruel smile broadened. 'I want to see if your relationship meets with my approval,' she explained. 'You tell me you're lovers. I'm not sure I believe it. I want you to prove it to me. Make love, now, whilst I watch.'

Kelly swallowed nervously. 'Now?' she repeated dumbly.

'Now,' Mistress Stacey told her forcefully.

Kelly turned to Helen, a look of barely concealed terror straining her features. She was shocked, but not surprised, to see a satisfied smile on Helen's lips. 'I told you never to say never,' her smile sang triumphantly. Kelly could feel her heart sinking in her chest.

'Come on, darling,' Helen said seductively. She allowed her arm to drop from Kelly's shoulder to her waist. 'We were about to settle down for the night anyway,' she said, directing her words somewhere between Kelly and Stacey. 'I'm not bothered if we have an audience, are you?' She smiled gleefully into Kelly's face, unperturbed by the passionate vehemence in the redhead's eyes.

'Of course not,' Kelly replied numbly. She could see no way out of the situation without having to endure one of Mistress Stacey's punishments. Considering the amount of lying she had done, Kelly doubted the mistress would show any leniency. Painfully aware of this, Kelly realised that her only option was to continue with Helen's charade. A single thought kept occurring to her over and over again: I'm about to make love with a woman. I'm about to make love with a woman and there's no way to avoid it. Her heart began to beat quickly with nervous trepidation.

The wave of panic disappeared when Helen took Kelly in her arms and kissed her. Her feelings of annoyance and anger evaporated as she remembered the arousal Helen had inspired. Helen's tongue eagerly explored Kelly's mouth. Her hands stroked the cool sensitive flesh at the nape of Kelly's neck before moving under her chin and cupping her face.

Hesitantly at first, then with more urgency, Kelly began to respond to Helen's touch. She did not simply accept Helen's passionate kisses. After a moment, Kelly began to return them. She had never enjoyed kissing throughout her marriage and eventually things had reached a state where it did not matter. Now, she put her heart and soul into the exchange, using her tongue and lips to explore Helen's mouth with an avaricious appetite. Her hands caressed Helen's face, then moved away, down towards her breasts. Within moments of the first kiss, she found herself stroking the soft, yielding orbs of Helen's tits.

'Please, ladies.' Mistress Stacey's commanding voice was harsh enough to stop them both.

They turned to face her uncertainly.

'Feel free to make use of the bed,' Mistress Stacey said kindly. She moved towards Kelly's dressing table and turned the chair around so it was facing the bed. She reached for the unwanted bottle of wine that sat on the dressing table, opened the top and sniffed it discriminatingly. 'I'll make myself comfortable here,' she said decisively, taking a swig from the bottle. 'You two carry on and enjoy one another,' she added, with a meaningful glance directed at Kelly.

'Thank you, mistress,' Helen said promptly. With a wicked grin, she turned to face Kelly and began to kiss her once again. They made their way clumsily to the bed, neither wanting to break the passionate exchange between their lips. Kelly stroked her hands eagerly over Helen's body, caressing each curve and contour. Distantly she realised the blonde was working on the buttons of her blouse. The garment was quickly unfastened and Helen made short work of the button and zip on her skirt. As they lay down on the bed together, Kelly realised she was almost naked. The sensation of Helen's hands, touching her thighs and cupping her breasts, was intoxicating. Kelly felt her nipples hardening furiously as the woman teased her flesh through the fabric of her bra. When Helen actually pressed her mouth against the orb and began to stimulate the nipple with her tongue, Kelly shuddered with pleasure.

Helen used her mouth first on one breast, then the other, pausing between each action to kiss Kelly warmly on the mouth. Her hands were never idle, delighting in the unexplored curves and contours of the redhead's body. She stroked her fingers softly around Kelly's waist before moving her hands slowly across the flat expanse of her stomach. The tips of her fingers brushed against the thin band of elastic at the top of Kelly's knickers.

Kelly sighed happily. Her fears and inhibitions were forgotten as she allowed herself to enjoy the pleasure that came from Helen's touch. Each careful caress of the blonde's hands transported her ever closer to a level of happiness she had never previously encountered. Lost in a world of ecstatic euphoria, Kelly barely noticed when Helen began to ease the thin cotton panties from her hips. She opened her eyes and smiled easily at her.

Helen returned the smile and pressed a kiss against Kelly's neck. In a discreet whisper, not intended for Mistress Stacey to hear, she said, 'I told you never to say never.'

Kelly laughed indulgently and pressed her own mouth against Helen's neck. As she kissed her softly, she replied in the same soft, prudent tone of voice, 'Don't gloat, just carry on doing what you're doing.'

Helen needed no further encouragement and moved her head away, turning her attention back to the redhead's breasts.

Kelly cast a wary glance in the direction of Mistress Stacey and was surprised when the woman winked knowingly at her. As Kelly watched, the mistress took a generous swig from the wine bottle. She wiped her lips dry with her wrist before turning her attention back to the show that the two trainees were providing. Stacey's legs were parted as she sat on the chair and Kelly realised the woman's skirt was raised sufficiently to show the pale, silky flesh of her thighs. The black triangle of her pants was clearly visible from Kelly's perspective and she watched as the mistress placed a purposeful finger to the gusset. The finger stroked gently along the fabric, outlining the shape of her pouting pussy lips.

Kelly sighed softly. She could have watched Mistress Stacey all evening, mesmerised by the woman's commanding beauty and cool air of detachment. She saw a second finger join the first and realised the mistress was using more pressure against herself. Glancing nervously into the woman's eyes, Kelly was shocked to see the mistress smiling broadly down at her. There was something predatory in Mistress Stacey's smile that made Kelly feel helpless and vulnerable. The sensation was arousing enough to unsettle her.

Kelly felt the front-clasp of her bra being released and turned her attention back to Helen.

The blonde was a capable lover and seemed determined to please Kelly. She had been rubbing her hands and lips over Kelly's body, slowly exciting the half-naked woman beneath her. Now it seemed that she wanted to do more.

Kelly's breasts spilled from their confines and she felt Helen's cool breath against them. The feeling was exhilarating and Kelly breathed a soft sigh of delight. The sound turned into a groan of pleasure when Helen's tongue flicked across her nipple. Unconsciously, she bucked her hips forward.

Helen shifted position on the bed. Kelly realised she was moving her mouth slowly down from her breasts. Using a series of soft, tender kisses, her lips travelled across Kelly's stomach and then lower. The notion of what she was about to experience was delightfully unsettling and Kelly savoured the moment with relish. She shivered when she felt Helen's warm breath on the hot flesh of her sex.

Helen pressed her nose into the fiery red flames of Kelly's pubic triangle. Gently, she nuzzled the sensitive flesh above her labia.

Kelly moaned excitedly. Her arousal increased when she felt the nose move further downwards and brush lightly against the moist folds of pink flesh. Helen's tongue ran slowly over the pouting lips, sending a shiver of joy through Kelly's body. The inner walls of her vagina began to contract hungrily, as though they were anticipating the new and unimagined treat they were about to enjoy. Helen moved her tongue deliberately up and down the outer lips of Kelly's pussy, inspiring wave after wave of enjoyment. Kelly shivered blissfully and released a contented sigh. The sigh became a moan of approval when Helen's tongue parted the lips and began to probe inside her. The tip of her tongue brushed against Kelly's clitoris. In a rush of unexpected delight, Kelly groaned with orgasmic elation.

'My turn,' Helen said pragmatically. She moved her legs carefully over Kelly's head, positioning herself so her pussy hovered above the redhead's face.

Kelly glanced uncertainly at the view between Helen's legs, mindful of Mistress Stacey's carefully watching eyes. Helen still wore her skirt but it was a short one and in this position it did not conceal anything. Kelly's face was mere millimetres away from the glorious haven of Helen's bare hole.

Shifting forward, she placed a hand on either side of Helen's buttocks and stroked the silky smooth flesh of her arse tenderly. As her hands continued to stimulate Helen's rear, Kelly saw the woman's labia slowly unfold. The lips of her sex were wet with arousal and Kelly inhaled deeply, smelling the sweet musky scent of the blonde's desire. All her inhibitions were now behind her and she felt driven by a single need. Not hesitating or even contemplating what she was about to do, Kelly pushed her mouth against Helen's wetness. Her mouth was suddenly full with the sweet taste of Helen's excitement. She drew her tongue carefully up and down the soft pink lips, savouring every sensation. The succulent sweet taste was incredible. The heady scent was intoxicating and the feeling of her tongue against the woman's sex was unbelievable. Unable to resist the temptation, she buried her tongue deep inside Helen's wetness. Kelly was not sure if she was doing it for Helen's pleasure, or her own craving to sample the woman's love juice. Regardless of her motives, the effects were the same.

Helen moaned softly in appreciation. Her face was still buried between Kelly's legs. Her tongue slid eagerly over the sensitive flesh she found there. Using her fingers to hold the lips apart, Helen rubbed her tongue deliberately over the exposed hood of Kelly's clitoris.

Trying not to think of the myriad prickles of pleasure exploding between her legs, Kelly concentrated her efforts on pleasing Helen. It seemed like the most natural thing in the world to nuzzle lovingly at Helen's hole and taste the sweet honey-like nectar of her sex. Her tongue probed inside and Kelly was delighted by the sensation of Helen's pussy muscles closing excitedly around her. She moved her hands so that they held Helen's legs and pulled the blonde towards her as she pushed her tongue deeper inside.

Helen squealed excitedly.

With her tongue forcing its way further up Helen's hole, Kelly felt the ecstatic shuddering of the blonde's body. Beneath Kelly's fingers, the muscles in Helen's legs trembled excitedly. She could feel the tingle of rapture that shimmered through the walls of Helen's pussy. Happily, Kelly realised she had caused the blonde's orgasm. When she tasted the honey-rich succulence of the woman's climax, Kelly realised she was not just sharing Helen's orgasm; she was enjoying another one of her own.

Greedily she drank Helen's creamy pussy-honey. She savoured the taste, indulgently licking the labia clean of every last drop. Breathless, she moved her face away from Helen's sex and turned to glance at Mistress Stacey. Kelly saw that, whilst her attention had been devoted to Helen, the mistress had moved her chair closer.

Again, she graced Kelly with a knowing wink, before drinking from the open bottle of wine. Kelly smiled quietly in reply, licking her lips unconsciously. She watched as Mistress Stacey moved the bottle down between her legs and stroked the neck of the bottle against her sex. The woman had moved forward on her chair and removed the black panties she wore. Kelly saw the tip of the bottle being pressed deliberately against the willing swell of the mistress's hole and she watched with voyeuristic fascination.

With her gaze locked on Kelly's, Mistress Stacey pushed the neck of the bottle into the welcoming depths of her tight pussy. She allowed herself a grim smile of satisfaction as it entered. Kelly continued to watch as Stacey pushed the bottle deeper, until it had accepted the entire neck. The lips of her vagina were spread wide over the body of the bottle and Kelly wondered incredulously how she managed to accept so much. As Stacey withdrew the bottle, Kelly saw the glass was glistening with pussy juice and she caught herself wondering how sweet that would taste.

Slowly, Mistress Stacey pushed the bottle back inside herself, then pulled it out. Her broad smile widened with mounting pleasure. She continued to frig herself as Kelly watched, employing the bottle like an over-sized dildo. When she tensed her legs muscles around the legs of the chair, Kelly realised the mistress was close to orgasm. Her smile was strained to a mask of agonised pleasure and a growl of deep-rooted satisfaction whispered from her lips. Tilting the base of the bottle forwards, she moaned loudly as the heady delights of her orgasm washed over her.

Seeing the flow of wine pour from between Mistress Stacey's legs, Kelly found her arousal reaching new heights. Again, Kelly found herself wondering how it would taste. It was an exciting thought. She watched Mistress Stacey lift the wine bottle to her lips and, after salaciously licking her own cream from the rim of the bottle, she drank another mouthful of wine.

Kelly watched and shivered with anticipation. She could have enjoyed watching Mistress Stacey all evening. She had never felt happier than she felt now. The mistress was gracing her with a kindly smile and Helen was carefully tonguing her vagina.

With her excitement mounting, Helen pushed herself into Kelly's face, forcing the redhead to enjoy the scent and taste of her sex.

Revelling in the heady aroma of the blonde's arousal, Kelly lapped eagerly at the pink folds of her pussy lips. Helen's fingers continued to hold her pussy lips apart as she ran her tongue over and around Kelly's pearl of pleasure. Occasionally she teased the nub of the clitoris with the tip of her finger whilst her mouth worked on the ultra-sensitive flesh of Kelly's inner lips. With her free hand, she began to tease Kelly's labia with the tips of her fingers. Wet with excitement, Kelly's hole was perfectly lubricated. When Helen pressed her fingers against the moist flesh, they slid easily into the redhead's eager pussy.

Kelly gasped breathlessly as she felt herself being penetrated. It was difficult to believe that sex could be this good. Kelly could feel three digits probing her hole as her lover skilfully tried to please her. The hand moved deep inside her, then pulled out, leaving Kelly with an aching emptiness that she longed to have filled.

After stroking the pads of her fingers around the wet entrance to Kelly's hole, Helen obligingly slid them back into the warm velvety depths of her pussy. Repeatedly she pushed her fingers deep inside then pulled them out again. With every withdrawal, she traced soft circles over the tender flesh of Kelly's inner lips.

Kelly's breathing deepened to a crescendo of mounting pleasure and Helen pushed her mouth on to the febrile nub of her clitoris. Her tongue darted over the tiny mound of flesh, stimulating wave after wave of furious delight through Kelly's body.

The redhead shrieked happily as a third orgasm rushed through her. Pressing her face delightedly between Helen's legs, she licked and nuzzled greedily. Her probing tongue delved deep between the soft folds of flesh and she lapped at the blonde's pussy juice. Her tongue pushed ever deeper into Helen's hole and she pressed her mouth against the swell of the blonde's sex. Helen screamed ecstatically as the climax washed over her.

Rolling to one side, Helen fell from Kelly's body and collapsed on to her back. She smiled fondly at the redhead.

Happier than she would have believed possible, Kelly could not stop herself from returning the grin. As they lay next to one another, Kelly could not stop her hand from tenderly stroking the soft flesh at the top of Helen's legs. She was thrilled, and pleasantly touched, when she felt Helen returning the caress.

'That looked like fun, ladies,' Mistress Stacey said kindly.

Kelly looked up and smiled at her. 'It was,' she agreed. She noticed Helen nodding agreement and grinned at her warmly.

'You must be ready for a drink now,' Mistress Stacey went on. 'Here, Helen, you can drink first.' Her instruction given, Stacey bucked her hips forward on the chair and inserted the tip of the wine bottle into her moist depths. Tilting the base upward, she poured part of the wine bottle's contents inside herself.

Helen climbed swiftly from the bed and knelt submissively before the mistress. Stacey slowly removed the bottle from between her legs and allowed the blonde to put her mouth there. Kelly watched as Helen drank greedily from Stacey's hole.

Her tongue pushed inside the woman and a mixture of wine and pussy juice poured over Helen's face. Unconsciously displaying her innate dominance, Stacey grabbed a handful of Helen's blonde curls and held her head firmly in position. Glancing at Kelly, Stacey offered her the wine bottle.

'Drink,' she commanded softly.

Eagerly, Kelly accepted the wine. She closed her eyes and inhaled the open top of the bottle, delighting in the fruity mixture of aromas that greeted her nose. The musky scent of Mistress Stacey's arousal mingled with the sweet aromatic fragrance of the wine. Hesitantly, she traced her tongue around the rim of the bottle, savouring the combination of flavours with a sly smile. She saw Stacey was watching her as she did this and Kelly tried to read the curious expression that glinted in her eyes.

Helen continued lapping at Stacey's hole, slurping noisily at her juices.

Kelly swigged from the bottle, mesmerised by the scene. She envied Helen the good fortune of being used in such a way and wished she was in her position. The thought stirred a longing inside her that quickly intensified into a burning desire. As these thoughts tumbled through her mind, she sniffed the top of the wine bottle and filled her nostrils with the scent of Stacey's pussy juice.

'Enough,' Stacey said abruptly. She pushed Helen roughly away.

The blonde released a small gasp of pain as her hair was unexpectedly tugged. Aware of her position, she moved away quickly, just as Stacey demanded. Placing herself on the bed, next to Kelly, Helen took the wine bottle and drank slowly from it.

'Well, you've proved to me that you are lovers,' Stacey said, leaning easily back in her chair. 'So I suppose I owe you both an apology for doubting you,' she went on.

Helen shifted uneasily on the bed, wary of the mistress's pliant mood. 'There's no apology necessary, Mistress Stacey,' she said, speaking quickly and quietly. 'Like I told you, we were about to settle down for the evening anyway. Neither of us minded having an audience, did we?' she asked, turning to Kelly for confirmation of this fact.

Surprised by Helen's unease, Kelly nodded confirmation. 'Of course we didn't mind. It was –'

She didn't get to finish her sentence.

Mistress Stacey broke in on her words sharply. 'Regardless,' she snapped. 'Your demonstration helped to clear up my misunderstanding and at least, if I don't apologise, then I should thank you for being so cooperative.' She smiled broadly at the two women and reached towards Kelly's dressing table. She calmly pulled the top drawer open and removed the hidden brooch that Kelly had secreted there. 'And whilst you're both being so cooperative, I wonder if either of you could tell me what this is doing here?'

Helen and Kelly exchanged a glance. Kelly felt her heart sink and wondered miserably what punishment she could expect. She had only gone through with the charade of being Helen's lover to avoid this confrontation. Now she saw she had gone through all of that and she was still going to be punished.

'Kelly!' Helen gasped. Speaking in a theatrical tone she said, 'How could you steal Mistress Stacey's brooch like that? Don't you know that stealing isn't just wrong: it's a punishable offence?'

Kelly stared miserably at the blonde, knowing that Helen was already building a barrier of protective lies for herself. It was hard to believe they had just shared so much pleasure and intimacy with one another. She studied the blonde's face, stunned by her hypocrisy.

'I haven't stolen anything,' she said softly.

Helen snorted in mock disbelief. 'It was found in your drawer!'

Kelly rubbed a nervous hand through her hair. She shook her head unhappily and glared at Helen. There was a dangerous light sparkling in the blonde's eyes and Kelly remembered her earlier threats of retribution.

Turning to Stacey, she nodded as though she were agreeing with some unspoken statement. 'Helen's right,' she whispered meekly. 'I stole the brooch. I took it, so I'm the one you should punish.'

Stacey raised her eyebrows doubtfully. 'You stole it?' A cynical smile played on her lips.

Kelly spat a vehement glare at Helen, then turned unhappily to Mistress Stacey. She nodded simply. 'That's right.'

Helen was shaking her head in a gesture of disgust, making tut-tutting noises at the back of her throat. 'I'm

66

surprised at you, Kelly,' she said piously. 'I thought you would have known better.'

'Helen,' Stacey said quietly.

Helen glanced innocently at the mistress. Her eyes were wide with pantomime naivety. 'Yes, Mistress Stacey?' she asked sweetly.

'Are you saying that you know nothing about this item?' Stacey asked calmly.

Helen put a hand to her chest, as though she was deeply shocked by the suggestion. 'Me?' she declared indignantly. 'Of course I didn't know anything about it. I promised you last time I wouldn't be taking anything from anyone. I'm a reformed woman, Mistress Stacey. You do believe me, don't you?'

Stacey shook her head sadly. 'I'd like to believe you, Helen. I really would,' Stacey said softly. 'Come to think of it, if I hadn't heard your conversation with Kelly before I came in here, I probably would have believed you.'

All the colour drained from Helen's face in an instant.

'I was glancing through the open door,' Stacey began. 'That's how I knew where it was hidden. Now, are you going to take your punishment properly, or will you try and wriggle out of that too?'

'Not the black room,' Helen said. Her voice was close to panic. 'Please, Mistress Stacey, not the black room,' she moaned.

Stacey smiled tightly. 'No, Helen. I'm not responsible for the black room this week so I wouldn't be able to enjoy your chastisement if I sent you there.'

Helen stared unhappily at her. There was an undercurrent of malice in Mistress Stacey's voice that told Helen she was really in trouble this time. 'Please, mistress,' she begged. 'Don't. I'll . . .'

Stacey ignored her. Turning her attention to Kelly, she said crisply, 'I've been watching your performance since you arrived here. You're an exemplary trainee and you've excelled in all your duties so far.'

Kelly considered saying thank you for the complement but she realised this was not the proper time.

'So far, you've managed to avoid punishment, haven't
you?' Stacey remarked.

Helen nodded.

'Until now,' Stacey informed her.

The mistress's mood changed in an instant. Her
muted tone and considered manner disappeared in the
blink of an eye. 'Both of you,' she snapped crisply,
'kneel down on the floor. I want your lying, bare arses
high in the air. Now!'

Not daring to disobey, Helen and Kelly knelt down
on the floor side by side. Kelly was still naked after
making love, whilst Helen remained partially dressed in
her loose blouse and short skirt. They both pushed their
heads to the floor and thrust their backsides high in the
air, exactly as Mistress Stacey had commanded.

'Is this your hairbrush?' Stacey asked calmly. 'Or has
this been stolen too?'

Kelly glanced over her shoulder. She didn't need to
look to know which hairbrush Stacey was referring to.
The large firm brush with its sturdy metal spikes was the
only one she had brought with her. Wondering if
Mistress Stacey was considering her appearance before
she administered punishment, Kelly replied, 'Of course
it's mine, mistress.'

The sound of a hand smacking flesh made Kelly
wince. It was not until Helen whimpered with pain that
Kelly realised who Mistress Stacey had chosen to
chastise first. The second blow landed smartly on the
swell of her own buttock and Kelly bit back an
anguished cry. She could feel her face burning crimson
with shame as she finally realised the true meaning of
the word 'humiliation'.

Stacey's hand whistled through the air again and
Kelly heard a ferocious smack, followed by Helen's
pained cry of remorse. The fourth blow landed on

Kelly's other cheek, leaving a stinging imprint that burnt as fiercely as the first.

'Did you really think you could get away with lying to me?' Mistress Stacey asked. She delivered two sharp blows, one for each of the trainees. 'Do you think I'm that gullible?' she asked, before administering two more.

'You can consider this a first warning, Kelly,' Stacey said, smacking her hard on the arse three times in quick succession.

'And as for you, Helen, you can consider this a last warning.'

Kelly heard Stacey's hand connect with Helen's backside in a staccato beat that must have lasted for a dozen blows or more. Helen's groans of anguish became ever more pained with each blow.

'Do you think you've had enough punishment?' Stacey asked sharply.

'Yes, mistress,' Helen sobbed.

'Yes, mistress,' Kelly agreed eagerly.

Stacey barked a sound of dry, cruel laughter. 'Perhaps you do,' she said coldly. 'But I've barely begun yet.'

Knelt on the floor, Kelly felt Stacey place a hand on her behind. She flinched from the touch, having expected another blow. When she realised the hand was not hurting her, she relaxed a little. The mistress slowly caressed her sore buttocks. Her brusque fingers rubbed the tender flesh of Kelly's arse. Earlier it would have been a pleasant stimulation. Now Stacey's touch rekindled flames on the sore flesh.

Kelly moaned softly. Her slapped backside hurt badly but she found the sensation curiously exciting. Her moans increased when she felt the fingers enter her.

'You're loving this, aren't you?' Stacey observed. 'It's a wonder you haven't come yet,' she snorted, a note of contempt tainting her words.

Kelly took a breath, intending to deny there was any truth in Stacey's accusation. If she was still aroused, surely that was because of what they had been doing before. It could not have anything to do with being punished, she told herself. Desperately she wished she could believe the inner voice that told her this, but the words lacked substance. Admittedly she had been highly aroused by the lovemaking she and Helen had enjoyed, but already that was a fading memory. Being totally honest with herself, Kelly realised her pussy lips were quietly tingling with impending orgasm. She also realised that there was only one possible explanation. She was getting pleasure from the pain and humiliation that Mistress Stacey was administering.

'Look how horny your arsehole is,' Stacey remarked.

Before Kelly could stop her, she realised Stacey was thrusting something into the dark canal of her backside. It was too stiff and rigid to be a finger, Kelly thought, lost in a dizzy wave of euphoria. It could only be the handle of the hairbrush Stacey had mentioned earlier. Her suspicions were confirmed when she felt the brush's lower spikes pricking uncomfortably against the tender flesh around her buttocks. Stacey had jammed the whole length of the handle into her and she was still pushing it deeper inside.

Kelly gasped breathlessly, aware that she was close to climaxing. Tears of embarrassment streamed down her face as she felt the first rush of pleasure sweep through her. The combination of humiliation and arousal was totally unexpected and Kelly was shocked by the intensity of her orgasm. She felt the brush being pulled from her bumhole, and wondered distantly what Mistress Stacey intended to do next. When she felt the sting of pain that pelted her arse cheeks, she realised the mistress's intentions immediately.

Whilst the handle of the hairbrush had made a good makeshift phallus, the spiked end was a far more formidable tool. The teeth bit into the reddened flesh of her arse like a barb. Kelly was breathless with the first blow, unable to believe she had experienced such a punishment. When the second blow connected she shrieked loudly. The pain was so acute and severe, she could not believe her body's response to it. The tremendous tingling in her vagina increased enormously. Each blow Stacey delivered seemed to augment her excitement. With the fourth and fifth blow the stinging was unbearable. Kelly did not believe she could take any more of the punishment but she did not want it to stop. She felt so close to orgasm she wanted the mistress to continue and push her beyond the brink of ecstasy.

Unaware that she was being so obliging, Stacey brought the hairbrush down again and again. When the orgasm struck, Kelly was debilitated by its intensity. She released a furious scream, unaware that the sound had been building inside her. Her entire body seemed to throb with pleasure as the climax exploded between her legs again and again.

Stacey placed a hand on Kelly's head and grabbed a fistful of long red locks. Tugging Kelly up from her knees, she pressed her mouth close to the trainee's ear. 'Consider yourself lucky,' she whispered passionately. 'Your punishment ends here.'

Kelly gasped an apology, distantly aware of the burst of pain in her pulled hair. Her words rushed out in a hurried sob that was barely intelligible.

'Good,' Stacey said, apparently satisfied with this response. 'I don't expect to have to punish you again.'

Not daring to incur the mistress's wrath again, Kelly stood meekly and watched as Stacey punished Helen. The blonde received the same treatment Kelly had experienced. When it was finished she was snatched from the floor by her hair.

'One of these days, you're going to upset me when I'm on duty in the black room,' Stacey said with controlled force.

Helen's apologies spilled quickly from her lips.

Stacey cut them short with a brutal slap to her face. 'Go to my room and wait there, in the darkness,' Stacey hissed angrily. 'When I've finished with Kelly I'll be along to punish you properly.'

'Yes, Mistress Stacey,' Helen replied timidly. She fled from the room without another word.

Stacey turned to Kelly. Her mood seemed to have softened and she was no longer acting like an austere disciplinarian. Kelly could feel a warmth emanating from the woman. It was a warmth that she found disturbingly comfortable, considering the treatment she had received.

'Lying to a mistress is wrong,' Stacey told her, pressing her lips to Kelly's ear as she spoke. 'And being bullied by the likes of Helen is wrong,' she went on. 'You're a decent trainee and you could do well here, but you still have a lot to learn.'

Kelly nodded, ashamed by her own behaviour and embarrassed that these facts actually needed pointing out to her. She was poignantly aware of her own nudity and her dishevelled appearance after the beating. 'I'm sorry,' she began. 'I realise you're right.'

Stacey silenced Kelly's words with a kiss. It was a soft, tender exchange, surprising Kelly with its subtle intimacy.

'Don't be sorry,' Stacey told her quietly. 'Just climb back into bed, and allow me to show you the right way of doing things.'

Kelly studied the mistress uncertainly. 'You aren't going to punish me again, are you?' she asked warily.

Stacey smiled indulgently into her worried face, then kissed her again. 'Not tonight,' she assured her. 'You've had your punishment for this evening. Now it's time for us to become properly acquainted. There's still some wine left in that bottle and I know how badly you wanted to drink it from me.'

Kelly smiled hesitantly. A frown crossed her face and

72

she asked, 'What about Helen? Didn't you say you were going to go and punish her?'

Stacey smiled indulgently and placed another kiss on Kelly's lips. 'Don't you worry about Helen,' she said gently. 'She's enjoying her punishment right now.'

Kelly raised a curious eyebrow, wondering how Stacey could be punishing Helen whilst she was in a different room.

'Right now, Helen is sitting alone in the dark, in the corner of my bedroom,' Stacey explained. 'She's expecting me to walk through the door and punish her at any moment.' There was a wicked smile creasing Stacey's lips. 'She's an intelligent woman with an active imagination. She knows I have a wide variety of punishments and she'll spend every minute torturing herself trying to guess which one I'll use on her.'

'Are you allowed to do that?' Kelly asked doubtfully.

'I'm a mistress. Here at the hostel I can do whatever the hell I please. Cross me again,' Stacey warned Kelly slowly. 'And you'll find out just how bad that can be.'

She smiled, breaking the moment's unpleasantness. 'But right now,' she said softly, 'I'm not in the mood to be cruel.' She placed her hand on Kelly's breast and caressed the tender flesh lovingly. 'Get into bed, and let me show you my mood.'

Smiling expectantly, Kelly obeyed.

Four

It was the type of seedy pub that Jo knew only too well.

The juke box was screaming at a deafening volume, playing a thumping back-beat bereft of melody. A noisy crowd of men barracked the bar, calling to make themselves heard above the music and their colleagues. Distantly, somewhere beneath these cacophonous sounds, a fruit machine whirred and sang happily, clanging coins into a metal tray.

No wonder people get hangovers, Jo thought darkly. It's nothing to do with how much they drink. It's down to the noise of the bar that they're in. She sniffed unhappily as she considered this thought, then wished she hadn't. Like the noise, the smell of the bar was all-enveloping. The scent of stale beer and pungent spirits was so thoroughly soaked into the woodwork that the smell filled her nostrils with every inhalation.

She was not dressed as a single woman should have dressed to sit alone in such a bar. Her skirt was short enough to reveal the top of her black, seamed stockings and she made no move to conceal this fact. The long-lined jacket of her suit was almost modest, yet Jo wore it with enough of the buttons unfastened to reveal her ample cleavage. A close observer, and there had been a few already, would have quickly gleaned that, beneath the jacket, she was wearing no bra and no top.

'What's a nice girl like you doing in a place like this?'

Jo glanced up at the awkward young man leering over

her. His was the fourth enquiry she had received in the past ten minutes. Fortunately, she was used to handling such attention.

'I'm waiting for the doctor who looks after me,' Jo said slowly. 'He says I shouldn't talk to men. He says that's why I ended up in that place last time.'

The young man took an unconscious step backward. His lip quivered uncertainly as he quickly tried to think of a way out of the situation. He was saved by a taller man, clapping him warmly on the shoulder.

'Go have a pint, Bill. On my slate,' the taller man said warmly. 'I'll take care of the mental patient here.'

Jo smiled up at the newcomer. 'You got my message, Nick.'

He settled himself on the stool opposite her. 'I got your message,' he said. 'What do you want to know this time?'

Jo tried to look shocked by his suggestion. 'Can't a girl ask her old boyfriend for a drink without having an ulterior motive?' she asked innocently. She placed a hand on her chest, drawing his attention to the unfastened buttons on her jacket.

Nick grinned in spite of himself. 'Not if you're the girl, Valentine,' he told her. 'What do you want to know?'

Jo sighed. 'Why don't we play this game properly?' she suggested, placing a warm hand on his. 'How's your love life, Nick?'

'Non-existent,' he said sullenly. 'Is it a difficult case you've landed?'

Jo shook her head and smiled at him reluctantly. She knew Nick well enough not to push him. 'I want two things off you,' she said boldly. 'Number one, and most importantly, I want you to remind me how good a lover you are.'

Nick smiled, his brown eyes appraising her favourably. 'I think I can accommodate you there,' he said smugly. 'What's the other thing you want from me? Information?'

Jo grinned broadly. 'I've got a missing person at the moment. I could use a little professional help,' she said tactfully.

'I'm not helping you to hack into the PNC again,' Nick said firmly. 'If that was what you wanted then I've got to say no right now.'

'The Police National Computer can't help me this time,' Jo said quietly. She knew this was true because Stephanie had hacked into the PNC network that afternoon and instigated a joyless search for Mr Rogers's errant spouse. Aware that Nick would not want to know about such illegal activities, Jo decided to keep this to herself. 'What do you know about the Pentagon Temping Agency?' she asked suddenly.

Nick studied her warily. 'The Pentagon Temping Agency,' he repeated slowly. He studied her curious face with measured concern. 'Stay away from them, Jo,' he warned her softly. 'You're out of your depth. Drop the case and forget you ever heard of them.'

Jo smiled uncertainly. 'Are you kidding?'

She and Nick had been lovers for two years and, in that time, Jo had come to believe she knew him as well as she knew any person. Studying the earnest frown on his face and the solemn line of his jaw, she wondered if he had a talent for practical joking she had previously overlooked. 'Come on,' she insisted, playfully. 'Tell me you're kidding. What's the joke?'

Nick shook his head. 'No joke,' he said solemnly. 'They're dangerous, Jo. Dangerous and apparently untouchable.'

Jo considered him carefully and tried to weigh up her options. If she pushed Nick on this subject she knew, from past experience, he would simply refuse to acknowledge the topic and she would get no information from him at all. Playing her hand carefully, she said, 'I suppose that's good in a way. Less talk about business leaves more time for us to enjoy one another.'

His smile was distrustful. 'I thought you just screwed me so I'd pass on information.'

Jo laughed lightly. 'It's never been just for that', she said. 'Take me back to your place and let's see if the old magic is still there.'

Needing no more encouragement, Nick stood up and gallantly offered Jo his arm.

A winter's night had fallen over the car park, leaving a cool yet clement darkness outside the pub. Jo rubbed herself against Nick as they walked out of the building and was not surprised to feel a bulge inside his trousers. 'You want me already, don't you?' she observed.

'Of course I do,' Nick said gruffly. 'You're the horniest thing on two legs that I've ever known.'

'Do you want me now?' Jo asked, her eyes shining excitedly up at him.

'Of course I do,' Nick said, puzzled by her question. 'I just said so, didn't I?'

'I mean,' Jo repeated, rubbing her hand firmly over his straining length. 'Do you want me now?'

Nick finally understood the meaning of her question when Jo pushed him into a dark alley behind the pub. He was about to say something: a protest as to why respectable police officers could not indulge themselves with their occasional girlfriends in public places. His words were lost when Jo pressed her mouth over his. The kiss was a passionate one, her tongue exploring his mouth as her hands held him close to her. She pressed the flat of her belly against the swell of his stiff cock, relishing the urgency of his arousal. When their mouths parted, her eyes were shining with increased excitement.

'Do you know what I've missed these last few months?' she asked.

Nick shook his head. 'No. What?'

'This,' Jo said quietly.

Regardless of the cool evening and the danger of their being discovered, Jo knelt down in front of Nick, unzipping his pants as she went. Her fingers plunged through the fly of his trousers and she removed his rock-hard dick from his pants.

Feeling the cool night air on his hot length, Nick gasped quietly. He could not believe he was allowing Jo to do this to him. If his desire for her had not been so intense he would have tried to stop her. He bit back a cry of delight when he felt Jo's lips pressing warmly against the swollen head of his glans.

Enjoying the taste of his cock, Jo allowed her tongue to trace along the huge length of Nick's member. It was a gorgeous cock. She fondly remembered it as being one of the best she had ever sampled. Nick's foreskin rolled back beneath the teasing of her tongue, revealing a huge purple end that glistened slickly in the glow of the streetlamp. Greedily, Jo swallowed it. Her mouth encompassed the wide girth of Nick's member and she sucked softly on the flesh as she guided it slowly to the back of her throat.

Nick groaned quietly. His initial nervousness had dissipated. He held her head fondly in his hands as Jo moved her mouth back and forth along his length.

Jo continued to suck him, enjoying the salty taste of his cock as it filled her mouth. She had never been a great lover of blow jobs but Nick was an exception. His stiff dick felt perfect in her mouth and the pressure of his swollen end, pressing against the back of her throat, always brought her close to the brink of orgasm. She squeezed the tip of his penis between her tongue and her palate, aware that he was pressing hard into her mouth as she did it.

Conversation drifted past them in a wordless drone. People entered and left the pub beside them, oblivious to their presence. Jo continued relentlessly. She noted a stiffening in Nick's cock when the sounds came too

78

close. Shrewdly, she realised his arousal was heightened by the fear of discovery. She continued to suck on him and tease his length with her tongue as she unfastened his belt. He only realised what she was doing when Jo began to pull his trousers down.

'Jo!' he exclaimed urgently. 'What the –?'

'I want to play with your balls,' she told him petulantly. To prove this was true, she began kneading his plums gently in one cool hand. Her fingers stroked through the downy hairs of his balls and she cupped his package appreciatively in her fingers. He was obviously enjoying her teasing, she realised, and it came as no surprise when she saw how close he was to ejaculating. His balls were a tight pre-climax bundle. She squeezed them softly in her palm, rolling the testicles together with a measured degree of care. It was a movement meticulously intended to bring him to the point. Her lips stroked his length and she showered it with tiny kisses. Each kiss caused Nick's entire body to stiffen tensely.

He's fighting it, Jo thought incredulously. He's on the brink of coming, and he's fighting it, she told herself. She rubbed her tongue over the end of his cock and lapped up the pearl of pre-come that had grown there. The sweetly salty taste of his juice was intoxicating and Jo felt herself shiver happily. Unable to contain her desire for him any longer, Jo placed her mouth around Nick's member and began to suck furiously on his length. As her mouth worked on his cock, her fingers stroked and caressed his balls in a quickening tempo.

'I'm going to come,' Nick hissed through gritted teeth.

Jo had not needed him to tell her this. Regardless of Nick's determination, she had other ideas of when he was going to climax. The rapid throb of his length in her mouth was sufficient to tell Jo he was on the brink. She felt dizzy with anticipation as she thought how good it would feel to have his seed spray against the back of her mouth. Greedily, Jo sucked harder. Her tongue teased under the rim of his cock's purple head, thrilling the glans deftly. She tasted another trickle of pre-come; and then he came.

She felt Nick's orgasm start in his balls. The base of his magnificent length shuddered against her bottom lip and suddenly it seemed as if his cock had grown inside her mouth. Nick pressed himself forcefully into her mouth until his cock was touching the back of her throat.

If she had been able to, Jo would have gasped for breath. A wave of exhilarated pleasure washed over her. The steady pulse of Nick's ejaculation began to thump inside her mouth. All she could taste was the heady flavour of his seed and the effect was instantaneous. Shot after shot of his jism filled her mouth and she swallowed it quickly. She savoured the flavour as greatly as she enjoyed the intimacy. Her own orgasm was not as powerful as Nick's but she did not doubt it was equally good. Every pore of her body seemed to sing happily as she gulped down the last droplet of his climax.

She moved her mouth away from his cock and smiled up at him. 'Just like old times, isn't it?' she said, licking her lips avariciously.

He grinned down at her, breathless from the exertion of his orgasm. 'Just like old times,' he agreed.

It took ten minutes for them to get back to Nick's flat. As she entered the doorway, Jo was reminded of the reason she and Nick had been unable to live together. The hallway was neat and uncluttered; the carpet was clean and recently vacuumed and all the visible surfaces glistened with the dull lustre of perfectly applied polish.

'I see you're still a neurotic,' she said, as he took her coat and placed it on a hook in the cubbyhole beside the door.

'It isn't neurotic to run round the place now and again with a Hoover,' he explained carefully.

His penchant for tidiness, and Jo's inability to accept it, had been the cause of the big argument that finally ended their relationship. The misery he had felt on the day she left his flat was still etched deeply on his memory and Nick did not want to scratch at that particular wound. He turned away from the cubbyhole and was amazed to see she was wearing only a skirt, stockings and shoes. He remembered her breasts fondly and was delighted to see his memory had not exaggerated their perfect beauty. The round orbs were slightly larger than was normal for a woman of her build and her areolas were a dusky rose-petal pink that darkened to red at her nipples. He gazed at them wistfully, momentarily transported to happier days when the sight of her nudity was not such a rare thing. A whirlwind of emotions began to swirl inside him, the most predominant of which was his growing arousal.

She swayed her bare breasts provocatively in front of him, rubbing the orbs playfully with her fingers as he watched. The notion that she was naked beneath the jacket had occurred to him when he first saw Jo in the corner booth at the pub. However, the fact seemed to have miraculously slipped his mind.

Now, admiring her half-naked body as she stood in his hall, Nick wondered how he could have overlooked such a thing. He did not waste any valuable time contemplating this thought. Instead, he pressed her forcefully against the wall and his mouth found hers. In an instant they were intertwined, kissing and caressing one another with furious delight. His hands fell on her breasts, carefully kneading them between his fingers and palm until Jo sighed happily in response.

His tongue pressed between her lips and Jo accepted it happily. His kissing was almost as exciting as the cool touch of his hands against her breasts. The occasional

brush of his thumb over the aroused swelling of her
nipples forced Jo to take deep breaths of laboured
excitement. She allowed him to taste her fully before
pushing her own tongue into his mouth and enjoying
the intimacy of kissing him. Her hands caressed his
cheeks and face. Her fingers ran through his hair and
she delighted in the tactile stimulation of his nearness.
Determined to extract as much pleasure from him as she
could, as well as the information she wanted, Jo rubbed
her hand eagerly against his swollen groin.

'I see you're almost ready for action again,' she noted,
a wry smile playing along her lips. 'Didn't I suck it
properly for you?' she asked teasingly.

'You did everything just right,' he said generously.
'But now it's my turn to please you.'

'Sounds OK to me,' Jo said glibly. She reached for the
zip at the side of her miniskirt and slowly unfastened it.

It came as no surprise to Nick when she stepped out
of the skirt and revealed she had been knickerless
throughout the evening as well. She had carelessly
allowed her skirt to pool untidily on the floor but, in his
state of high arousal, Nick overlooked this.

Jo stood proudly before him, dressed only in a pair of
stiletto heels and hold-up stockings. Her long dark hair
cascaded over her shoulders in a waterfall of lustrous
ebony waves. The dark tresses seemed to stress the
golden hue of her gorgeous tanned body.

She could see the longing in Nick's face and she
teased a hand against her breast obviously. She used her
other hand between her legs as he watched.

'You are one hell of a saucy bitch,' he told her, his
breath laboured with desire. Without waiting to be
prompted, he knelt before her. Placing a hand on each
thigh, he pressed his nose against the dark hairs of her
pubic triangle and nuzzled her gently. His tongue
slipped almost casually against the soft swell of her sex
and he licked the exposed flesh gently.

Jo sighed softly.

Nick allowed his tongue to separate her lips, then drew it back and forth along them, savouring the taste of her desire. Occasionally he would rub the tip of his tongue over the hood of her clitoris, extracting a shiver of excitement from her.

'I want you inside me. I want to feel you inside me,' she hissed.

'Come with me,' Nick said quietly, standing up and taking her hand.

Jo followed him wordlessly until he paused outside a door and then pushed it open. 'The bathroom?' she said, trying to remember the layout of this apartment.

'The bathroom,' he agreed, with a knowing smile. He flicked the light switch and led her into the room.

Like every other part of Nick's home, the bathroom was scrupulously clean. With the newly installed Jacuzzi bath in one corner, Jo thought the room looked like a photograph from an Ideal Home catalogue. She allowed Nick to lead her to the bath and obeyed him instantly when he turned the taps on and suggested she undress completely. She kicked the stilettos into one corner of the room and sat on the edge of the bath to unroll her stockings.

Nick watched her lovingly, mesmerised by the moist pout of her vagina, which she so blatantly directed at him. The lips of her labia separated gently as he watched, and he could see a silver glimmer of wetness glistening there.

Jo cast the unrolled stockings in carefree directions, enjoying Nick's desire for her with a typical lack of thought for the consequences. She stroked her thighs self-indulgently after removing the hosiery then, more for Nick's benefit than her own, she teased a finger against the wetness of her hole. The ferocity of her own desire came as something of a surprise to Jo and she was pleasantly surprised by the dampness that coated her finger when she removed it.

As Nick watched, she placed the finger to her lips and inhaled the musky scent of her own arousal. It was a fragrance that she invariably marvelled over. As Nick watched, she stroked the finger against her mouth, coating her lips with the sweetly scented pussy honey. Her tongue brushed against the finger, kitten-like at first, then with a greedier, avaricious urgency.

Nick watched her silently, his arousal becoming stronger and stronger. 'Before I spoil what I have planned for you,' he began slowly, 'would you do me the honour of climbing into the bath?'

Jo shrugged. 'How might you spoil it?' she asked, standing up and pressing her face close to his.

He could smell the fragrance of her pussy juice on her breath and her lips. The scent was so stimulating he could feel his cock twitch in eager anticipation. 'You might make me so horny I decide to just pin you to the floor and screw you here and now,' he whispered quietly.

'That would spoil things, would it?' Jo teased, moving her mouth closer to his.

Unable to resist the temptation any longer, Nick pressed his mouth against Jo's and kissed her passionately. He savoured the taste of her pussy-sweetened lips, feeling his cock twitch demandingly in the confines of his pants. Determined to resist the charms of her nakedness, he plunged his tongue deep into her mouth and embraced her tightly in his arms. The swell of his erection pressed uncomfortably into the flat of Jo's stomach but neither of them seemed to care. The excitement of their kiss teetered on the brink of greater intimacy.

With a gasp of self-annoyance, Nick broke the embrace and stepped away. He smiled uncertainly at Jo, hoping the expression would reassure her. Unable to find the words necessary to sum up his feelings, he pointed at the bath and widened his grin. 'Please,' he said quietly.

Obligingly, Jo stepped in. The water was, as she expected in Nick's home, the perfect temperature and the feeling of the warm liquid against her excited vagina was stimulating enough to enhance her arousal. 'Don't tell me you've taken to washing your women before you use them,' she teased carelessly.

'I believe it was that type of sarcasm that got us both to move our separate ways,' he reminded her softly.

Suitably chastised, Jo mouthed an apology and watched as he picked up a bar of soap. He pushed it into the bubbling waters of the Jacuzzi, then began to lather Jo's body. He started on her arms and shoulders, allowing her to be coated with the luxuriant cream of the soap before rinsing the lather away with bath water. He deliberately ignored her breasts and pussy at first, concentrating on the subtler erogenous zones of her neck, waist and thighs.

Jo was thrilled by the unexpected pleasure of Nick's ministrations. The lathering was an incredible stimulus to her skin and she could feel her arousal intensifying as he swirled the soap carefully over her body. The water was just on the right side of warm for her liking and, as Nick rinsed the creamy lather away, Jo felt each pore of her body tingle with renewed desire for him. He carefully washed her entire body this way before bringing the soap gently against her breasts.

Jo moaned happily.

He began to rub the soap into her breasts with calculated pressure. Each orbit of the bar circumnavigated her areolas, missing the hyper-sensitive flesh by millimetres. He kneaded her orbs with the soap, until the moment to rinse finally came. Then he cupped his hands with water and carefully poured it over her.

Jo could not believe she was so close to orgasm without having being properly touched. Her eyes were closed and she had rested her head back, enjoying the stimulus of Nick bathing her. When she felt the soap finally pressing against the hardened bud of her nipple she opened her eyes and stared at him.

Nick smiled into her face. 'Lie back and enjoy it,' he said. 'It's no blow job in the pub car park, but I'm hoping you'll enjoy this more.'

'I'll try,' Jo conceded, resting her head back and closing her eyes. 'I'll try,' she told him.

He rubbed the soap over her breasts, again concentrating on the delicate flesh of her nipples. His touch was firm, yet gentle, and he teased them to a state of sensitivity that was so vehement it bordered on being painful.

Jo struggled to maintain a proper control over her breathing. She was deeply aroused by the delicacy of Nick's touch and she could not recall ever having felt so pampered. A huge climax welled within her and Nick's subtle indulgence alone would have been enough to push her beyond the pinnacle of pleasure. When he poured a handful of warm water over her bared breasts, Jo gasped and uttered a guttural cry of satisfaction. A fiercely satisfying orgasm exploded inside her, sending shivers of pleasure through Jo's body.

She shook her head slowly, bewildered by the easy way in which Nick had coaxed the orgasm from her. Blinking her eyes open she glanced at him and saw the satisfied smile on his lips.

'Stay still,' he told her softly. 'It gets better.'

Ordinarily Jo would have raised a cynical eyebrow. However, her delight was so complete she simply nodded and lay back in the bath, allowing Nick to do to her exactly as he wished. Before she realised what was happening, she felt Nick's bar of soap moving down between her legs. He had already washed her legs, right up to the tops of her thighs, and she wondered what he intended to do with the soap now. When she felt the bar rubbing gently against her exposed labia, she realised exactly what he intended. For the first time, she noticed

86

the shape of the soap. Rather than being the traditional unspectacular oblong shape, this bar was round, smooth and cylindrical. As soon as she realised its shape, Jo guessed it had only one real purpose: it was a makeshift phallus.

The end of the soap pushed gently against the swollen lips of her vagina. They were beneath the water and Jo would have expected them to be less responsive than normal. Perversely, she found her lips tingling with anticipation the moment the soap pressed against her. Her body's eagerness to accommodate it was completely unexpected. Her lips parted as though they had been expecting a treat like this and Jo groaned delightedly as the bar of soap filled her. The slippery sensation contrasted peculiarly with the soap's hard, bonelike feel. Jo felt a wave of ecstasy rush through her as Nick began to slide the length in and out of her hole. Not only was the makeshift phallus exciting her beyond belief, the warm bubbling bath water was creating a suction that truly enhanced Jo's delight. The wide girth of the soap seemed to fill her and its slow entry into her body caused wave after wave of delighted sensations to explode deep in her love canal. As Nick increased the speed of his penetration, Jo felt dizzy with excitement. She grasped the sides of the bath with both hands and braced herself for the impending eruption of pleasure. Bucking her hips hungrily towards the soap, she rode it furiously, trying to keep tempo with the swift pace of Nick's movement. The slippery length penetrated her so easily she could have screamed with pleasure. This feeling, along with the unfamiliar sensation of the Jacuzzi and the warm water, caused an orgasm to sweep over her with unnerving alacrity.

Jo had never anticipated that sex could be so good without having to work hard at it. When the orgasm struck she felt herself temporarily lost in a blissful haze of euphoria. Every muscle in her body seemed to tremble in unison. Her inner muscles clamped together with a furious climactic force and pushed the bar of soap rudely from her body. Such was her delight, Jo barely noticed. Her head, breasts and clitoris felt as though they were tingling with the most wonderful version of pins and needles imaginable.

'Are you OK?' Nick asked, smiling warmly into her upturned face.

She returned the smile. 'That was sensational,' she told him, struggling with laboured breath.

His grin widened. 'It's not over yet,' he said quietly. He took the soap and, once again, moved it between her legs.

Jo was allowed a moment to wonder what he intended to do with it now. As he pressed the soap against her, she realised exactly what he had in mind. The phallus-shaped bar of soap prodded lewdly against her anus. Jo gasped in surprise. Suddenly her eyes were wide open and she was staring uncertainly at Nick.

'Relax,' he soothed. 'You'll enjoy it.'

Comforted by his easy tone of voice, and eager to participate in whatever plans he had in store, Jo did as Nick instructed. She separated her legs slightly, allowing him full access to her backside as he pressed the soap firmly against her. Aided by her advanced state of arousal and the water's soapy consistency, the cock-shaped soap plunged into her without a moment's hesitance. Jo let out a scream of delight as the slippery phallus slid deep within her forbidden darkness.

Nick held the base firmly and used the soap like a dildo. He slid it back and forth with a languid, unhurried action that came close to driving Jo insane. She desperately wanted to feel the bar plunging roughly in and out of her. Such a raw, passionate motion would have satisfied the ravenous hunger of her carnal appetite.

Instead, Nick seemed to slow his pace deliberately,

building her pleasure up slowly and steadily. With one soapy hand, he fondled her breasts, his fingers slipping over her nipples with a lubricated friction that she found devastating. His hand slid lower, beneath the bubbling waters of the bath and into the forest of curls on her pubic mound. As though he were sensing her needs psychically, Nick plunged a finger between the lips of Jo's vagina.

It was an intensely erotic feeling. He continued to ride her arse with the bar of soap, still using his slow, carefully measured pace. But now, his fingers added something else. The dull friction was so thoroughly arousing she felt breathless with emotion.

She and Nick had been lovers previously but he had never been this good. If he had been, she doubted their relationship would have come to an end. It occurred to her that she was supposed to be trying to pleasure him, so he would give her the information she so desperately wanted. Pragmatically, she put this thought to one side and concentrated on the myriad enjoyable sensations that were spiralling through her body. Her breath deepened to a ragged, animal pant and she squeezed her pussy muscles tightly around his fingers.

Nick smiled tightly and continued to tease her with his leisurely rhythm. Deep inside her pussy, his fingers pressed against her velvety warmth. They massaged her g-spot occasionally before sliding out of her lips, then sliding back inside again. Now and again, he would press his fingers against the bulge of the phallus as it entered her.

Jo panted hungrily, desperate for him to push her over the brink of orgasm. 'Please, Nick,' she begged him. 'Just a little faster, please.'

'Anything to oblige,' he told her honestly. He pulled the phallus back, until the tip of its head was at the rim of her anus. Jo could feel the muscles of her sphincter contracting slowly at the same moment as he thrust it back inside her. The bar of soap plunged roughly into her, then he pulled it out, repeating the process with swifter and swifter movements. Jo's breathing matched the quickening tempo of his penetration. Before he had completed a dozen thrusts, she heard herself scream elatedly as a quake of Richter proportions ploughed through her body.

'Good?' Nick asked, curiously.

'Don't stop,' Jo hissed through gritted teeth. 'Faster. More,' she implored him urgently.

Nick continued, his pace becoming furious as he pushed the phallus vigorously in and out of her anal canal. Repeatedly he pulled it from within her, allowing the sphincter to tighten before pushing it back inside her. Each time he did this, Jo shrieked excitedly and urged him to continue. His fingers remained inside her but they were no longer content to gently rub the sensitive inner flesh. Instead, Nick began to slide them in and out of her pussy with the same hastening pace he was employing with the soap. Unconsciously, he adopted a rhythm where his fingers slid into her vagina as the soap pulled out of her anus. When the soap pushed inside her, Jo felt his fingers sliding from between her lips. It meant that she was not without something inside her. She was constantly being filled, either by the delicious bar of soap or Nick's expert fingers. She doubted he could have gone faster had he tried, yet still she heard herself urging him to increase the speed of his actions.

When the huge orgasm finally hit her, Jo roared with guttural satisfaction. The sound came from some unplumbed animal depths deep within her. Wave after wave of delighted explosions caused shiver upon shiver to course through her body. The intensity was so ferocious Jo felt sure she would leave fingernail marks embedded in the porcelain sides of the bath. Nick continued to plunge the phallus and his finger into her, but she brushed his hands away, fearful of how intense another orgasm might prove to be.

'Screw me, Nick,' she whispered. 'Get in here and screw me,' she told him hoarsely.

Needing no further prompting, Nick quickly stepped out of his clothes and lowered himself into the bath with Jo. He knelt between her legs, then slid himself backwards, until the tip of his eager cock was pushing against her belly. Jo grabbed Nick's length in one hand and took a moment to admire the wide girth and the desperate throb of his pulse. Beneath the water his cock felt harder than usual and she wondered if this was a phenomenon caused by the bath water, or a symptom of his arousal. Either way, she knew she was going to enjoy having such a rigid dick filling her hot, wet hole.

He kissed her lovingly on the mouth and she responded in kind. His hands found her breasts and massaged them deftly, caressing the curves and swell of her orbs with infinite tenderness.

Jo sighed wonderingly, unable to believe her body could still be so responsive after so many powerful orgasms. She guided his cock between her legs and rubbed the tip slowly against her pussy lips. The swollen end of his dick was the only part of his cock that did not feel like it had been carved from stone. Its pliant pressure against the tenderness of her labia was urgent and she once again found herself on the edge of an earth-shattering orgasm. Pulling Nick's foreskin back as far as she could, Jo gripped the base of his shaft and guided him into the heat of her wet opening.

They groaned in unison, unable to find words to express their mutual pleasure. Nick rode slowly in and out of Jo's tight, warm hole, his cock seeming to swell with each thrust. Jo kept a tight hold of his cock, keeping his foreskin held back as he pushed into her. It was a technique she knew he had always appreciated in the past but this was not her only reason for employing it. The sensation of his cock inside her was divine. Her feelings for Nick had not disappeared when they parted and she was determined to make this as good an evening for him as he had made it for her.

They enjoyed one another with furious abandon. Nick's cock filled Jo each time he pushed into her. When he withdrew, the pressure of the water against her labia seemed to reinforce her emptiness. Jo helped to accelerate his swift pace by bucking her hips on to him. Water splashed over the sides of the bath as their urgency intensified. Jo heard herself screaming for him to ejaculate as another orgasm threatened to blast its way through her body.

When Nick did climax, his seed shot deeply into her, burning her heated warmth with the vehement force of his excitement. Jo barely heard his howl of delight, drowning the sound with her own cry of gratified bliss. Her earlier orgasms had been far more intense but this one was better. The pleasure was so deeply fulfilling it outshone the others and made them pale in comparison.

They held one another tightly for a while, content to lie in the bath together, entwined the way true lovers should be. When Nick began to kiss her softly on the cheeks and forehead, Jo realised she had fallen into a light daze.

'I can't believe how much I've missed you,' Nick whispered in her ear.

'I can't believe I moved out of this flat when you're so bloody good,' Jo told him earnestly.

Nick moved away, a bashful smile playing over his lips in spite of the intimacy they had just shared. He stepped out of the bath, reached for a towel and passed it to Jo as he helped her out.

She smiled, touched by his unfashionable chivalry, and accepted the towel gratefully. And now you have to work him for information, she told herself cynically. The thought seemed perversely cruel, particularly after he had pleased her so adeptly with little thought for his own enjoyment. She tried to dismiss this notion but it kept recurring to her as she towelled herself dry. Each movement of the rough cotton against her body inspired a memory of the pleasure he had given. As she towelled her breasts dry, the nipples responded to her touch. Her legs shivered when she pressed the towel against them and, for a moment, she hesitated before putting the cloth between her legs.

'Earlier,' she began, hating herself furiously for the conversation she was trying to instigate. 'Earlier, you said the Pentagon Temping Agency was a group I should stay clear of.'

Nick nodded. 'They're dangerous,' he said. 'Dangerous and powerful.'

She studied him, chilled by the flatness of his voice. Exaggeration was not in Nick's nature. 'I'd feel awful if I gave up on this case though,' she persisted.

'Missing person?' he asked, rubbing a towel between his legs and then moving it over his chest.

'A woman, yes,' she said.

He nodded. 'They don't just take women, but they seem to prefer them. The link between the Pentagon Agency and a handful of missing persons is well known in the office but we can't convince any of the hierarchy to invest time or money in an investigation.'

Jo winced as she realised what Nick was saying. 'Jesus! That stinks of corruption somewhere,' she told him.

He nodded, a dour smile on his lips. 'It does, doesn't it,' he agreed unhappily.

'So what happens to these women?' she asked, not sure if the question came from genuine curiosity or her investigator's professional interest. 'Do you find bodies, limbs, what?'

He grunted bleak laughter. 'Something like that might give us a lead,' he said miserably. 'But whatever happens to those missing persons is far worse than you can imagine.' He fixed Jo with a cold glare and said softly, 'To date, they are all still listed as missing persons.'

Jo shivered uneasily.

Five

Lying alone in his hostel bed, Russel smiled quietly to himself. He was happily enjoying the same dream again. Technically, he couldn't decide if it was a true dream or his mind replaying, and exaggerating, a treasured life experience. In all honesty, he would not have cared which category it fell into. All that mattered to Russel was that, for a few fleeting moments, he was reunited with his beloved Mistress Byrne.

'You're properly bound now, Russel, aren't you?' Vanessa asked in a delightfully sultry whisper. She was wearing a business suit as she spoke to him. The buttons of her blouse were unfastened enough to reveal a tantalising glimpse of cleavage. The skirt she wore was a modest length but it was short enough to entice him with the glimpse of stocking tops he could see.

Asleep, his head moved up and down on the pillow as he nodded confirmation. 'I'm properly bound, Mistress Vanessa,' he assured her softly.

She smiled in response and teased the hem of her skirt upwards, allowing him to see her naked pubic bush. 'Is this what you want, Russel?' she asked softly. 'Do you want to play with my pussy?'

He sighed heavily, aware that his cock was a raging limb that demanded to be touched. 'Yes, mistress. Yes!' he implored her. He was so lost in the dream, so acutely involved in this regular nightly homage to Mistress Vanessa, he did not even realise he was no longer alone in bed.

'You've been a naughty boy though, haven't you?' Vanessa teased coquettishly.

Russel frowned, puzzled. 'Please, mistress,' he begged. 'I haven't done anything un . . . untoward.'

She shook her head sadly, a frown of disapproval creasing her lips as she unfastened her blouse further. 'You've been having wicked thoughts about the girls you're working with, haven't you?'

'No,' he began hurriedly. 'I haven't –'

'Don't lie to me,' she hissed sharply. She drew the belt in her hand back and flicked it down swiftly at his groin.

There was no pain, unfortunately, Russel thought, but he flinched from the gesture anyway.

'You've been having dirty little thoughts in that cesspool you call a brain.'

He sniffed sadly and nodded. 'I'm sorry, mistress,' he told her earnestly. 'I'm truly sorry.'

'Sorry . . . isn't . . . good . . . enough!' she told him, punctuating each word with a crack of the belt to his inner thighs. 'I want to hear you beg for forgiveness.'

He considered explaining the situation, then thought better of it. After all, she was the one who had suggested he enrol with the Pentagon Agency in the first place. He did not doubt that, when she suggested he join, Vanessa knew all about the place and its credo: 'ultimate temps for the demanding executive.'

He had listened to Mr Smith's induction speech. The man had said a lot of things about the strict regime employed and the disciplined environment. All the time Russel had been trying wilfully to understand the man's point. It had not taken long for him to understand exactly what Mr Smith was alluding to.

During his first lesson at the hostel, he had witnessed an example of the Pentagon Agency's strict regime and disciplined environment. A fellow colleague, who had made the mistake of backchatting to a tutor, had been paddled until she sobbed for mercy. Russel had watched the spectacle in a haze of wonder. Part of him had wanted to rush to the front of the class and stop the punishment.

Another part of him had been too aroused to dare moving. He had wondered what it would be like to be a victim of the tutor's punishment. The prospect was deeply exciting. The idea of being spanked on the bare backside, in front of a group of his peers, left Russel shivering with excitement. It was that part of his mind he listened to, trusting its appreciation of the natural order between dominants and submissives.

'You've been watching the other girls,' Mistress Byrne told him. She used the strap with merciless accuracy. 'You've been excited by them,' she pointed out, seemingly blessed with an ability to read his mind. 'That's a punishable offence, Russel,' she told him sternly.

In his sleep, Russel shook his head in silent dispute of his mistress's words. It's not an offence, he wanted to say. Mr Smith said fraternising with female trainees was acceptable, as long as it didn't mature into . . .

His silent words were cut short by another blow from the belt. It did not matter what Mr Smith had said. The truth was: Mistress Byrne was correct. He had been watching the other girls and indulging in lewd thoughts. If she told him this was a crime, then that was sufficient for Russel. In his mind, and in his heart, there was no difference between what Mistress Byrne told him, and what was expected of him. The two were indivisible.

In spite of the blows this dream vision had delivered, he still felt his cock thrusting upwards. More than that, his cock was experiencing feelings that were new to him. There was a delicious moist friction that he could not account for. His length felt as though it were being encompassed in a warm, wet passage. The moist heat that surrounded him was so warm, wet and thrilling he wondered if he was going to embarrass his mistress again by ejaculating on her. He closed his eyes and prayed that he would not commit this sin again.

When he opened them, he was staring down at the blonde head that hid his cock from view. The woman going down on him bit back a soft murmur of appreciation and continued to ride his length with her mouth.

Russel bit back a protest, unsure if this was still his beloved dream, or a bizarre reality he had fallen into. Mistress Byrne could not be sucking his cock. That was wrong, and forbidden. She was a mistress and as such she was permitted to have him do her bidding. She would never lower herself to taking his cock in her mouth. That was not the behaviour of a dominatrix.

Perplexed by this paradox, Russel tried to find a rational explanation for it. His mind was still trying to come to terms with it when he felt the explosion fire from his balls. His cock pumped and pumped and, to his chagrin, Russel realised the woman sucking him was swallowing his seed.

He groaned unhappily, wishing he knew what was going on.

'It felt like you really enjoyed that,' she said, glancing up at him from his dick. A trickle of white semen dribbled from her lower lip and she licked it up avariciously as she smiled at him. 'You taste nice,' she added, with a sly smile.

Russel stared incredulously into Helen's face, wondering how she had managed to get into his room. 'Why did you do that?' he asked, unable to stop his voice from faltering.

'To make you come,' Helen told him honestly. 'Now it's my turn,' she said, taking his failing length between her fingers and teasing it playfully. 'Do you think I can suck him hard for a second go?' she asked curiously. 'I reckon I can.'

'I don't want a second go,' Russel told her, a tremor

of unease creeping into his voice. 'I didn't even want the first. Get off me.'

Helen stared unhappily at him. As she assessed the frightened pallor of his expression her smile widened. Her pale-blue eyes glimmered with Machiavellian glee as she quickly formulated a plan. Her smile broadened. 'Play with me, Russel, and do as I say, or I won't be your friend.'

'I don't want you to be my friend,' he told her grumpily. 'I want you to leave.'

Helen frowned theatrically. 'That's not very nice,' she told him sadly. 'Do you really want me to leave and tell people our secret? I don't think it will go down well.'

'What secret?' Russel asked, puzzled.

Helen's pantomime smile could not conceal her expression of triumphant accomplishment. 'We've just cohabited, Russel,' she pointed out. 'That's against the rules here, or didn't you know?'

Russel knew perfectly well that this was the truth. The thought had been in his mind only a few moments ago, although he could not recall if it had been in his dream or not. 'I didn't . . .' he began.

Helen shook her head solemnly. 'If you want me to go, then I'll leave now, and tell the security guard along the corridor what we did. I'm sure he'll tell one of the mistress's what you did with me.' She moved as if to get off his single bed.

A dozen things flashed instantaneously through Russel's mind. He saw Mistress Byrne standing before him, naked and holding a strap. She was smiling at him and assuring him that if he completed the Pentagon Agency's course, he would be her slave for ever. He also saw the austere Mr Smith, telling him that cohabitation with female trainees would lead to expulsion. This warning, Vanessa's desirable smile, and his longing to be her treasured slave, were all feelings and images that tumbled through his frightened mind in a hectic, helter-skelter blur.

Scared of the repercussions, Russel put a hand out to stop her. 'Wait,' he begged.

Helen's smile widened. 'You want me to stay now?' she asked slyly. 'Do you think that's wise?'

Russel caught a breath in his throat and studied her in the semi-dark of his room. He had seen Helen throughout the week and come to regard her as a steel hand in a velvet glove. Even from a distance, Russel had sensed it would be wisest not to get involved with her. She exuded an air of danger that he shied away from. He would have been happier if he could have avoided all contact with her. However, he realised that things were not going to happen that way.

A sense of self-preservation made him keep a hold of her arm as they spoke. 'What do you want from me, Helen?' he asked quietly.

She smiled, a disarmingly pleasant expression. 'I want us to be friends,' she told him, patting the hand that held her arm. 'I want us to be good friends,' she amended, giving the words their own intimate meaning.

Russel's smile faltered uncertainly. 'But you've just told me male and female trainees aren't allowed to indulge in relationships with each other.' He wondered if it would be possible to argue his way out of this situation. He doubted it would be, but he could see no other option. Unless he could discuss this rationally with her, Russel knew he would have to go along with whatever Helen wanted.

Helen leant forward on the bed and placed a kiss on Russel's mouth. He could taste his own semen there and tried not to think how arousing the flavour was. The last time he had tasted that flavour had been when he licked his own seed from Mistress Byrne's bare breasts. That had been an experience so memorable he realised he was still dreaming about it. The memory was enough to make his cock twitch excitedly.

'There are ways around that,' she told him, her voice

barely controlling the devilish giggle at the back of her throat. 'Here,' she said, 'watch what I do, and learn.'

Russel felt powerless to resist as he watched Helen begin to undress. She stepped out of her shoes, then began to unroll her stockings, taking time to display her legs as she removed the nylons. After this, she pulled her blouse off, unfastened her skirt, and stood before him in only her bra and pants. Mesmerised by the beauty of her sylphlike figure, Russel could not wrench his gaze away. When she removed her bra and slid her panties down to her ankles, he realised his cock was already rock-hard again.

'Now.' She smiled encouragingly at him. 'Step one wasn't so difficult, was it?' She looked at his solid dick and drew a finger lovingly along his length. 'It looks to me as though you really enjoyed it,' she said, rolling the tip of her finger over the swollen head of his knob. 'I wonder if you'll enjoy step two as much?'

His wary frown deepened. The sensations she inspired in him were infuriatingly arousing and he fought against his body's longing for her. 'Step two?' he asked doubtfully. 'What's step two?'

Helen smiled easily. Again, he found it disarming, especially considering her nudity.

'Step two is where you put these clothes on,' she said simply.

Russel gaped in horror and shook his head. 'No way!' he declared. 'I'm not doing that,' he told her firmly.

Helen simply shrugged. 'OK,' she said, making her way towards the door. 'I'll probably see you when they bring you out of the black room. Bye bye, Russel.' Heedless of her nudity, Helen reached the door, placed her fingers on the handle and began to tug it open.

Russel watched all this nervously. Naturally he had heard of the black room. It was the source of punishment so severe it could not be kept quiet, especially in a place like the hostel. The whispered stories Russel had heard were chilling. He had already decided to avoid the black room at all costs.

He suspected Helen was trying to bluff him. Common sense told him it would be wisest to let her walk out. She would have nothing to gain by getting him in trouble. If she tried that, and then the mistresses heard his side of the story, Helen could face severe retribution.

His only worry was that she might make good with her threat anyway. From what he had seen of Helen he already knew she was unpredictable. 'Wait!' he called, almost falling out of bed as he tried to stop Helen from opening the door.

She turned to face him, an unsurprised smile teasing her lips. 'Yes?' she enquired sweetly. She put on a curious expression, as though she genuinely wondered what he intended to say.

Russel took a deep breath and sighed heavily. 'I'll do it,' he told her solemnly. 'I'll do step two.'

Helen grinned as she walked slowly towards him. 'Of course you will,' she said knowledgeably, caressing her breasts as she moved. 'I thought you'd want us to be good friends.' She moved her hands from her breasts and placed one on his rigid length. The other hand went to her pussy and she teased the lips open as Russel watched. 'You want to put this gorgeous piece of machinery in here, don't you?' she asked, lowering her voice to a soft, husky whisper.

Russel nodded, not trusting himself to respond verbally. He did not like Helen, but his body ached to possess her.

She rolled his foreskin back and forth over the swollen head of his glans. Her fingers stretched to circumnavigate the wide girth of his manhood. With her other hand she teased the lips of her tight, pink hole wide apart and plunged her finger deep inside. When she removed the finger, she pushed it under Russel's nose and told him to lick it.

Obedient as ever, Russel did as she instructed.

'You want to stuff this beautiful cock of yours in here, don't you?' she asked softly. 'Like this,' she elaborated, moving her pussy closer to him and rubbing the wet lips of her labia over the throbbing purple end of his dick.

Russel groaned with excitement, wondering how close he was to climaxing again.

'Not yet, though,' Helen told him, a mischievous smile twisting her lips. She rubbed his cock once more against her pussy lips, delighting in the hot, wet friction. 'You haven't dressed up yet,' she reminded him. 'And according to the rules, I can't make love to you unless you're another female.'

'Do I have to do this?' Russel asked unhappily.

'No,' Helen said, her finger still playing with the lips of her vagina. 'You can refuse to dress up and play my game if you want to. It will just mean you don't get to screw me, and you spend some time in the black room.' Her smile was as cruel as any Vanessa had ever graced him with. 'The choice is yours, Russel.'

Blushing furiously, Russel stepped from the bed and began to sort through the discarded pile of Helen's clothes. 'Which items?' he asked dully.

'All of them,' she said. 'Knickers, stockings, bra, skirt and blouse. And don't ladder my stockings, or you really will upset me.'

Mortified that he was obeying her, Russel picked up the knickers and tried to decide which way they went on.

'Sniff them first,' Helen snapped crisply. She flopped on to his bed and smiled up at him as she issued the command. One finger toyed idly around her moist lips whilst the other teased a nipple between the index finger and thumb. 'Sniff them and tell me how good I smell.'

Russel's length hardened furiously. He sniffed the gusset of Helen's pants and inhaled the enticing aroma.

Maddeningly, he felt his balls tighten with anticipation and he sniffed them a second time, without her having to command it. The fragrance was soft, sweet and musky. It was a reminder of the scent he had caught on her finger, before licking it clean. For a moment he felt intoxicated by her bouquet.

'Put them on then,' Helen instructed lazily, still playing with herself. 'There'll be plenty of time for you to enjoy the source of that scent later on.'

Reluctantly, Russel moved the pants away from his nose and stepped into them.

Helen watched him critically as he dressed, her finger moving with a quickening tempo as her appetite for him increased. He was not the handsomest of men. His thin frame and boyish looks gave him an androgynous appearance that was unremarkable, save for the huge cock between his legs. She watched as he tried to conceal this huge member in the skimpy white-cotton panties she had been wearing, and suppressed a smile when she saw how impossible this was going to be. Unmindful, Russel rolled the stockings on to his legs and then fastened the bra around his narrow chest. He slipped into the blouse Helen had worn, before pulling her skirt on.

Helen bit back a sigh of delight as she studied him. His cock was still twitching at the front of the skirt, creating a give-away bulge that was far from discreet. However, she had to concede that he made a fine-looking woman. His legs were too shapely for a man. Clad in the sheer black stockings, they looked desirably good. She glanced at his face and saw that he was crimson with a combination of humiliation and embarrassment.

'There's some lipstick in my blouse pocket,' Helen told him, her fingers tickling frantically on her exposed clitoris. 'Put some on,' she gasped between deep breaths.

For a moment, Russel could not move. He was

captured by the vision of Helen masturbating as she watched him. An expression of eagerly anticipated delight strained her features as the first trembling of an orgasm swept through her. Every muscle in her body seemed to tense and she bit back a groan of deep, guttural excitement as she climaxed.

Russel felt his cock stiffen hungrily as he eyed the glistening slickness of her wet hole. A part of him wanted to grab his cock and jam it into her as vigorously as she would allow. He did not doubt it was something Helen would want, and he felt sure they would both enjoy it.

However, Helen had not asked him to do that and Russel was already beginning to learn his place in life. It was a place where such impulsive desires were not allowed, not for him anyway. His role was to do as his superiors told him and even though she was just a fellow trainee, Russel realised Helen was still superior to him. He watched the last tremor shake itself from her body, then moved to the mirror at the room's dressing table. Without studying his reflection, he applied the lipstick to his mouth, coating the lips adequately with the garish red colour.

'What a lovely young woman you are,' Helen said, giggling nastily. She climbed off the bed and walked swiftly over to him. Without shoes on, they were the same height and she had no trouble planting a kiss on his painted lips. Her tongue explored his mouth as her hands went behind him. She cupped his buttocks with her palms and squeezed him against her. The swell of his jutting dick pressed rudely against the flat of her stomach. Lasciviously, she rubbed her naked stomach against him, feeling the length throb hungrily against her.

'Why, tell me, young woman,' she began theatrically, 'what is that bulge at the front of your skirt?'

Russel frowned uncertainly. He did not know what to

say and knew he was just the plaything in Helen's game. He tried a hesitant smile and a half-shrug, then watched helplessly as Helen knelt down and began to lift his skirt.

'My God!' she exclaimed in mock-horror. 'It looks like you have a cock down here,' she told him. 'It looks like a cock, and . . .'

Russel felt her fingers teasing his rigid member from the cotton panties it was stuffed in. She gripped it firmly at the base and allowed her fingers to roll slowly back and forth along the entire length. He bit his lower lip in anguish, fighting to stave off the impending climax.

'. . . and it feels like a cock,' Helen told him. She paused for a moment.

Russel felt her tongue tracing lazy circles around the head of his knob. Her hot breath warmed his length with a slippery wetness that he knew was as good as her pussy would be. The tip of her tongue teased its way into the hole at the top of his prick, then she took him in her mouth and began to ride him with her face.

'Good heavens!' she gasped, standing up to face him. 'It tastes like a cock, too. It really must be a cock. You're a man!' she declared.

'You know I'm a man,' Russel replied sullenly. 'It was your idea to dress me up like this.'

Helen slapped him sharply across the face. 'How dare you suggest such a thing?' she said sternly. 'You're a man dressed up as a woman, and you need punishing for that.'

'No,' Russel began quickly. 'That's going too far. You're not punishing me. I'm not having that.'

'You'll have whatever I tell you,' Helen told him menacingly. 'Unless,' she added with forced sweetness. 'Unless you want me to get one of the mistresses to punish you instead? I could enjoy that just as much.'

Russel watched helplessly as Helen moved towards the door of his room and reached for the handle again.

Let her go, a part of his mind encouraged him silently. Let her go, and get the punishment over and done with.

And never see Mistress Vanessa Byrne ever again, he thought miserably. He was left wondering how he could have been so stupid as to let her get so close to the door again.

'Wait,' he hissed angrily.

Helen turned to face him, her sly smile broadening. 'Wait? Why? Do you want me to punish you, rather than one of the mistresses?'

He nodded dumbly.

'Say "Yes please",' Helen told him.

'Yes please,' Russel replied sullenly.

Her smile widened and she moved away from the door. 'I think there's a reason why you want me to punish you, rather than one of the Mistresses. I'm right, aren't I?'

He nodded.

'You probably think I'll go easier on you than they would, don't you?'

'No,' he began. 'I just . . .'

'Well, I won't,' Helen assured him, not listening to his reply. 'If anything, I intend to punish you as severely as I can.'

Russel trembled inwardly. He wished his cock would behave normally when he was subjected to news like this. He thought it would have been appropriate for his excitement to dissipate at the threat of punishment. Instead, he found his dick standing harder than ever. Miserably, he realised that a part of his mind was eagerly anticipating the correction Helen had planned for him.

'What are you going to do to me?' Russel asked warily.

Helen smiled and rubbed her hand against the thrusting stiffness of his erection. It was a huge cock and she found herself unable to resist the urge to touch it and play with it. 'I could do a lot of things to you, if I wanted,' she told him. 'But I wouldn't do anything that would stop this cock from being hard, you do know that, don't you?'

Unhappily, Russel nodded. Helen wanted him as desperately as he wanted her. The only difference between their desires was that Helen wanted to humiliate him before they did anything. It was a difference that he did not particularly like, but he was happy to accept it, considering the prize that awaited him at the end of the evening.

'Now bend over, raise your skirt, and drop your knickers,' Helen told him crisply. 'I want to see your backside.'

Russel's cheeks burnt so fiercely it felt as though they were ablaze. Ashamed by his own servility, and mortified by the arousal which it inspired, he did as he was instructed and bent over. His nose was close enough to the hem of Helen's skirt for him to detect the faint aroma of her perfume on the garment. Again his cock twitched hornily. He had not bothered to remove the pants and he felt Helen's fingers tease the fabric away from his buttocks and tug them slowly downwards.

She stroked the downy hairs that covered his arse with a tenderness that bordered on being loving. Her fingers played carelessly around his anus, touching the rim heedlessly, before delving into the feathery swatch of his pubic bush. She cupped his balls in her hand and squeezed them gently in her palm. 'I wouldn't want to hurt these, either,' she told him earnestly. 'Although I could, if I wanted, couldn't I?'

'Yes,' Russel murmured quietly. For the first time, he was beginning to realise that the threat of pain was almost as powerful an aphrodisiac as the actual experience. Being rolled between Helen's fingers, his balls felt decidedly vulnerable, yet he felt his excitement mounting.

She moved her hand away and began to stroke his long cock. Her wrist brushed against his arsehole as she did this, thrilling him with the unexpected stimulation.

'You like that, don't you?' A dark smile crossed her lips. 'I can see why.' 'I'm tickling your bum-pussy, aren't I?'

'I . . . I . . .' Russel faltered. His cheeks felt bright red with shame and he could not have thought of anything sensible to say even if Helen had not interrupted him.

'Don't bother denying it.' She laughed gaily. 'The clothes suit you, just like they suit your desires. You want to be screwed up there, don't you?'

'No,' Russel denied furiously. He tensed himself against the threat of an orgasm which longed to burst out of him. Every muscle in his body tightened in anticipation of the climax but, for the moment, his willpower seemed to have the upper hand. The moment passed without him ejaculating. Russel realised it had been close.

Helen appeared not to have heard him. 'Mistress Stacey has a strap-on dildo in her rooms,' Helen told him in a discreet whisper. 'Perhaps I should go and get that, then come back here and give you a good hard shagging.'

'No', Russel gasped, wishing her words were not so arousing.

'Perhaps I should ask her to come back here and use it on you,' Helen suggested coyly. 'She's had more experience of wearing it and I bet she'd know just how to use it up this tight little bum-hole of yours.'

'Please! No!' Russel implored her. 'Don't get Mistress Stacey. Please?' There was a pathetic, faltering note in his voice as he finished this last sentence, turning it from a request to a plea.

'But feel how eager you are for it.' She slid a finger smoothly into his arse, parting the hole easily.

Russel groaned as he fought against his climax again.

His cock felt as though it were about to burst, and he knew that if Helen deigned to touch it at that moment he would shoot his load all over the skirt she had made him wear.

She slid the finger inside him as deep as it would go. When she slowly pulled it from him, the movement forced a shiver of delight to course through his entire body. 'Sniff it,' she commanded, holding her finger in front of his nose. When Russel moved his head disobediently away, she grabbed his hair and forced his head close to the finger. 'Sniff it, I said. Now!'

Tears of shame pricked at the corners of Russel's eyes. Obediently, he did as Helen told him and sniffed the finger she had used inside him.

'Recognise the scent?' Helen asked softly. 'It's the aroma of a hole that needs satisfying, isn't it?'

Russel groaned and stammered a reply. 'It . . . It is,' he agreed.

'Do you want me to fuck your bum-pussy?' Her lips were a whisker away from his ear and Russel felt the delicious warmth of her breath against his neck. 'Do you want me to use my fingers, and fuck your bum-pussy?' Helen asked again.

'Yes!' Russel gasped excitedly. 'Oh! Please! Yes!' he implored her, wanting this more than anything he could recall.

'OK,' Helen said obligingly. 'I guess I can do that for you. Move over to the mirror and stand in front of it: Legs spread slightly, hands on either side of it.'

Russel moved as she asked, shuffling his feet in small steps because Helen had not given him permission to step out of the panties that pooled around his ankles. He stood in front of the full-length mirror, the raging force of his erection lifting the skirt he wore so that his penis pressed against the cool glass surface.

'You're very obedient,' Helen observed quietly. 'I'm going to enjoy having you around the hostel.'

Russel sighed, knowing this had all seemed too good to be true. 'I thought you promised it would just be this one night,' he said softly. He could see her in the mirror behind him and was aware of the cruel tinge to her smile.

Helen's grin widened. She caressed the cheeks of his backside before replying. 'Are you telling me you don't want to feel this again?' She asked the question as she slid her index finger slowly into his wanton arsehole.

Russel bit back a cry of ecstasy. He could feel himself on the brink of orgasm, a position Helen seemed to have held him at throughout the evening. The pleasure that emanated from his anus was stronger than any he had enjoyed before. If he had been forced to endure this humiliation in front of Mistress Vanessa, his fantasy would have been complete.

Thoughts of Mistress Vanessa made his cock shiver impetuously against the mirror. He knew she would be offended if she discovered what he and Helen had been doing, but that thought brought pleasures of its own. She would be angry, but she would not be upset. He could imagine that she would punish him for this misdemeanour and that realisation thrilled him beyond belief.

'You're close to coming, aren't you?' Helen noted. 'Do you think another finger might help?'

Before Russel could reply, he felt her index finger slide from its warm haven inside him. His sphincter tightened on the finger's egress, sending a thrill of pleasure through his body. The thrill was nothing compared to the joy he received when Helen shoved her index and middle fingers inside him. She pushed them roughly into him, unmindful of the sensitive tissue inside. He was wet with his own arousal and the digits easily pushed his tight hole wider as they slid deeper and deeper into his backside.

Russel gasped for breath, aware that his climax was

imminent. Helen's fingers moved in and out at a maddeningly slow pace. The fingers of her other hand moved tentatively between his legs, toying lazily with his balls. The combination of sensations was more than he could take and Russel bit back a cry of desperation. He dared to open his eyes and glance at the reflection of himself in the mirror.

He did not really look like a woman, he was not foolish enough to convince himself of that, but, nevertheless, he found his mirror-image arousing. He looked at how his cock had pushed itself free of the skirt and was pressed urgently against the mirror. He could see his legs and he had to admit that Helen's stockings looked very good on him. The shapeliness of his calves and the slenderness of his thighs was feminine enough for him to wear the nylons without looking foolish. He also thought the blouse looked good on him, along with the hint of bra he could glimpse inside the open buttons.

'Quite a pretty little thing, aren't you?' Helen observed. She smiled knowingly at his reflection.

Russel started to reply and then realised Helen was trying to insert a third finger inside him. He tried to protest but she shushed him with her soothing voice.

'Take it easy,' Helen insisted. 'You're not the first young woman I've ever deflowered,' she laughed. 'I think I know what I'm doing. And I think three fingers is enough for you to remember that this has happened.'

Russel did not really think this evening would be one he could ever forget, but he did not tell Helen this. His thoughts were focused on the debilitating pleasure she was inflicting up his arse. His bumhole felt full to bursting, as did his balls. He felt as though he was being stretched to the brink of tolerance.

He felt the orgasm begin in his balls. A pulsating throb of pleasure released itself from somewhere between his anus and his scrotum. His dick stiffened and, before he realised it, he was shooting semen all over the mirror. A giddying whirl of pleasure rushed through him as he came. The muscles of his arse tightened forcibly around Helen's fingers as the climax washed over him.

'Very good,' Helen said encouragingly. She removed her fingers slowly from him, then moved so that she could kiss Russel's face. She drew one hand through the semen that covered the mirror and tasted it avariciously.

Russel watched as she licked it from her fingers. A salacious smile rested on her lips.

'You taste nice,' she told him, scooping up another fingerful of his seed from the mirror. Before Russel could stop her, she had smeared the seed over his lips. She wiped her finger all around his mouth and then pressed her mouth against his.

As she kissed him, Russel heard her moan softly. He wondered if she was deriving her pleasure from the actual kiss, or the taste she had put there. He did not have time to ponder these thoughts before Helen began tugging him towards the bed.

'Screw me now, Russel,' she implored him, holding his cock in her hand. 'Screw me before this gorgeous monster of yours goes limp.' She fell on to the bed, pulling him on top of her as she went. Her hand guided his length towards the welcoming warmth of her hole.

Within moments of him climaxing, Russel realised he was on the brink of having Helen.

She groaned quietly as his dick prodded at the sensitive flesh of her pussy. It was a large cock and Helen knew it would be a tight fit. As it began to slide between the lips of her labia, Helen realised just how big it was. Russel's cock filled her. The vast size of his girth was the broadest she had ever experienced. She gasped breathlessly as he pushed it slowly inside her. She had never felt so full and the stimulation was so total it was sublime. Each and every inch of her inner muscles were being forced apart by the mammoth length that pushed into her. The tip of his knob began to nuzzle at the neck of her womb and she bit back a scream of surprise. She had been unaware that an orgasm could steal over her so unexpectedly.

Russel rode her with inept deliberation. He was an inexperienced lover. Vanessa was the first woman he had ever seen naked. Helen was the first who had ever encouraged him to do something like this. Nevertheless, what he lacked in experience, he made up for in obedience and enthusiasm. He pushed himself deeply into Helen before pulling back, then pushed in again at a pace that would have been too eager for a man with a smaller cock.

Thrilled by the pressure of his enormous manhood, Helen did not care about his pace. Each inward thrust forced Helen to experience a climax of devastating proportions. Wave after wave of delight swept through her as he rode her. The intensity of each orgasm increased until she feared how powerful the next would be.

His strokes quickened swiftly, as did Helen's orgasms. She struggled to keep her pleasure silent, mindful of the ever alert security presence in the hostel. As Russel neared his own orgasm, Helen was too exhausted to care. She felt his cock twitch inside her and distantly heard Russel moan a soft sigh of joy.

The sound was only faint: her own orgasm was so ferocious she was deafened by the sound of the blood pumping savagely in her temples. If he had not worn her out with his stamina, Helen knew she would have screamed ecstatically as this final orgasm struck.

Russel pulled his cock from her slippery hole, aware that Helen was smiling coyly at him.

'Was that all right?' Russel asked uncertainly.

Helen smiled through her exhaustion. 'Adequate,' she said, after a moment's pause. 'We'll have to try it again some other night. In fact, we'll keep trying it until you get it right.'

Russel frowned again when Helen mentioned a repeat performance. He began to remove the items of her clothing that he still wore, taking off the stockings first, then the skirt, blouse and bra. 'What if we get caught?' he asked unhappily.

Helen shrugged, putting the clothes on as he took them off. 'If we get caught, we end up in the black room. I doubt it's such a big deal,' she told him, trying to sound confident about this.

Russel doubted this was true, but did not say anything. 'What if I don't want to do it again?' he asked, not daring to look at Helen.

She leant across the bed and planted a tender kiss on his cheek. 'Why, Russel, darling, if you really don't want to do it again, that's not a problem.'

He glanced up at her hesitantly, aware that her voice was too sweet and pleasant to be proposing something he would like.

Helen gave him a guileless smile. 'If you really don't want to spend a night like this with me again, the solution is simple.' Her pleasant smile turned into the bitter expression of cruelty he was used to seeing on her face. 'Under those circumstances, I'd just have to force you,' she explained.

Russel stared at her, unable to keep his unhappiness from surfacing on his face.

Helen finished dressing and stood up in front of him. A mischievous light glinted in her eyes and she reached for the hem of her skirt, lifting it up in front of him. 'Take my knickers off, Russel,' she commanded briskly.

Russel frowned miserably, but knew better than to argue. He slowly removed her knickers.

'Well done,' she told him, helpfully stepping out of the underwear. 'Now put them on, and keep them on until tomorrow night. I'll be back to reclaim them then. I hope you'll be ready for me,' she added with a broad grin. 'I might even bring a friend to share that gorgeous rod of yours.'

Russel frowned at the pants he held in his hand, wondering if he should do as Helen wanted. His own feelings ceased to be an issue when she said crisply, 'Put them on now, Russel. I might decide to check if you're still wearing them sometime tomorrow, and I'll make you very sorry if I discover you're not.'

Hurriedly, Russel began to slide the skimpy cotton panties over his feet and up his legs. He started to phrase another question for Helen, hoping he could find a way of dissuading her from her plans. However, when he had finished putting the knickers on, he realised she had already left the room.

Six

Stephanie and Jo sat in the parked car trying to avoid looking at one another. Unusually for them, Stephanie sat in the driver's seat, with Jo as the passenger. Although the engine was still, the air conditioning ran noisily, filling the car with a cool, necessary breeze. A bright, cheerful Mozart symphony spilt from the car's CD player, rushing along at its own vigorous pace.

Nick's words came into Jo's mind: 'You can't listen to Mozart and stay miserable.' She would have liked to have him sitting in the car now. An impenetrable silence had fallen between the two women. The atmosphere was heavy and neither one of them was listening to the music.

'This is ridiculous,' Stephanie said dourly.

'This is our last chance,' Jo replied in a solemn voice.

It was a beautiful summer's day. Sunlight filtered its way through the canopy of heavy foliage lining the avenue. An elderly woman, tall, dignified and refined, walked slowly down the street, holding the leash of a poodle. Trimmed into a show-cut, the dog looked just as tall and dignified as its owner.

The woman and her dog were the only pedestrians the two investigators had seen. Aside from them, the avenue was deserted. The fronts of the executive abodes in this area were shielded by lush, verdant shrubbery. Each had a long driveway, and Jo guessed this would reinforce the sense of seclusion. It seemed like the ideal place for an organisation like the Pentagon Agency. Whatever they were up to, they had no worries about discretion. Jo had already decided that each property enjoyed a good deal of isolation.

She kept her thoughts to herself. Stephanie was already unhappy with this stage of the assignment and Jo did not want to worry her partner any further. She also suspected that Stephanie had worked out all these things for herself.

'Nice street,' Jo remarked simply. 'You and I could retire if we came trick-or-treating here next Halloween.'

Stephanie snorted derisively. 'You have a more optimistic view of the future than I do. I can picture you still being on the missing-persons list by then.'

'I'll be all right,' Jo replied softly. She reached out, intending to squeeze Stephanie's hand reassuringly. Jo realised the gesture was a mistake as soon as she had started it. Stephanie had her hands in her lap. As she clumsily reached for her friend, Jo felt her fingers brushing against the cool, creamy skin of Stephanie's thighs. She had still not dared to reveal her feelings, even though the longing had not abated. Her need for Stephanie was transforming into an emotion so powerful it was almost tangible.

They had been working diligently on the Rogers case for the past week, but Jo had still found time to discreetly study Stephanie's body. Long nights at Stephanie's apartment, discussing possible leads and different perspectives, had meant they were spending a lot more time together. Those nights had been torture, and Jo had fought to keep a tight reign on her feelings when they were inevitably stirred.

She had managed to keep her desires secret so far but, as she put her fingers in Stephanie's lap, she turned again to the idea of confessing exactly how she felt. It was a ridiculous notion and she discounted it before it had properly formed.

The sudden closeness was too much. She simply squeezed Stephanie then moved her hand away. 'I'll be all right,' she repeated huskily.

'Surely there must be another way,' Stephanie implored her. 'This can't be our only option.'

Jo shook her head. 'We've been over it and over it, Steph,' she said quietly. 'Every lead we've had has drawn a blank. Nick either can't or won't help us. None of our usual contacts are in the same league as this Pentagon Agency and your computer seems to point to this street as being the next location for our enquiries to continue.'

'Is it worth it?' Stephanie asked.

Jo grinned. 'Only if you want to eat next month,' she replied. 'You dealt with the Pentagon Agency yourself when we were making enquiries. You've hacked their database, and seen the name Kelly Rogers on their records, yet still they've denied all knowledge of her. Add that to the little I managed to get out of Nick, and we've got all the makings of a lead that is being well and truly covered up. When you consider those names that were in the agency's database, and cross-reference them with the PNC's list of missing people, you begin to realise how big this thing is.'

'Which is why I think it's too big for us,' Stephanie said tiredly. 'What's wrong with passing it all over to the police and sitting back whilst they do the work?'

Jo grinned. They had been through this several times before. 'There's only three things wrong with that,' she said quietly. 'First, the police won't do the work; Nick told us that much. Second, our client doesn't want the police involved, slimy little wretch that he is. And third, if we do that, we don't get paid.'

Stephanie shook her head, knowing she was not going to make Jo change her mind. 'You won't let me talk you out of this, will you?'

'No.' Jo smiled sadly. 'But that's only because I know

119

I'll be all right. You seem to forget, I'm a born actress. This is going to be the perfect role for me.'

'You'll need to be a born actress,' Stephanie said unhappily. 'You're not the type of person these people usually recruit. That application form we completed wasn't just assessing your temping skills. That form was designed to get a specific psychological profile.'

'Which is why we took so long filling the damned thing in,' Jo reminded her. 'And we must have done it right, otherwise I wouldn't have managed to get this interview with Mr Smith.'

Stephanie looked away, not trusting herself to say anything about the doubtful Mr Smith. She had no trace of a man called Smith being involved with the Pentagon Agency. The name was so obviously an alias she was worried by its blatancy.

'So how come you're going undercover as the temp, and I'm relegated to back-up?' she asked eventually. 'When it comes to typing, they'd call you ham-fisted if you used more than two fingers. Your shorthand is illegible and your spelling is atrocious. Why aren't I going undercover as the temp?'

Jo grinned. 'Because it's a temping agency,' she explained. 'I can make crap coffee, be rude on the telephone and turn up late better than anyone else you know. Try and distinguish my behaviour from a temp's in any way at all and I'll let you do this damned assignment.'

'And you still insist on going in naked?' Stephanie enquired.

Jo nodded. 'Figuratively, of course,' she said with a grin. 'According to the form I filled in, I'm Jenny Vaughan. I have a limited social circle, so I have no need for my laptop, filofax or mobile phone. If Mr Smith thinks I will be a suitable candidate then my two weeks' residential training course will begin immediately. I'll do my damnedest to contact you each night, at your home, around eleven. I'll find some way of doing it from the phones they have inside, but I can't risk taking a phone in with me. That would look far too suspicious.'

'It still sounds too dangerous to me,' Stephanie said with despair in her voice. 'What if something goes wrong? What if they turn nasty? Do you think Jenny Vaughan can handle this situation if it starts turning bad on her?'

Jo shook her head. 'Of course she couldn't, spineless bitch that she is.' She gave Stephanie a knowing grin. 'If things get out of hand, Jenny Vaughan is going to disappear and Jo Valentine will take over.'

Stephanie shook her head. 'Perhaps, when we got that psychologist to look over the application form, we should have booked a therapy session for you and your schizophrenia.'

Jo glanced at her watch and then confirmed the time with the dashboard clock. 'I haven't even got time to insult you for that little jibe,' she said quickly. 'If I don't set off now, Jenny's going to be late for her interview, and Jenny is always punctual.' Seeing the frown of concern on Stephanie's face, she leant across the gear stick and planted a soft, tender kiss on her cheek.

She had intended it to be platonic and reassuring. Instead, Jo found herself amazed by the emotion this simple kiss inspired. A charge of excitement seemed to bristle against her lips. She glanced into Stephanie's eyes and saw an expression there that she had only dreamt of seeing previously. The glint of desire and anticipation in Stephanie's mellow brown eyes seemed to mirror the longing Jo knew was in her own. She paused, uncertain of what to do next. She wished she had the time to talk about this with Stephanie, but the case in hand intruded impatiently on her thoughts.

'Take care,' Stephanie said quietly, putting a hand on Jo's.

Again, Jo sensed that electric tingle of attraction. She had considered making some light or witty comment before leaving the car: 'I'll get out of this in one piece, or my name isn't Jenny Vaughan' was the line she had intended using. Now, wondering if Stephanie really was aware of her feelings, and daring to hope she might feel the same way, Jo doubted the joke would be appropriate.

'I'll take care,' she said, swallowing down the lump in her throat before she spoke. 'We'll talk tonight, OK?'

Stephanie nodded and watched Jo climb from the car. Not trusting herself to watch her walk away, she started the car's engine and drove quickly away.

Jo watched the car drive swiftly down the impossibly still avenue. A faint smile creased the corners of her mouth. She wondered how close she and Stephanie had come to confessing their feelings for one another. 'It's going to happen one day,' she told herself. 'And, the sooner I can solve this case, the sooner Stephanie and I can get down to discovering one another.'

It was a warming thought and she carried it with her into Mr Smith's interview room.

Tall, broad, dark and commanding, Mr Smith exuded an air of controlled power that was positively chilling. He conducted the interview with a crisp voice that sounded uncompromisingly austere. His steel-grey eyes studied Jo relentlessly, frowning darkly on the rare occasions when she dared to meet his gaze.

Jo realised that if she failed to meet with Mr Smith's exacting standards, she would be banished from his office with no hope of ever returning. It was an intimidating thought and she struggled valiantly to answer all his questions with the most suitable answers.

'Perhaps you'd like to know a little bit more about our organisation,' he said eventually. There was an undercurrent of a foreign accent in his voice but so subtle it was barely more than an inflection. 'Here at the Pentagon Agency we strive to provide a very special kind of temp for our more discerning clientele. We employ ordinary temps for a lot of our tasks but those whom we train here at the hostel are destined for our exclusive client list; an inner pentagon, if you will,' he said, testing an unfamiliar smile across his lips. 'Aside from selecting candidates with a high degree of administrative skills, we are also looking for a particular type of person. A person who embodies the corporate image of a Pentagon Agency temp.'

Jo nodded, a sweet, understanding smile on her lips. Occasionally she glanced at Mr Smith whilst he spoke but, on the whole, she studied the painfully neat surface of his desk, seeming to be too timid to dare to meet his gaze.

'We're called the Pentagon Agency because we were originally founded, ten years ago, by a group of five business associates. All of us knew what we wanted from a temping agency. None of us knew where to find it. We decided to join forces and train temps to our own standard of excellence.'

'It sounds like it was an ideal arrangement,' Jo said politely. 'Were you one of the founders?'

He nodded. 'As I said, there were five of us who set up the company and we worked very well together. Each of us contributed something unique to the company: marketing skills, specific legal knowledge, recruitment and training techniques, amongst other things.'

Jo nodded, not daring to ask what these other things might be. The way Mr Smith alluded to them made it clear there would be no detailed discussion on the subject. She did not mind. She was learning more about the Pentagon Agency.

'Four of the founders remain the same today as they did at our commencement. The fifth member, our man

123

with the specific legal knowledge, sadly passed on several months ago.'

'My condolences,' Jo said quietly.

Mr Smith exercised his tight, humourless smile. 'His replacement is just as knowledgeable. He is also equally in tune with the rest of the directorship, in terms of what he wants for the company. It is down to his foresight and acumen that we are currently enjoying a period of expansion, allowing us to employ and train a greater number of temps than ever before.'

'Does that mean you're accepting my application for training?' Jo asked cheerfully.

Mr Smith smiled sardonically. 'I'm not a hundred per cent sure yet, Miss Vaughan. According to your previous-employment record and your application form, you seem perfectly suited for training with the inner pentagon. However, I have reservations that you would be uncomfortable with some aspects of the training.'

Jo swallowed. 'What are your doubts?' She kept her voice quiet. 'Perhaps I can assuage them?'

His smile resurfaced, as though he had anticipated her saying something like this. 'I'm not sure it's as simple as that,' he explained slowly. 'Here at the hostel, we employ a strict regime and a disciplined environment. I'm not sure you would be happy with it.'

Jo smiled disarmingly. 'If you've read my CV you'll notice I was educated in an all-girls boarding school from twelve to twenty-one.' She watched Mr Smith pick up her papers from his desk and glance at this piece of information. 'Now, I'm not trying to say we endured KGB-style training whilst we were there.' She grinned. 'But there was little tolerance for unruly, or inappropriate behaviour.'

'They used corporal punishment?' Mr Smith asked. He seemed intrigued.

Jo nodded. 'The headmistress used to cane naughty girls. She didn't have any of these special tawses or paddles you hear about nowadays. All she relied on was an old birch cane.' She smiled, hoping the expression looked like genuinely fond recollection. 'God, could she use that cane!'

'You sound as though you appreciated the benefits of that environment.'

'I did,' Jo agreed. 'It was a harsh, strict regime but it instilled a sense of discipline in us and I don't think that's a bad thing, do you?'

Mr Smith ignored her question, apparently considering his words carefully before he gave voice to them. 'You enjoyed this environment five years ago, when you were still a schoolgirl?'

'I wouldn't have used the word enjoyed,' Jo told him, grinning as she said it. 'But I lived happily within the restrictions that were imposed on me.'

'Do you think you could live under such restrictions again?' Mr Smith asked, deliberately. He fixed Jo with a determined expression, the grey steel of his eyes reading her innermost thoughts as she considered his question.

'Are you asking me if I would allow myself to be caned?' Jo asked hesitantly. 'Is that part of the strict regime you employ here?'

'You don't sound as offended or shocked as I would have expected,' Mr Smith told her.

Jo shrugged. 'You're training a group of relatively young people to be disciplined and conscientious. Corporal punishment was the only way of doing that when I was at school. I don't see that much has changed since then.'

Mr Smith laughed suddenly. It was a hearty, genuine sound and, in that moment, Jo knew she was on the verge of being offered a position with the Pentagon Agency. Considering all the talk about caning and corporal punishment, she wasn't sure she wanted to be offered the post but Jo realised she was in no position to haggle over such niceties. She still had a job to do and there was only one way to do it. Whether she liked it or not, Jo knew she would have to stay at the hostel.

She had already discovered more about the Pentagon Agency and its structure during her thirty-minute interview with Mr Smith than through a week's research from her own office.

At the back of her mind, she knew that if Stephanie had heard the conversation, she would have been dragging Jo from the hostel as if the place were on fire. It was a warming thought, reminding Jo how strongly her partner cared for her. Trying not to think about Stephanie, Jo gave Mr Smith a winsome smile.

'Are my ideas so amusing, Mr Smith?' she asked coolly.

He shook his head. 'Not at all,' he said reassuringly. 'They reflect our company policy so closely it's quite disturbing, to tell the truth,' he explained. 'Please, don't think me a cynic, but are you sure you don't consider yourself beyond caning? You're a mature woman, in her mid-twenties, surely you're beyond having your bottom spanked?'

Jo held herself stiffly in the chair. Calmly, she studied Mr Smith, trying not to show him how uneasy she was with this line of questioning.

Nick had suggested something similar to her before their relationship ended. As far as Jo could recall, it was one of the many reasons for the relationship ending.

'If you want to hit someone, go back to the police station and visit the drunk tank. You can beat up a couple of piss-tags down there,' she had told him sharply. 'Half of them probably won't remember tomorrow. The other half probably deserve it anyway. Just don't think you're playing spanky-spanky games with me.'

Looking back on the incident, Jo realised it was that particular conversation that had been the beginning of the end. After that, their relationship had gone into a slow, downward spiral.

She did not consider herself a prude: sexually she was happy to try anything. However, the whole idea of spanking and sexual power games left her cold. Determined that Mr Smith would see none of this in her face, Jo managed a smile. 'I don't consider myself beyond appropriate punishment,' she told him quietly. 'And I suppose it depends on the circumstances as to what punishment is appropriate.'

His smile was unsettlingly confident. 'Please don't think I doubt your honesty or integrity,' he began, shifting position in his chair. 'But I'm still not sure you appreciate the exact regime we employ here.' He paused, his eyes flickering hesitantly. 'Would you be greatly offended if I asked you to prove your acceptance of our discipline?'

Jo forced a warm smile to her lips. 'I'd be happy to put your mind at ease by doing just that,' she told him calmly. 'Do you want me to stand anywhere in particular?'

He was already climbing from his chair, a frown of consternation creasing his brow. Jo watched as he reached inside the large cupboard behind his desk and slowly withdrew an old birch cane. She swallowed nervously. Her anxiety increased when she caught a glimpse of the faraway expression in Mr Smith's eyes. He was considering the birch cane with a misty-eyed appreciation that bordered on affection.

Jo wondered how dangerous a man had to be before he started to look at a stick in such a way. It was a notion that gave her serious cause for worry, reminding her again how vulnerable her position was.

The cane sliced the air with a vicious whistle.

Jo flinched, startled by the sound. She glanced up from her thoughts and saw Mr Smith was idly brandishing the long birch cane in her direction.

'Just stand up and hold your hand out,' Mr Smith snapped crisply. A bitter smile twisted his lips. 'I imagine it will be just like old times for you.'

Jo wondered if he was trying to be pleasant with this comment. She could not be certain because of the subtle inflection of his Teutonic accent. Holding her hand out, she smiled calmly at him and nodded agreement. 'Yes. Just like old times.' The smile remained on her lips as she watched Mr Smith test the cane across the tips of her fingers.

His smile broadened as he noted the apprehension on her face. He barely looked at her hand. Instead, he watched her face as he whacked the cane across the tips of her fingers.

Jo sucked in her breath, shocked by the exquisite pain that flared in her hand. She stared sharply at Mr Smith, unable to stop an angry glint from lighting her expression.

He laughed, his accent giving the sound a cruel note. 'If you had glared at your headmistress like that, I doubt she would have let you get away with it.'

Jo forced a natural smile to her lips. She tried to ignore the throbbing explosion of pain in the ends of her fingers. 'As I recall, she didn't let me get away with it,' Jo replied.

Almost casually, he smacked the cane across her fingers again, renewing the flare of pain. Jo winced, but held her hand steady. This time, she managed to keep all venomous emotions from appearing on her face.

'Good,' Mr Smith told her. 'Now if you'd care to bend over, I'll show you how we usually administer punishment here at the hostel.'

Jo raised a surprised eyebrow in Mr Smith's direction. 'Bend over?' she asked hesitantly.

His broad smile seemed to accommodate her reluctance. 'You do want to be accepted for a trainee position here, don't you, Miss Vaughan?' he asked, the hint of a threat barely tainting his words. As he waited for Jo's reply, Mr Smith tested the cane's pliancy by bending it between both hands.

'Of course I want to be accepted,' Jo told him truthfully. In all honesty she would have done anything to get a positive lead on this case. It was the most beguiling one she had ever had on her books, not to mention the most lucrative. As far as Jo could see, this was going to be the only way forward and if that meant indulging Mr Smith with his sadistic little game, then so be it. Actually solving the puzzle of the missing Kelly Rogers and collecting the fee were going to be compensation enough, she decided.

Besides, being totally honest with herself, she supposed she was enjoying the unfamiliarity of the whole episode. At the back of her mind she almost wished she had taken Nick up on his offer when he had originally suggested it. The spreading warmth between her legs told Jo that she would have thoroughly enjoyed it.

Moving slowly, Jo bent over, her head close to the meticulously neat surface of Mr Smith's desk. She shoved her backside out as she bent, trying not to think of the vulnerable position she was placing herself in.

Mr Smith stepped calmly behind her. He placed a hand on her rear and stroked her arse through the fabric of her short skirt. There was nothing particularly sexual about his touch. His hands simply traversed the contours of her rear. He did not try to tease the crease of her sex with his fingers or touch the sensitive valley that led to her anus. His touch was barely discernible through the strained fabric of her skirt.

Jo found the heat of her arousal increasing.

'Feel this.' His voice was almost conversational, hardly the tone she would have expected from a man brandishing a cruel birch cane. The wood whistled smartly through the air, three times in quick succession.

Each time Jo felt the cane strike her backside she bit back a small cry of surprise. There was no real pain in the blow but the anticipation of pain was more than enough.

'You can hardly feel anything, can you?' Mr Smith noted, as though he had expected this much.

'I felt enough,' Jo replied, hoping the answer did not sound too flippant.

There was a note of dry laughter in Mr Smith's voice when he next spoke. 'Somehow, I doubt that. What you just felt was a lover's caress. The way we employ discipline here is slightly different. Let me show you.'

Before Jo could raise a word of protest, she felt Mr Smith's hands return to her backside. This time she was perfectly aware of what he was doing.

He made no attempt to conceal his intention. His fingers grabbed the hem of her skirt and pulled it roughly upwards.

Jo felt the fabric being drawn against the flesh at the top of her thighs. As a minor draught cooled the tops of her legs, she realised there was only a thin pair of satin knickers protecting her arse from the cane. When she felt Mr Smith's fingers tugging at the waistband of the pants, she knew that in a moment even that minimal protection would be taken from her.

Surprisingly, her thoughts turned to Stephanie. She wondered how quickly her partner would have put an escape plan into action if she had known what Jo was subjecting herself to. She sincerely doubted Mr Smith would have been able to raise his birch again before Stephanie stopped him.

Thinking practically, Jo realised Stephanie was oblivious to her predicament. She knew Mr Smith was going to chastise her unless she stopped him herself. Considering the importance of this case, Jo knew that such a thing would not be happening. She needed to get the job he was offering and this was the only way.

He tugged the pants over her hips, then drew them slowly down her legs, to her ankles.

Jo was aware of his fingers stroking the sensitive flesh of her arse cheeks and legs. She felt a trickle of moisture dampen her pussy lips.

As before, it was a completely asexual touch that did not seem intended to arouse or stimulate her. His fingers carefully avoided the heated crevices and depths she displayed, concentrating on the moonlike orbs of her arsecheeks instead. In spite of his avoiding her erogenous zones, Jo could feel her stimulation mounting.

'You have a nice arse,' he murmured softly. 'Beautiful, unmarked cheeks,' he told her, still stroking the skin. 'I imagine you're very sensitive here.'

'I've never really thought about it,' Jo told him quietly. 'I suppose you're right.' She tried to keep her voice calm and even.

'Shall we test that supposition?' he asked coolly.

Before Jo could respond she heard the cane whistle through the air and felt the wicked birch bite her arse. A red-hot wire of pain stung her backside. The blow was cripplingly painful but the sensation that followed was even more debilitating. Jo gasped for air, suddenly unable to breathe. She realised she was clenching every muscle in her body as tight as she could. When she released the tension from her body she felt a thrill of pleasure rush through her. It was not the orgasmic explosion of joy she normally experienced from sex, but it was just as satisfying. Her breath had deepened to a ragged pant, a sound she normally associated with heightened arousal.

She did not think it was so peculiar to be making such a sound now. Mr Smith's cane was not the fierce implement of punishment she had imagined it would be. She found herself hoping he would continue with his demonstration, then dismissed the idea with self-loathing. That was not the way she should be thinking in this situation.

As though he were anticipating her needs, Mr Smith delivered three rapid blows with the cane one after the other. His force and swiftness were matched only by his accuracy. Jo did not doubt that each blow landed on exactly the same spot. The initial pain she had experienced was severe. However, it was barely more than a tickle compared to these three rapid blows from the birch. The pain was augmented with each strike, leaving her breathless as the last hit reached its mark. An explosion of exquisite pain erupted from the raging stripe across her arse. The thrill of pleasure that coursed through her body this time was tremendous. Jo felt her knees wanting to buckle as the waves of joy washed over her. Her excitement was so intense that she wondered if she was going to lose control of her bladder. When she felt the spray of her own ejaculation spatter against her inner thighs, she wondered if this was what had happened.

A groan of ecstasy escaped her lips. She could sense the warmth of Mr Smith's smile as he appraised her chastised arse. His hand caressed the orbs of her arse again, this time stroking along the raised, reddened flesh his punishment had caused.

'There are ways to vary this punishment,' he explained, his tone of voice showing no signs of his own arousal. He could have been discussing something as dry and uninteresting as palaeontology or clinical psychology. His interest in the topic seemed so detached it was almost mechanical. Perversely, she found his lack of sexual interest for her was also a spur for her passion.

If Nick had caned her when he suggested the game, Jo knew that he would have been powerfully aroused by it. Thinking about it, she knew that his arousal would have somehow spoilt the eroticism of the moment. There was something infuriatingly exciting about Mr

Smith's cool detachment. Her vagina and arsehole were being proudly displayed to him and he had so far chosen to ignore their existence. Instead he had simply chosen to cane her with a will that seemed merciless.

She doubted Nick would have been able to punish her as torturously as Mr Smith had just done. Nick's hand would have been tempered with tenderness whereas Mr Smith seemed to lack all traces of compassion.

'Several members of staff here prefer to redden their victims before they punish them,' Mr Smith explained, oblivious to the tangents Jo's mind was following. 'They use paddles and beat the offending trainee's backside until it is red. Then they cane them. They claim it enhances the pain.'

Jo nodded, darkly excited by the thought of enduring such a punishment.

'Personally, I prefer to mark pale skin, like yours,' Mr Smith told her. He drew his finger purposefully along the bright-red line that marked her arse. The pressure he applied was sufficient to make Jo gasp softly. 'I doubt anyone could make a mark that hurts as much as that. Do you agree?'

Jo nodded again and heard herself gasp a meek yes in response.

'It turns you on as well, doesn't it?' he asked, the inflection of his accent suddenly becoming more pronounced. He slid a finger along the lips of Jo's exposed labia, inspiring a wealth of stimulating pleasure.

'Here,' he said, thrusting the finger under her nose. 'Lick my finger clean. It's sodden with your juices.'

Obediently, Jo did as he asked. She licked the pussy honey from his finger, amazed there was so much there. The taste of her own arousal was a sweet fragrant one that she felt comfortable and familiar with. On the cool finger of the austere Mr Smith, it seemed to taste better than ever and she was happy to comply with his request.

When he pulled his digit away from her mouth, Jo avariciously licked her lips, relishing the last taste of the cream that remained there.

'You are a very responsive pupil,' Mr Smith told her. 'I'm beginning to think you will be an asset to us here at the Pentagon Agency. Let me try something else. Stay where you are.'

Not daring to incur his wrath, Jo remained bent before the desk. Valiantly, she tried suppressing the shivers of pleasure that trickled through her body. There was a moment's silence. She tried glancing from the corner of her eye to see what he was up to. He was standing directly behind her and she knew she would not be able to see him without moving her head. Not daring to imagine what this something else might be, Jo braced herself for another caning.

Instead, she was pleasantly surprised to endure the familiar feeling of a cock sliding between her legs. The length pressed against the swollen lips of her labia then, with a forceful push, it was filling her completely. She groaned loudly, delighted by the unexpected turn of events. His cock pressed firmly against the tight inner walls of her pussy. She felt it slide deep inside her, then pull out so the tip nestled against her clitoris. As he entered her a second time, Jo realised he was squeezing the flesh of her arse with his fingers. Whether by coincidence or intent, his hand seemed to have caught the tender line of flesh he had been caning.

Jo suspected it was deliberate but she could not fault the response it inspired. A scream of delight roared from her as he plunged his cock deep inside. The intensity of her excitement was so strong she felt her inner muscles clenching greedily on his length. An orgasm exploded powerfully inside her. Her breathing deepened again and she braced herself for another entry as his cock pulled out of her.

This time he did not push it back into her vagina.

Before Jo knew what was happening, she smelt the familiar scent of her own juices delightfully close to her nose. She opened her eyes and saw the length of Mr Smith's cock only inches from her face.

'Lick it clean,' he told her stiffly.

Jo did not hesitate. She took his cock in her mouth and allowed the tip of her tongue to roll around the head of his knob. She wrapped her lips tightly around his length and tried to suck the organ into her mouth. The swollen purple end of his cock pressed heavily against the back of her throat but she barely noticed. The combined taste of his arousal and her own secretions was a fantastic flavour which she could not seem to get enough of. She used her tongue as best she could, sucking hungrily on the length so she removed every last trace of her juices from him.

'Very good indeed,' he said coolly, removing his dick from her mouth.

Jo gasped with surprise. Even though she had been sucking his cock with as much passionate fury as she could muster, he still sounded barely interested. His appraisal was nothing more than a courtesy. Again she was stimulated by the ambivalence he showed to her. She was trying to form these thoughts into some semblance of order when she realised he was behind her again.

His hands clasped her arse, inspiring a furious rebirth of the deep-rooted pain he had planted there. She felt the round end of his stiff dick poking between her legs and steadied herself for his entry. The thought of what he might be intending was darkly arousing.

He moved his fingers so they caressed the rim of her anus. Using the thumb from each hand, he spread the tight little hole wide open. His thumbs slowly slid into the dark warmth of her backside.

Jo groaned softly.

With his thumbs inside her, he pressed his cock

against her pussy lips, thrusting forward more forcefully than before. A low groan of satisfaction escaped him.

Jo felt the strength drain from her body as a rush of pleasure swept through her. She did not know what caused the joy to hit her, if it was a single stimulant, or a combination of all of them. His thumbs felt sublimely good up her arse. His cock was magnificent between her legs. The burning sting of her striped backside was still a white-hot pit of agony, but this too was enough to leave her breathless with pleasure.

Mr Smith's small, almost reluctant cry of satisfaction made Jo feel warmer than she would have believed. To suffer at the hands of Mr Smith's indifference had been enjoyable. However, to know he was receiving some pleasure made Jo feel as though she was better at being submissive than he had anticipated.

His cock pushed forcefully into her, then slid back, so that the tip had almost escaped the tight confines of her pussy. Then he was pushing back inside her. His thumbs tugged roughly against the inner walls of her anus, stimulating a wealth of pleasure that pushed her further towards orgasm.

Jo screamed happily as the thrill of pleasure filled her. She pushed herself on to his length, trying to accommodate as much of his manhood as she could. She could feel the hungry pulse of his length throbbing deep within her. The sensation left her feeling hotter than ever.

'Very good indeed,' he told her, removing himself from her warm confines. He slid his thumbs free at the same time, then walked around his desk and settled himself back in his chair.

Jo noticed that he had not bothered putting his trousers back on and she wondered what else he had in store for her. She did not dare allow her imagination to dwell on this topic for too long. She was aware that she was likely to explode in delight again if she pictured a particularly exciting image.

136

'Come around here and lick me clean again,' he told her briskly.

Jo needed no more encouragement. She hurried around to the side of his desk and knelt in front of him. Her fingers traced the length of his cock before she took it in her mouth and began to suck it again.

'Raise your arse,' he commanded brusquely.

Jo did as he asked, continuing to tease his length with her tongue and lips. She pressed her lips against the end of his organ and then slowly moved her head down on it, encompassing the entire length with a soft, gentle sucking. She was beginning to wonder why he had wanted her to shove her arse up in the air when she felt the first blow.

Using his bare hand, Mr Smith delivered slap after slap to the cane-burnished cheeks of Jo's backside. He was as adept with his bare hands as he was with a cane. Each blow produced a loud, hard crack that rippled through her body. The pain was formidable, inspiring an excited reaction from Jo that made her suck on his length with a furious hunger. Every time his bare hand connected with the naked flesh of her exposed arse, Jo realised she was using her mouth more diligently on his length. Her desire to please him increased with the amount of pain he inflicted.

Similarly, the pleasure she received from his punishment only seemed to grow. Each slap from his bare palm inspired a wave of delight to erupt inside. The first had been hard and uncomfortable, causing a searing red-hot explosion in her cheeks. The second had been just as fierce. It had inflamed the sensitive skin caused by his first blow. The beating went on in this manner until Jo thought she could tolerate it no longer. The sensations were so intense she felt giddy. She knew she was close to passing out with the thrill of orgasmic pleasure. Fervently, she worked her mouth on Mr Smith's cock, sucking as furiously as she dared.

137

When she felt the explosion of semen in her mouth, Jo shivered excitedly. His seed sprayed thickly in her mouth and she swallowed it quickly, careful not to spill any. With each swallow, she felt a thrill of climactic pleasure engulf her.

Mr Smith continued to spank her backside, adding to her pleasure with the ferocity of his blows. He released a soft, satisfied groan and Jo felt herself being immersed by another wave of glorious pleasure. She was pleasing him, just as much as he was pleasing her, she realised. The notion brought with it a sense of accomplishment that was almost physical. As soon as he had climaxed his cock fell flaccid. Nevertheless, Jo continued to lick it, savouring the last droplets of his come and licking his shaft clean. She did not stop until he pushed her head gently away.

When she glanced up at him, Jo realised Mr Smith was smiling fondly down at her.

'You have the makings of a star pupil,' he said earnestly. 'I don't usually go to such lengths when I'm interviewing trainees.' He put his cock away and pulled his trousers back on. 'I'm glad I made the exception for you.' Casting an almost offhand glance at her half-naked body, he said, 'You can get dressed now.'

Jo realised from the tone of his voice that this was a command and not a request. Hurriedly, she moved away from him and began to straighten her clothes. She dressed herself quickly, aware that he was watching her with an impatient eye.

'There is only one more thing,' Mr Smith said. 'You are now fully aware of the sort of punishment we administer here at the Pentagon Agency, wouldn't you agree?'

Jo could not stop a blush from colouring her cheeks. She smiled demurely at him. 'I'd say that was a fair assessment,' she said shyly.

He nodded, his manner crisp and businesslike. 'That

has two advantages,' he told her. 'Primarily, you will be on your best behaviour from now on, aware of what is in store for insubordinate actions.'

Jo tested a wry smile on him. She was still feeling a little unsettled by her acceptance and enjoyment of his chastisement. The pleasure she had received was far greater than she would have believed. However, as enjoyable as the experience had been, Jo did not intend repeating it ever again.

'And secondly,' Mr Smith went on. 'You will now have no compunctions about signing your acceptance of our doctrine.' He pushed a stiff-looking, white document across the desk to her. Holding a pen out with his other hand, he smiled tightly at her. 'Sign at the bottom,' he said, 'and you will be accepted as a trainee.'

Without a moment's hesitation, Jo took the pen from him and was about to sign the document. She took a moment to mentally correct herself: she had been about to sign the page with her real name rather than the pseudonym she was working under, but Mr Smith did not notice the hesitancy. With the name Jenny Vaughan written, she smiled up at him, trying not to show how triumphant she felt.

Now she was inside the Pentagon Agency it would only be a matter of time before she had found Kelly Rogers.

'Congratulations,' Mr Smith said, offering her his hand. 'Now, if you want to go and have your medical examination, I'll organise a room for you here at the hostel.'

Jo's broad smile widened. 'Thank you,' she told him.

Seven

Helen sighed unhappily. 'You two are a right pair of miserable bastards to work with,' she growled moodily. 'I thought this assignment would have been fun with the three of us working together.'

'Shut up, Helen,' Kelly snapped. Her attention was focused on the typing in front of her. 'I don't have time for your stupidity right now.'

Helen snorted rudely in reply. She turned to Russel at his monitor and tested a winning smile on him. 'What about you, big boy?' she asked coquettishly. 'Are you in the mood for some fun?' She reached a hand beneath his desk and stroked his inner thigh.

Russel stopped her hand from making its way up to his groin. 'Not here,' he hissed forcefully. 'Why don't you stop messing about and get on with your work?'

Helen snatched her hand from Russel's, glaring at him with hostile intent. 'What the hell's wrong with you?' she demanded. 'You were great fun last night. Now you're acting like a real bore. I thought it would have been fun being on an assignment with you. What's wrong? Have you got the hots for that bitch who runs this dump?'

Russel glowered angrily at Helen. 'I don't think you should be calling Miss Byrne a bitch,' he said quietly. 'It shows a distinct lack of respect.'

'Well, that's because I harbour a distinct lack of respect for the overbearing cow,' Helen said emphatically. She watched the flare of anger erupt in Russel's eyes and giggled triumphantly. 'I knew it!' she declared happily. 'You do have the hots for her. You want to get into her knickers, don't you?'

'Keep your voice down,' Russel hissed, his cheeks flaring bright crimson. 'Someone will hear you.'

'Perhaps I want someone to hear me,' Helen suggested wickedly. 'Perhaps I want our conversation to be overheard, so that the word gets back to her. Hadn't you thought that's what I might be doing?'

'Give it a rest, Helen,' Kelly snapped tiredly. 'Lets just get the work done. This is mine and Russel's first time out and neither of us wants to screw up.'

Helen sniffed disdainfully. 'Still trying to be teacher's pet? They don't think any better of you if you suck up to them like that.'

'I'm not sucking up to anyone,' Kelly told her crisply. 'I'm just getting on with my job. I think that's what you should be doing.'

Helen glared angrily at Kelly. She seemed on the brink of saying something, then hesitated, a wicked smile shaping her lips. 'Why don't you and Russel come to the stationery room with me? I bet we could have a laugh in there.' She forced her tone to sound encouraging.

'Make a sentence out of these words, Helen,' Kelly said wearily. 'Fuck off, and stop bothering me.' Her fingers sped over the keyboard before she stopped and cursed the mistake she had just made.

'Russel's wearing a pair of women's knickers,' Helen told Kelly cheerfully, pretending she had not heard her rebuke. 'Do you want to see them?'

'You said you weren't going to tell anyone about that,' Russel hissed suddenly.

Helen ignored him. 'Do you want to see them?' she asked Kelly again. 'He looks quite saucy dressed in women's clothes. I bet you'd get a real buzz out of seeing him.'

Kelly shook her head, trying to force her concentration on to the work in front of her. 'I don't have the time or the inclination,' she said, trying to sound totally unenthusiastic about the proposition. 'Why not ask one of the regular employees here? Perhaps they'd be interested in what you have to say.'

Helen seemed to consider this. 'I would,' she said thoughtfully. 'But I don't think they'd get the same personal thrill out of it that you might experience. You see –' she leant closer to Kelly and whispered '– I don't think they'd be able to identify the real owner of those panties as well as you could.'

There was an undeniable meaning in Helen's words that Kelly could not miss. She stopped typing at the computer and turned to face Helen. She glowered menacingly into the blonde's smiling face. 'What are you talking about, Helen?' she hissed, clenching her teeth tightly together. 'What are you trying to say?'

Helen moved back in her chair and glanced innocently at the typing in front of her. Suddenly her concentration seemed devoted to the work she had been asked to do. She looked like the ultimate in conscientious administration. 'This is quite an impressive word-processing package,' she said quietly. 'Wouldn't you agree?'

Kelly leant over from her seat and put a hand on the lapel of Helen's jacket. 'What did you mean before?' she asked sharply. 'That comment about my being able to identify the owner of the pants he's wearing?' She nodded her head in Russel's direction.

Helen's smile was reptilian. 'I'm sure you can work it out for yourself,' she said coolly. 'He's wearing a pair of women's knickers. They're not mine. Take a guess at who they belong to.'

'You bitch,' Kelly snapped angrily.

Helen's grin widened. 'I'm worse than that,' she assured her. 'And if you don't do exactly as I say, I'll have Mistress Bitch Byrne do a strip-search on Russel. If she finds what he's wearing, the pair of you will be enjoying your own separate stints in the black room.'

'I'd tell them they're not mine,' Kelly replied quickly. She wished there had been no uncertainty in her tone but she heard it tainting her words.

Helen appeared to be concentrating on her work. Her fingers occasionally pecked at the typewriter keyboard. 'They'd probably believe you,' she said encouragingly. 'It's not like you have your name written in the back, is it?' She smiled at her own joke. 'And, admittedly, you are probably the only person in the hostel who has that colour of emerald-green underwear, but that's hardly proof, is it?'

'You bitch,' Kelly breathed, stunned by the ease with which Helen had managed to manipulate her. 'You've got him wearing a pair of my knickers? What if someone finds out?'

Helen smiled. It was a knowing expression that Kelly found totally infuriating. 'Do you want to take Russel and me into the stationery cupboard, so that you can resolve this matter?' she asked. She phrased her question so that it sounded like a harmless, almost innocent, suggestion.

Kelly stared at her again, not daring to utter an insult and not knowing what else to say. She wondered idly if Helen was a good chess player. The woman had a knack for thinking ahead that went beyond anything Kelly had found herself capable of. Considering the game-play she had indulged in over the past few days, Kelly wondered if Helen ought to be renowned for her Grandmaster status.

'What if I say no?' she asked coldly. It was a stupid question and she supposed that, at the back of her mind, she already knew the answer to it.

'You won't,' Helen told her. 'You know the potential repercussions aren't worth it.' She made an attempt at

143

the beginning of the typing in front of her, then turned to face Kelly. 'Russel's wearing a pair of your panties. That's a cold, hard fact. As cold as a witch's tit, to use the vulgar expression.' She smiled tightly, just to show she was still amused by the situation rather than annoyed by it. 'If he's caught wearing them, he'll be in the shit, and the owner of the pants will be too. I think I'll escape without any punishment, but I doubt if you could make the same claim.'

'I'd say you made him wear them,' Kelly told Helen hotly.

Helen nodded sagely. 'I expect Russel would say the same thing,' she agreed. 'That could work one of two ways. Either the authorities back at the hostel would believe you, or they'd wonder why your stories fitted so perfectly. I wonder who they'd choose to believe.'

Kelly stared at the blonde incredulously. 'You bitch!' she gasped.

'I do have a record for unruly behaviour,' Helen said, speaking as though she had not heard Kelly. 'So there is a possibility that they might believe you. On the other hand, he's wearing your knickers and that fact would count for quite a lot.'

'You fucking bitch,' Kelly gasped, unable to control her rising temper.

'You don't know the half of it yet,' Helen said, a smug grin twisting the corners of her lips as she spoke. 'I'll see you in the stationery cupboard.' She paused as she climbed out of her chair and nodded in Russel's direction. Speaking to Kelly, she said, 'Bring your knickers with you. You wouldn't want to be caught without them, would you?'

Kelly caught herself from uttering a sharp retort, knowing that such a response would do no good now. She watched Helen climb from her desk and saunter out of the office, heading in the direction of the stationery cupboard. Unhappily, she noted that Russel had watched her egress with a miserable frown on his face.

'What do we do now?' he asked.

Kelly sighed. 'I guess we do whatever she tells us to,' she said miserably.

Vanessa Byrne cradled the telephone between her shoulder and her ear. 'Sorry, Stacey,' she said quickly. 'I'm trying to do my nails and talk to you at the same time.'

'I'm sorry to interrupt you during such a busy period,' Stacey said dryly. 'How are the new trainees shaping up?'

Vanessa smiled warmly. 'Don't tell me you're worried about your fledglings leaving the nest,' she teased. 'Or do you think I'm going to gobble them up before you can get them back tonight.'

'That latter thought had occurred to me,' Stacey remarked sarcastically. 'I was just checking they were OK.'

'They're OK,' Vanessa assured her. 'Kelly and Russel are a pair of decent hard-workers. Good-looking and very eager.'

'And Helen?' Stacey asked crisply.

'Deadwood,' Vanessa said simply. 'I would say she needs a little more discipline. Do you want me to deal with that?'

'No,' Stacey said quickly. 'I doubt you could do any better than we've been able to here at the hostel. I'd appreciate it if you could keep a close eye on her today. If she's breached any of the rules, I'll take care of her.'

'You're in the black room this week?' Vanessa asked curiously.

'Mr Smith and I are there all week,' Stacey assured her. With a note of bitterness, she added, 'I've had a feeling that Helen and I would be meeting in there one day. I guess I'm going to be proved right.'

'I guess you are,' Vanessa said, her voice suddenly tense. 'I've just glanced into the office,' she explained down the telephone. 'It looks like all three of them have disappeared.'

Stacey's voice was a shriek of disbelief. 'All three of them!'

'Give me a minute to let this polish dry,' Vanessa said crisply. 'If they're not back at their desks, I'll go and find them.' Impatiently, she blew on her wet fingernails.

The stationery cupboard was only a small room, just large enough to house a photocopier. The walls were lined with shelves that strained beneath the weight of letterheads, forms and various types of envelope. With the three of them inside and the door closed, they filled the room.

'Whatever you're doing,' Kelly hissed, 'make it quick.'

Helen's smile was enigmatic but her tone was harsh. 'Don't try bullying me, Kelly,' she replied tersely. 'I've been dominated by professionals and they still haven't cowed me. Don't think you'll manage to succeed where they've failed.' She stared defiantly at the redhead, daring her to take issue with the statement.

Kelly stared uncertainly at Helen, wondering if she had heard correctly. She had tried to fathom her own reasons for becoming involved with the Pentagon Agency and her easy acceptance of their regime. In her own mind she felt comfortable with the new role she had adopted. She wanted to serve and the staff at the agency allowed her to be servile. It was a simple equation and she had assumed that each of the trainees was there under the same terms. Hearing Helen's defiant words, Kelly realised that the blonde's feelings were not so straightforward.

Helen wanted to be forced into submission, Kelly guessed. Rather than simply enjoying the control of a dominator, Helen actively sought the fierce punishment which Kelly shied away from. Aware that this was neither the time nor the place for such thoughts, she reluctantly snatched her gaze away from Helen.

Spurred on by her victory in the argument, Helen glared angrily at Russel. He was standing timidly in one corner of the stationery room, looking as though he wished to be forgotten. 'Take your trousers off,' she snapped. 'Now!' she added with unnecessary force.

Russel stared at her with a beseeching expression. 'What if someone comes in?' he asked.

Helen shrugged, not caring. 'If someone comes in, then they'll see your cock. Get your trousers off,' she snapped. 'The longer you take, the more chance there'll be of us being missed.'

Kelly felt her stomach groan at the thought of them being missed. It was not the thought of being punished that upset her. She had derived a lot of pleasure from the chastisements she had received so far. Although she felt uncomfortable admitting it to herself, she would have happily enjoyed another caning from Mistress Stacey. However, the thought of being punished by Vanessa Byrne was another matter entirely.

'Make it quick, Russel,' Kelly snapped. 'Perhaps we can get out of this without being caught if you hurry.'

Helen grinned, delighted that the pair were now obeying her. 'We don't want to make it too quick,' she cautioned. 'Part of Russel's charm is his stamina.'

Kelly glared angrily at her. 'What do you want us to do, Helen?' She found her gaze would not focus on Helen. Instead her attention was drawn to Russel as he removed his trousers.

His legs were muscular and well shaped, she noted: a sign of his obvious physical capability. As her gaze moved upward she saw that the hem of his shirt covered his manhood and whatever underwear he was wearing. He began to unfasten his shirt from the top and had moved down to the waistline of the garment when Helen caught Kelly's attention.

'Here,' she said sharply. 'I want you to lick this.' She was holding the hem of her skirt up to reveal the shaved flesh of her pubic mound. Her fingers played coquettishly with the delicate-pink folds of skin.

Kelly tried to appear nonchalant as she studied Helen's pussy but it was a struggle to maintain the facade. The situation was already arousing her, in spite of her unhappiness.

'You know you want to taste it,' Helen teased, sliding a finger deftly inside her own hole. 'You couldn't seem to get enough of it the other night.'

Kelly's cheeks flared crimson as she recalled the evening when she and Helen had performed for Mistress Stacey. The memory inspired a thrill of warm pleasure to trickle down her spine. Reluctantly, she moved towards Helen and knelt down in front of her. As Helen spread the lips of her pussy, Kelly tongued her hole carefully.

Helen sighed deeply. 'That's it,' she breathed encouragingly. 'Get me good and wet for him. I'll do the same for you afterwards, if you want,' she promised. 'He's got this gorgeous thick cock and he really knows how to . . .' Her words broke off to be replaced by a sigh of enjoyment as Kelly continued to tease her sensitive labia.

In spite of her anger, Kelly could not deny that she was feeling highly aroused. The flavour of Helen's pussy juices was positively intoxicating. As the cream filled Kelly's mouth, the scent filled her nostrils. The musky aroma of the blonde's arousal was so darkly stimulating that Kelly quickly became aware of her own desires. Helen's talk of them both having Russel was incredibly arousing.

Before she realised what she was doing, Kelly found she had thrust a finger into Helen's pussy whilst she greedily slid her tongue around the woman's clitoris. She would not have believed it was possible to derive so much pleasure from such a submissive act but the tingling in her own pussy confirmed her feelings.

Surreptitiously, she slid her other hand between her own legs and rubbed the heel of her palm against the heavy ache of her longing. She wished she could have employed her fingers, or had Russel tease her in the way she was pleasuring Helen. However, she did not want Helen to be aware of the powerful effect she was inducing. Before her passion could grow any greater, Kelly felt her hair being tugged, pulling her away from Helen's pussy.

'Enough for now,' Helen told her. A contented smile rested broadly on her face. 'I'll let you do some more of that later,' she assured Kelly.

Staring past Kelly, Helen snapped her fingers and pointed at the wet hole between her pussy lips. 'Screw me, pretty boy,' she told Russel sharply. 'I'm just about ready for you.'

Kelly watched as Russel moved unhappily forward. His cock was a formidable length and the idea of having it inside her was thrilling. She saw the tip poke at the edge of Helen's lips, then he was pushing himself forcefully into her. Helen gasped breathlessly as the cock filled her hole. She suppressed a deep-rooted groan of satisfaction as his shaft spread her lips apart.

Kelly realised she was still rubbing the aching seat of her desires as she watched this. Aware that she could now employ her fingers to pleasure herself, she raised the hem of her own skirt and slid a hand quickly inside her panties. She would have begun to caress the delicate folds of skin there if she had not noticed the knickers that Russel still wore. They were so flimsy that they simply hung around the rampant cock rather than restraining it.

Before, Kelly had been marvelling at his length and wishing she could enjoy it. Now, her thoughts were caught by one realisation. The panties were white. Not only were they white, they were also the satin type that Helen favoured. She breathed a sigh of relief. The pants were not the emerald-green pair Helen had pretended they were. Russel was wearing a pair of Helen's white knickers.

Helen had been lying.

For an instant she was torn between two options. Her libido wanted her to stay in the stationery room with Helen and Russel. The passionate sex they were enjoying was deeply arousing and Kelly knew that she would be able to enjoy the feel of Russel's cock if she remained. However, the fear of being caught was still at the forefront of her mind. Now that she knew Helen had no evidence to incriminate her, Kelly felt as though she had won a reprieve.

You can finger yourself as you think about this back at the hostel, she told herself sensibly. Get out now, before someone comes in here and discovers the three of you.

It was a sensible warning and she heeded it well. Standing up, she straightened her skirt, wiped the last remainder of Helen's pussy juice from her lips, and made for the stationery-room door.

'Where the fuck do you think you're going?' Helen asked, her words made ragged as Russel pounded his cock repeatedly into her.

Kelly glanced back over her shoulder and treated Helen to a cursory smile. 'He was wearing a pair of your knickers, not mine,' she said quietly. 'You've got no hold over me, Helen. Just enjoy what you've had out of me, and we'll leave it at that.' Before Helen could say a word that might stop her, Kelly slipped through the door of the stationery room and closed it behind her.

Her relief at getting away from Helen was so great she almost began to run down the corridor in her urgent quest to get back to her desk.

'What the fu –!'

Kelly didn't realise she had bumped into the woman until she heard the angry exclamation. A shower of hot liquid sprayed across her chest, scorching her breasts and then chilling them a second later. She bit back a gasp of pain, apologising profusely to the woman she had collided with. 'I'm sorry,' she began. 'That was all my fault, I –'

'You stupid fucking bitch!' Vanessa Byrne growled angrily. She was glaring furiously down at her blouse. Like Kelly's, it too was sodden with spilt coffee. A scattered pile of saturated papers had pooled at her feet. Her face was as dark as thunder when she looked up and met Kelly's fearful expression.

Kelly bit back her initial feelings of distaste as she looked into Vanessa's eyes. Meekly she repeated her apology. 'I'm sorry,' she began. 'I didn't –'

She got no further. 'You're going to be sorry,' Vanessa told her. She slapped her open palm across Kelly's face. 'Why weren't you at your desk?'

'I . . .' Kelly began, too stunned to think coherently. 'I . . .'

'And where are those other two cretins hiding?' Vanessa asked sharply.

Kelly considered pointing at the stationery room but fear stayed her hand. She had already seen how cunning and vindictive Helen could be when cornered. The way she had tried to avoid punishment for the stolen brooch was a perfect example. Kelly knew that she had only avoided discipline because Mistress Stacey knew all about Helen and her habits. If Vanessa Byrne was to be the judge, Kelly doubted she would see through Helen's convincing lies.

'Aren't they back at their desks now?' she asked, shaping her words so she did not actually lie.

Vanessa slapped her face again. 'Pick up my papers and take them back to my office,' she snapped. 'I think you need to be properly disciplined.'

151

Kelly considered saying a word in her own defence but she could see the resolution on Vanessa's face. Knowing that she would only make the situation worse for herself if she continued to talk, Kelly bent down and began to collect the coffee-soaked pages from the floor.

'You pathetic little bitch,' Vanessa snarled. 'You've ruined this top, you know. Black coffee doesn't come out of Armani silks. How could you be so fucking stupid?'

Hating herself for being humiliated by Vanessa, Kelly mumbled another apology. A hand struck her backside with a gun-shot retort. The sound echoed around the narrow corridor. Kelly felt tears of pain sting her eyes.

'The word "sorry" won't get the stain out, will it.' Seeing Kelly had collected the last of the pages, Vanessa grabbed a fistful of her hair and dragged her from her knees. 'Let's get to my office and see if you can properly make amends.' Still holding a swatch of Kelly's hair, Vanessa tugged the redhead back to her office.

If Kelly had felt embarrassed and humiliated before, it was nothing compared to the shame she felt as Vanessa led her down the corridor and through the main typing pool. Tears of shame rolled down her cheeks. She was surprised they did not evaporate into steam as they struck the burning heat of her blush-tarnished cheeks. Typists and secretaries glanced up from their work to watch the spectacle of Kelly being led through their midst like an errant schoolgirl. They each glanced down and hurried on with their work before Vanessa could turn her gaze on them but Kelly saw the look of delighted excitement in their eyes. She shivered at the obvious disgust they harboured for her and experienced a moment's self-loathing that she knew should have been directed at Vanessa Byrne.

Vanessa all but hurled Kelly into her office, slamming the door closed behind herself. She graced the redhead with a scornful expression before jamming her finger on to the desk intercom. 'I'm taking no more calls this afternoon, Sally,' she snapped into the machine. 'And you'll have to cancel both my remaining appointments.'

'Yes, Miss Byrne,' Sally's voice replied meekly from the machine.

'Close the blinds,' Vanessa snapped, directing her words at Kelly. 'I'll be in the en suite when you've done.'

'Yes, Miss Byrne,' Kelly said quickly. 'I'm sorry I spilt the coffee on you. It was a genuine accident. I didn't –'

'Whilst you're closing the blinds, why don't you shut up?' Vanessa broke in rudely. 'Hurry up now.'

Unhappily, Kelly closed the Venetian blinds in the office. She would rather have been punished by anyone other than Vanessa Byrne. She despised the woman vehemently and would have made this fact known, if she had thought it would help. However, she knew that it would do no good. She realised the quickest way to get the punishment over and done with was to obey Vanessa's every instruction. Hurrying into the office's en suite bathroom, she was greeted by the sight of Vanessa completely topless.

'Look at my tits!' Vanessa declared impatiently. 'They're bright red because of you, you stupid little slut. Have you seen?'

Kelly could not stop herself from looking at the round orbs of Vanessa's beautiful breasts. They were not bright red, as she claimed, but the hot coffee had given her flesh a rosier hue than seemed usual. Kelly found her gaze focusing on the stiff nipples at the centre of Vanessa's pale-pink areolas. She found the woman's arousal quite unsettling.

'I'm sorry, Miss Byrne,' she began quietly. 'It was an accident. I didn't do it deliberately.'

'Wash my clothes,' Vanessa snapped. She tossed the blouse and bra she had been wearing at Kelly. 'And take your top off too. I can see you've spilt coffee on yourself, you stupid girl.'

Kelly said nothing. Instead, she began to unfasten the buttons on her blouse as she took Vanessa's clothes to the sink.

'Take your bra off too,' Vanessa commanded. 'It looks sodden.'

Reluctantly, Kelly complied. She stood at the sink with the clothes in her hand, painfully aware of her reflection in the mirror. Her breasts, like Vanessa's, were also a darker shade of pink than normal. She also realised her nipples were standing erect and Kelly tried convincing herself that this too was because of the hot coffee which had doused them. Behind her, she could see Vanessa gently teasing her own nubs as she watched Kelly bend over the sink.

'If that stain doesn't come out I'll dock the cost of a replacement one from your salary,' Vanessa informed her. 'The same goes for the bra, you understand?'

'I understand,' Kelly replied softly, hating the sound of Vanessa's voice more than ever. She focused her concentration on the clothes and filled the bowl with warm water. Using a bar of hand soap that was on the edge of the pristine sink, she washed the clothes furiously in the water until she felt certain the stain was gone. She worked on Vanessa's blouse and bra first, before tending quickly to her own clothes.

'There are coat hangers for my blouse and bra in that cupboard,' Vanessa said, pointing. 'Drape your own over the radiator. They'll dry there.'

Kelly obeyed. 'Is that all, mistress?' she asked quietly.

Vanessa laughed darkly. 'I hardly think so,' she replied. 'You haven't tended to my injuries yet, have you?'

Kelly was about to ask her what injuries she meant, when she remembered the fuss Vanessa had made about her scalded breasts. She glanced at the woman's bare tits, aware that Vanessa was happily caressing her injuries.

'What do you want me to do?' she asked.

Vanessa shook her head. 'You've hurt yourself, haven't you?' she observed, nodding towards the red marks on Kelly's chest. 'I'll show you what to do.'

She moved towards the sink and ran a bowl full of hot water. Taking the soap Kelly had used to wash the clothes, she began to rub a lather between her hands. She stopped when she had a fistful of white bubbles. 'They say that warm soapy water is good for burns,' she explained. 'So I want you to do this for me.' She placed her hands on to Kelly's left breast and began to rub the lather into the skin.

Kelly gasped softly, surprised by the sensitivity of her own flesh. She stood resolute as Vanessa massaged the soap thoroughly into her, aware that the woman was paying more attention to her nipple than was necessary. It was a disconcerting feeling. Vanessa manipulated her areola and nipple with skilled dexterity, rolling the nub of flesh between her fingers. Reluctantly, Kelly felt her arousal increase, in spite of her hatred for the woman who was stimulating her. She could feel her chest's rise and fall becoming more and more laboured as the pleasurable sensations began to fill her.

When Vanessa changed breasts and began to knead the right one, Kelly released a guttural moan of pent-up delight. She hated Vanessa and she hated herself for enjoying what was happening. However, she could not stop herself from submitting to the woman. Her arousal was so total she could feel the well of an orgasm building up inside.

'You're enjoying this, aren't you?' Vanessa observed.

'Yes, Miss Byrne,' Kelly replied stiffly, her words made ragged with desire.

'You'd like me to do this on your pussy, wouldn't you?' Vanessa breathed softly, placing her mouth close to Kelly's ear.

155

Kelly closed her eyes, not knowing what to say in reply. She would have loved to have Vanessa perform the same intimate massage on her vagina. At the same time, she was loath to have the woman touching her. It also occurred to her that Vanessa Byrne was equal in rank to Mistress Stacey. Therefore she was far too superior to perform such an act on a trainee like Kelly. As she stood with her eyes closed and these thoughts tumbling through her mind, Kelly realised Vanessa had moved her hands away.

Before she had a chance to open her eyes, she felt Vanessa's soapy palm rubbing against the gusset of her panties. Her short flared skirt was no hindrance to the woman and Vanessa seemed happy enough to massage Kelly's flesh through the fabric of her knickers.

Kelly bit back a sigh of delight. She felt her pants become sodden with hot soapy water and relished the bizarre sensation it inspired. Having another woman caressing her in such a way was intensely stimulating. The pants rubbed against her swollen lips, creating a subtle friction that was devastating. Unconsciously, she placed a hand on the side of the sink to steady herself. The welling orgasm that had built inside her was close to release and, as Vanessa continued to rub the liquid against her crotch, Kelly felt the strength of her impending climax swell to even greater proportions.

She tried to fight against the sensations, not wanting to be brought to the pinnacle of pleasure by Vanessa Byrne of all people.

Vanessa's fingers worked their way beneath the gusset of Kelly's panties. The sensation of the woman's warm fingers stroking her wet, wanton pussy lips was too great for Kelly to struggle against. In spite of her reluctance, an orgasm swept through her, forcing her to shriek with ecstasy. Waves of pleasure rushed through her body, starting at her clitoris and emanating outward and upward. Her nipples ached with the dull throb of satisfied pain.

'There.' Vanessa smiled, straightening herself as she stepped away from Kelly. 'That was good, wasn't it?'

Kelly paused for breath before replying. 'You're right, Miss Byrne,' she said softly. 'Do you want me to tend to your burns now?' she asked.

'Of course,' Vanessa snapped briskly.

Kelly moved to the sink and began to soap her hands as she had seen Vanessa doing. When she had a rich creamy lather between her fingers, she turned to the woman and hesitantly moved her hands towards Vanessa's breasts.

'Perfect,' Vanessa breathed warmly. Relishing the sensation of warm soapy hands massaging her tits, she smiled happily at Kelly. 'That feels perfect.'

Despite her dislike of the woman, Kelly had to agree. Vanessa's skin felt creamy smooth beneath her fingers. The velvety feel of her flesh against the slippery palms of Kelly's hands was a powerful aphrodisiac. For a moment, Kelly was startled by the erotic stimulation she was experiencing. Her hands moved slowly and deliberately over Vanessa's huge, heaving orbs, rubbing brusquely against the tender skin. She did not go out of her way to stimulate the woman's nipples, aware that she was meant to be tending to the mistress's burns rather than her sexual needs. The heel of her palm and the tips of her fingers stroked them occasionally, and each time the touch incited a groan of satisfaction from Vanessa.

Vanessa put her hands on Kelly's bare arms as she continued kneading her breasts. Her grip was hard and firm and Kelly was left in no doubt as to who was in control of the situation. 'Get more soapy water,' Vanessa breathed quietly. Even through her whispered tones, the undercurrent of a threat was still clearly audible.

Kelly responded immediately. 'Yes, Miss Byrne,' she said.

157

She moved to the sink and began to raise a lather between her hands again. When the creamy suds spilt between her fingers she moved them towards Vanessa's breasts.

The woman stopped her.

'Let's try it a different way this time,' she said stiffly. Scooping a handful of suds from Kelly's palm, she smoothed the soap across the redhead's breasts.

Kelly gasped, surprised by the intensity of the stimulation.

Vanessa smiled into her shocked face. 'Do the same for me,' she whispered. 'Wet my tits with your soap.'

Kelly obeyed instantly. She began to massage the soap into Vanessa's heaving breasts, aware of the urgent hardness in her nipples. Her hands moved faster than before and this time her concentration was focused on Vanessa's areolas. Her fingers teased the woman's nipples, rolling them between thumb and forefinger with a measured degree of pressure. The soapy lather created a fluid friction that was rich with erotic power.

'No,' Vanessa whispered, tearing the word forcefully from her mouth. She had her hands on Kelly's arms and this time she pulled the redhead towards herself. 'This is what I want,' she told her firmly.

Kelly was aware that their naked torsos were touching. The creamy lather they had been applying to their breasts rubbed wetly between their uniting flesh. She could feel the hard pressure of Vanessa's nipples scratching urgently against her own. Vanessa held her tightly by the arms, pressing herself fully against Kelly's body. When Vanessa tightened the pressure of her fingers in the tender flesh of her arms, Kelly looked up, wondering if she had caused offence.

Vanessa pressed her mouth against Kelly's. Her kiss was passionate and intoxicatingly erotic. She forced her tongue into Kelly's mouth and explored it fully.

It was the most exciting kiss she had received from

any woman, Kelly thought. Helen's kisses had been passionate but lacking in intimacy. Mistress Stacey seemed to prefer not to overindulge in such obvious stimulation. Feeling Vanessa's tongue explore her mouth, Kelly felt a wave of excitement building inside. The emotions that stirred were intense and she shivered physically in Vanessa's arms.

'You like this, don't you?' Vanessa observed, moving her lips slowly against Kelly's face as she spoke. 'You're really enjoying it, aren't you?'

'Yes, Miss Byrne,' Kelly breathed huskily.

Vanessa pressed her body more fiercely against Kelly's. Their soap-lathered breasts rubbed determinedly together, giving and receiving a myriad starburst sensations of scintillating excitement. Vanessa adjusted her position, placing one foot between Kelly's legs. Then, using her thigh, she rubbed softly against the heated centre of Kelly's sex.

Kelly groaned loudly.

'You don't deserve such kind treatment,' Vanessa observed.

Kelly did not bother replying. Instead she pressed her mouth against the other woman's and extracted a kiss from the sweetness of her lips. Their mouths were locked in a bond of arousal that could not be broken. As their tongues explored one another, Vanessa continued to rub her leg against the aching seat of Kelly's longing. She kept her fingers pressing into the redhead's upper arms, exerting as great a control over her as was physically possible.

When their mouths eventually parted, both women gasped excitedly for air.

'You like kissing me?' Vanessa asked breathlessly.

Kelly nodded.

'Then kiss me here,' Vanessa instructed, forcing Kelly down on her knees. 'If you're half as good with your tongue down there, I'm in for the best afternoon of my life.'

Kelly hesitated as she stared at Vanessa's pale pubic bush. The woman had lifted her skirt to reveal she was knickerless and Kelly could already smell the warm musky scent of her arousal. She tried not to think of her hatred for Vanessa Byrne. Considering the eager appetite of her own arousal, it was not a difficult thing to overlook. However, she hesitated, aware that she was acting like a slave for a woman she deplored. The fact that she was enjoying it only added to her confusion as she vacillated about what to do.

Vanessa was in no doubt about what Kelly should be doing.

'Hurry up and lick it,' she commanded sharply. 'You don't want me to get impatient, do you?'

There was enough warning in her words for Kelly to make an instant decision. She pressed her wet hands against the soft milky flesh of Vanessa's upper thighs and buried her tongue into the woman's cleft. The scent of her excitement was dark and overwhelming. Her pussy honey tasted like nectar and Kelly lapped at it greedily. She pressed her tongue hard against the woman's clitoris and then ran it slowly along the length of her labia.

Vanessa groaned happily. 'You are too good for words,' she moaned softly. Her fingers toyed with Vanessa's hair, tugging the locks roughly.

Kelly gasped with pain but did not stop licking. She could feel her excitement mounting into something tremendous and she knew from recent experience that discomfort and pain would only help. Her tongue probed as deeply as it could into the warm folds of Vanessa's hole. She savoured the sweet taste of her juices, pausing occasionally to inhale the fragrant aroma. Occasionally she would tease Vanessa's clitoris with the tip of her tongue, enticing it from under the hood of tactile flesh it hid beneath. She was aware that Vanessa was close to climax and this realisation brought with it a disturbing arousal. Feeling sure that she was close to her own orgasm, Kelly pressed her mouth against Miss Byrne's hole with hungry determination.

She lapped the tip of her tongue against the mistress's clitoris, coaxing the tiny pearl of pleasure from the confines of its hood. Catching the flesh between her lips, she sucked gently on it. She did not know if the mistress would approve of what she intended to do but her arousal was so great she did not care. All that mattered was pleasing the mistress. Kelly knew that if she did, she would be pleasing herself. Her teeth pressed lightly against Vanessa's clitoris and she nibbled softly on the swollen nub of flesh.

'God! That's good,' Vanessa gasped. 'I'm close. Carry on.' She had a fistful of Kelly's hair in one hand and tugged it roughly as she gave this command.

Kelly squealed uncomfortably but continued as she had been told.

'For punishment,' Vanessa went on, her words ragged with arousal. 'For punishment, I'm going to piss on you,' she explained. 'You'd agree that was acceptable, wouldn't you?'

Kelly could not believe what she had heard. The thought of being used by someone in such a way was abhorrent to everything she had ever believed. The idea of being used like that by Vanessa Byrne, of all people, was even more galling.

Nevertheless, Vanessa's words were exciting enough to push Kelly close to the brink of orgasm. She tongued furiously at the woman's pussy, pushing her head hard against Vanessa's pubic mound. Her hair was now being pulled so hard she wondered if it would come out at the roots but she did not care. All that mattered in that moment was pleasing Miss Byrne. It did not matter what Miss Byrne did to her. She could tug fistfuls of her hair out, piss on her and then beat her arse red raw with a riding crop. Kelly knew that her own orgasm

161

depended on Vanessa climaxing. The boiling heat of her own arousal was so fierce it negated everything else.

Vanessa tugged Kelly's head sharply away from her sex and stared down at her. From her position on the floor, Kelly thought the woman looked truly formidable. 'You didn't answer me,' Vanessa pointed out. 'You don't mind if I punish you like that, do you?'

'No, Miss Byrne,' Kelly replied, her cheeks crimson with shame as she realised what she was agreeing to. 'I don't mind,' she whispered.

Vanessa pushed Kelly's head back to its position at her pussy lips. 'What a servile little slut you are,' she muttered absently. Closing her eyes to enjoy the moment more fully, she repeated the words fondly, gripping Kelly's hair more tightly with each word. 'What a lovely, servile little slut you are.'

Kelly could have screamed with agony as the pain in her head intensified. Her cheeks still felt scarlet with humiliation, but the fire that burnt there was only stoked by Vanessa's insults. She could not tell if it was the pain, the eroticism of the moment or the servility of her position that aroused her most. It was a devastating combination for someone like her. Whatever the cause, she felt herself being propelled towards orgasm at a lightning pace. She knew the climax was going to be a forceful one.

Above her, she could hear Vanessa's moans becoming lower and more guttural. The woman was as close to coming as she herself felt.

Kelly continued to work her tongue furiously on Vanessa's pussy, delving inside her, then tracking a wet course along the length of her lips. She felt the clitoris pulsating beneath her tongue and in that moment she knew Vanessa was about to orgasm.

She moved her head slightly away, intending to inhale the sweet fragrant scent of the woman's explosion. Before she could experience this aroma, she felt a spray

162

of warm liquid spatter against her face. Startled, she opened her eyes and saw the golden stream of Vanessa's piss shooting into her face.

Vanessa was groaning happily with delight. Her head rocked from side to side and a broad smile creased her features as the waves of pleasure flooded her body. Her fingers were still buried in Kelly's scalp but they no longer pulled her hair. Instead they merely held her still.

Kelly knelt beneath Vanessa's stream, unable to believe she was subjecting herself to such a punishment. She could feel the spray flooding over her, warm at first but quickly cooling. The sweet-scented stream of golden yellow bounced against her nose and chin. Her nostrils were filled with the florid fragrance of Vanessa's piss. Not knowing why she did it, Kelly thrust her tongue out, catching the mellow warmth in her mouth and savouring the dark intimacy of its taste. Incredulously, she felt the thrilling rush of her own climax. It exploded inside her body, transporting her to a realm of exhilarating joy. She was in a place where humiliation and pleasure were so entwined they were indistinguishable. It felt divine.

Delirious with pleasure, she moved her face forward into the never-ending jet that shot from between Vanessa's legs. The waves of warm liquid flowed over her face as she licked hungrily at Vanessa's wet hole. The pleasure was intensified by her own eager acceptance of the punishment. She felt the second thrill of an orgasm ripple musically through her body as she licked at Miss Byrne's sodden hole.

She glanced up at Vanessa's face and saw the woman was wearing a distant smile. It was a stark contrast to the cruel smile that usually rested on Vanessa Byrne's lips. Kelly also thought the woman looked as despicable as ever and she was once again reminded of her hatred for the woman.

She experienced a moment's self-loathing as she

realised how easily Vanessa had pleased her, in spite of their mutual antipathy. She also felt a moment's shame as she realised how torrid and base her own actions had been.

It was not that she considered she had done anything wrong. In her own mind it was a simple equation: she was being used, therefore she was useful. She had given pleasure to someone, therefore she was pleasing. It did not really matter what she thought of Vanessa Byrne, just as it did not matter what the woman thought of her. All that mattered was that she had begun to accept her new role in life. She was submissive and servile and, whilst she was not happy about those facts, she could not deny them.

Accepting the situation did not just make life easier, it also made it a lot more pleasurable. She moved her mouth back between Vanessa's legs and began to lap lovingly at her.

'Good girl,' Vanessa breathed, tugging Kelly's head away. She was smiling down at the redhead, a soft smile lighting her lips. 'You took your punishment like a good girl.'

'Thank you, Miss Byrne,' Kelly said quietly.

'There's a change of clothes in that cupboard,' Vanessa said, pointing. 'Get yourself cleaned up and back working in the office. If you're not there in twenty minutes, I'll have to punish you again.'

Obediently, Kelly did as she was told.

Vanessa went to the cupboard and selected a change of clothes for herself. She cast a wary glance in Kelly's direction as she stepped out of the short skirt she still wore. A wry smile twisted her lips and a look of recognition lit her eyes. She paused on the brink of saying something, then stopped herself.

She was used to thinking fast and making quick, yet solid, decisions. Even after the pleasant distraction of the afternoon, her thoughts were still crystal clear and her mental process was as sharp as ever. If Kelly was the person whom Vanessa believed her to be, she thought it would be more prudent to keep the knowledge to herself. The idea excited her and her smile broadened.

She washed herself quickly then stepped into a change of clothes. Her mood was brighter than it had been in days. Leaving Kelly in the en suite, Vanessa returned to her office.

Kelly could hear the woman talking on her intercom, barking commands and bawling irrefutable statements at her subordinates. She detested the sound of the woman's voice and felt her loathing rise again. The memory of their intimacy was washed from her mind as easily as the remnants of their lovemaking were washed from her body. She was still aware that Vanessa was her superior and if the woman gave her an instruction she would have willingly obeyed it.

But she still hated the bitch.

'Change of plan, Kelly,' Vanessa snapped, appearing in the doorway of the en suite bathroom. 'I want you in my office in two minutes.'

Knowing better than to argue, Kelly simply nodded and began to towel her body dry. She quickly stepped into a change of clothes and rushed into Vanessa's office as she had been asked.

'Kneel on the floor, beside me,' Vanessa said sharply.

Blushing with embarrassment, Kelly knelt down. She knew the woman was going to invite other people into the office and the shame of further public humiliation left her feeling cold. Having Vanessa frogmarch her through the crowded typing pool had been a debasing experience. Kelly realised that whatever the woman had in store for her now would be just as belittling.

Vanessa pressed the intercom on her desk. 'Send them in, Sally,' she snapped. 'All three of them.'

Kelly closed her eyes, wishing she could be somewhere else. The shadow of humiliation brought with it a dark arousal that she both loved and detested. It flavoured her excitement with an unsettlingly sweet taste.

In the darkness of her closed world, she heard the muted shuffle of footsteps against the luxurious carpet of Vanessa's private office. When she heard the office door close she dared to open her eyes, so that she could brace herself for what was about to happen.

Staring at the room full of people, Kelly could not believe what she was seeing. Mistress Stacey sat in the chair facing Vanessa's desk. Standing beside her were Russel and Helen. Both of the trainees looked nervous.

'Have you got a problem, Vanessa?' Stacey asked calmly.

'Yes,' Vanessa replied crisply. 'A major problem if we're being honest. One of the trainees is in need of a visit to the black room.'

Stacey frowned. 'What's been happening?' she asked, casting a cursory glance over the three trainees. Her gaze rested on Kelly. 'Is it her?' she asked.

Kelly swallowed nervously.

She wanted to stand up and defend herself. It had not been her fault. She had accidentally bumped into Vanessa. It had not been deliberate or intentional. It had been a simple accident and she had been well and truly punished for it. She did not think she deserved a trip to the black room. That was taking things too far. Miserably, she closed her eyes and waited for the damnable Vanessa to condemn her.

'No,' Vanessa said. 'Kelly and I had a little run-in earlier, but we've sorted all that out, haven't we, Kelly?'

For a moment Kelly could not reply. She was so overwhelmed with relief that the effects were physical. She was not going to be sent to the black room and that thought took precedence over everything else. The sense of release the thought gave was almost palpable.

'Kelly?' Vanessa repeated, the word sounding cold and stark.

'I'm sorry, Miss Byrne,' she said quickly. 'Yes. It was all sorted out. I am truly sorry for . . .'

'Kelly isn't the problem,' Vanessa said, speaking over the submissive before she could finish her sentence.

'Then who is?' Stacey asked tersely. 'If one of the trainees is slacking off, I need to know, Vanessa.'

Vanessa smiled tightly. 'You are in a dominant mood today, aren't you?' she observed wryly. 'I pity the poor thing who's going to end up in the black room with you this evening.'

Stacey rolled her eyes. 'Cut to the chase, Vanessa,' she said dryly.

Vanessa smiled. 'You know how security conscious I am around this place, don't you? We have guards, we have stock controls, we have password-protected databases –'

'This isn't cutting to the chase, Vanessa,' Stacey observed.

'– and we have security cameras.'

Russel and Helen exchanged a nervous glance. It was a subtle gesture but it was noticed by both Stacey and Vanessa. From her position, kneeling at Vanessa's side, Kelly saw the exchange as well.

Vanessa continued. 'I keep the stationery room monitored because it's one of the areas where we can lose a lot of stock. I've caught a couple of petty thieves in there before today. But I have to say the tape I've just received makes the whole monitoring system well worth the money I spent on it.' She smiled broadly at Helen.

Stacey was frowning darkly. 'What have you been up to Helen?' she asked quietly.

Vanessa broke in. 'This is the tape,' she said, handing a VHS cassette across the desk. 'You'll see exactly what she was doing. I trust you'll reward her accordingly.'

Stacey took the tape, her frown deepening. 'Was she alone?'

Vanessa shook her head. 'She'd taken Russel and Kelly with her but the dialogue leaves you in no doubt about who the instigator was. I'm sure you can still whip *him* into the sort of shape I'm wanting.'

Stacey nodded curtly and stood up. 'I'm sorry they were such a disappointment to you,' she said stiffly. 'I'll take them back to the hostel now and see if I can sort things out.' She snapped her fingers, capturing the attention of all three trainees at once.

Vanessa placed a steadying hand on Kelly's shoulder. 'Can you leave this one with me?' she asked. She smiled warmly at the redhead. 'She intrigues me.'

Stacey hesitated before replying. She cast an unhappy glance between Kelly and Vanessa, obviously wanting to refuse this request. 'It goes against company policy,' she said carefully.

Vanessa smiled. 'Some of the things you do in the black room go against company policy,' she remarked. 'But I'm not going to tell anyone about them.'

Stacey glanced at the woman, wondering if this was a threat. 'OK,' she said eventually. 'But go easy on her, or I'll have you in the black room.'

Instead of taking umbrage at the remark, Vanessa smiled indulgently. 'If I was going to let anyone take me into the black room, it would be you.' She waited while a reluctant grin surfaced on Stacey's face. 'After all –' she grinned '– I know that, in the black room, you have a reputation for being the wickedest.'

Eight

Jo sat cross-legged beneath the doctor's desk, cradling the telephone in her lap. The room was pitch-black and her eyes were only just beginning to adjust to the lack of light. It was not the most ideal place to use but she had no other options. The commonroom payphone was out of order and there were no other accessible telephones in the building. This was her only choice. She desperately needed to talk to Stephanie. She was already an hour past the contact time she had specified for herself. The simple problem of having no telephone was not going to defeat Jo Valentine.

Straining her ears in the silence, Jo listened for any sounds that could indicate potential trouble. It was after midnight and she knew all the trainees should be in bed by now. However, there were a handful of guards patrolling the hostel's corridors, reinforcing the strict security with a heavy-handed presence. She doubted they would be thorough enough to search unlit rooms that were supposedly unused. Paid security was never that good. However, Jo's well-developed sense of self-preservation told her that in these circumstances she had to err on the side of caution.

Satisfied that she was so far undetected, Jo cradled the handset of the telephone between her shoulder and her ear. She carefully dialled Stephanie's number. In the silent darkness, the whisper of the dial tone was a deafening roar. Even though she knew this was just a cruel trick her nerves were playing on her, Jo felt her stomach do a nervous somersault. Admittedly, she had every reason to be nervous. The hostel was not a place for the faint-hearted. Her first day had already revealed that much.

She knew she should have suspected something after the incident with Mr Smith. Initially she had dismissed him as an exploiter: a lech who willingly took advantage of every new and vulnerable trainee. It had not taken her long to realise that he was motivated by a darker agenda.

Her thoughts were interrupted by the ringing tone in her ear. Mentally, she could picture the cordless phone in Stephanie's apartment with its shrill tone. The thought was a small sliver of comfort in a bleak night. The phone was answered on the third ring.

'Jo, is that you?'

'Steph, I'm sorry it's taken so long to call you,' Jo began.

'You're whispering. What's wrong? Are you in trouble? For Christ's sake, tell me you're out of that place.'

Jo was taken aback by the note of panic she could hear in Stephanie's voice. Her partner was normally so cool and level-headed that Jo drew on her resilience for inspiration. For the first time since she had met her, Jo heard a ragged edge in Stephanie's voice.

'Christ, Steph!' she exclaimed softly. 'I'm OK. Keep a hold on things.'

'Are you still in there?' Stephanie insisted. 'Tell me you're not.'

'Of course I'm still here,' Jo replied, puzzled and more than a little unnerved by Stephanie's reaction. 'This is an undercover operation, remember. Much as I'd like to do it from the Presidential suite at the Hilton, that isn't a practical solution.'

'She's still in there.'

Jo heard Stephanie say the words to a third person. In the dark, a frown furrowed her brow as she tried to imagine who Stephanie might be talking to. 'Who's with you, Steph?' she asked carefully. 'Is someone putting pressure on you? What's happening?'

Jo struggled to control the rising surge of panic that welled inside her chest but the emotion continued to grow. She focused her thoughts clearly on the problem at hand and tried to ignore the mounting tide of her own fear.

'Tell me, Steph,' she said softly. 'What's happening?'

'You have to get out of there,' Stephanie said quickly. 'I've been doing some research. Nick's been helping me and it turns out that place is a black hole. People go in there and just disappear off the face of the planet.'

'Is Nick with you now?' Jo asked quickly.

'Yes. I called him here when you didn't ring me at eleven. He's concerned about you. He said he'd warned you not to touch this case.'

Jo sighed with heartfelt relief. She could now see Stephanie's panic for what it really was. Nick had been talking to her and filling her head with his stupid ideas about the dangers of the Pentagon Agency. Because she was alone, and had been given the time to dwell on these thoughts, Stephanie's natural concern had blossomed into terror.

If she had been in the same room as Nick, Jo would have kicked him in the balls.

'I know what this place is, Steph,' Jo said quietly. 'It's nothing more than a training ground for submissives. I've almost got the case sorted. I should be out within a day or two.'

'Get out now, Jo,' Stephanie implored her. 'I'm worried about you, Jo. I don't want you being there.'

Jo smiled. Her heart missed a beat as she realised how strong Stephanie's concern was. She must feel something for me, Jo thought, elated by the notion.

She's really worried. That has to be more than just friendship, she decided: that's love.

'I can think of lots of places I'd rather be,' Jo said quietly. 'But if I don't get a result on this case Mr Rogers isn't going to give me the rest of the pay packet I'm expecting.' She considered adding that she had already earnt both the remaining envelopes, and then thought better about fanning the flames of Stephanie's concern. 'Kelly Rogers is a resident here at the hostel. I haven't seen her yet but I've spoken to a guy called Russel who was with her this afternoon. She should be back tomorrow. I can talk to her then.'

Stephanie groaned wearily, an anguished sound that Jo found painful to hear. 'You're not listening to me, are you?' Stephanie cried. 'It's dangerous, Jo. Get out of there.'

Jo tried to think of soothing words or an explanation that would placate her partner. Admittedly they employed a strict regime at the Pentagon Agency, but Jo felt sure she could handle any situation that arose. She realised a lot of the trainees were painfully submissive but that was only to be expected. It was not a sign of danger.

The telephone crackled and hissed in her ear, then Jo heard a man's voice shouting sternly.

'Will you listen to your bloody partner, Valentine? You don't know what you've gotten yourself into. Get out of there now, while you still can.'

Jo glared menacingly at the telephone. 'Fuck off, Nick,' she snapped tiredly. 'I'm not in the mood for you. Be a good boy and tell Stephanie that I'll be OK, then piss off out of her apartment and leave us all alone.'

'I'm saying this for your own good,' he said stiffly.

'And I'm saying this for your own good,' Jo said angrily. 'The next time we meet, make sure you're wearing a steel-plated cricket box.' She would have said more. A stream of insults was poised on the tip of her tongue and she could have happily torn a strip off Nick with all of them.

A flickering of light in the waiting room warned her the security guards were being more conscientious than she had anticipated. Speaking in a stiff whisper, she said shortly, 'I'm hanging up now, Nick. Goodnight.' Without waiting for a response, she replaced the handset firmly, careful not to make a sound.

There were two of them, both male. Jo guessed that neither of them expected to find anything out of the ordinary. Their conversation was muted but the little Jo could glean sounded mundane enough to ease her worries. This was simply a part of their regular night-time routine, she realised. They were expecting their patrol to be as dull and uneventful as it always was. Somehow, Jo doubted this evening would be either dull or uneventful.

Stealthily, she placed the telephone on the floor. Her concentration was focused on the two male voices in the waiting room and she strained to make words from the whispered mumbling.

'. . . can't do anything about it,' one voice said quietly. 'But if they make the league next year then . . .'

The other grunted something Jo could not hear. The beam of his flashlight was moving back towards the waiting-room door and she held her breath, hoping it would continue in that direction.

'Wait a second, Terry. Shouldn't the doctor's door be locked?'

Jo bit her bottom lip and frowned. She had left the door slightly ajar after breaking into the doctor's surgery. It was a modern security lock and she had not trusted her ability to pick the damnable thing a second time. They would almost certainly enter the room and Jo did not doubt they would discover her third-rate hiding place beneath the desk. She knew that some sort of action was required and she quickly turned over the available options in her mind.

'Perhaps the doctor forgot to shut it on her way out?' Terry suggested. The beam of his flashlight hit the door and a thin ray of torch-light pierced the black gloom of the surgery.

'I don't reckon she's the forgetful type,' the first guard replied. 'I think we ought to check it out.'

'Overzealous bastards,' Jo thought sourly. She raised herself from the floor and slid easily into the doctor's chair. In one hasty motion she reached beneath the hem of the short skirt she wore and removed her knickers. Without thinking about the consequences, she stuffed them in one of the drawers on the doctor's desk.

There was always a way out of any problem, Jo thought, a smile twisting her lips. And she realised that, if she played this situation properly, she might get something out of it herself.

The door opened and the two men entered warily. The beams of their flashlights cut brilliant lines of light through the darkness. Jo stayed perfectly still as the torch beams criss-crossed and illuminated the walls and corners of the room. The brilliant white light touched on her, then moved on. For a moment she was filled with the hope that she would remain undiscovered. It was only a small hope, tinged with the sad realisation that she might miss out on her intended fun if that did happen. However, even before Terry placed his fingers on the light switch, she realised her discovery was inevitable.

'Hello, boys,' she said, blinking against the light that flooded the room.

'Who the hell are you?' the first guard asked incredulously.

Jo watched him glance at his colleague, as though the other man might know who she was. She suppressed a small smile of amusement as the man shrugged helplessly.

'You keep an eye on her, Bob. I'll go and fetch the night supervisor.'

'Hold on a second, boys,' Jo said softly. She climbed out of the chair and settled herself on the doctor's desk, allowing the hem of her skirt to rise almost casually. Her warm smile was lewd and eager as she studied the two men. Terry, by the door, was tall and broad, struggling to keep his powerful athletic body in the confines of his security uniform. His colleague Bob did not have as imposing a physique but he still looked more than capable.

'Do either of you two like to gamble?' Jo asked, reaching into the breast pocket of her blouse.

Bob and Terry exchanged a wary glance.

'Gamble?' Bob asked. 'I've been known to have the odd flutter.'

'Should I fetch the supervisor?' Terry asked from the doorway.

Bob waved a silencing hand in his direction. 'Hold on a minute. We're in no rush.' Smiling at Jo, he asked, 'Why are you talking about gambling?'

Jo grinned into his eager face. She held the double-headed sovereign in one hand and tossed it carefully into the air. She caught it lazily and then tossed it again. 'We all know that I shouldn't be here,' she explained. 'I was wondering if you wanted to toss for my future. If it's tails, you can put the handcuffs on me and frogmarch me to one of the senior night staff.'

A broad grin split Bob's face in two. He eyed Jo's legs hungrily then shifted his gaze to meet her eyes. 'And if it's heads?' he asked curiously.

Jo pretended to think about what to do if this was the outcome. 'If it's heads,' she said carefully, 'I suppose I would have to show you how grateful I am that you haven't turned me in.' To emphasise her meaning, she made a show of crossing her legs. For an instant her pubic bush was on full display to the pair. It was only

175

a fleeting moment, but it was long enough to have its effect on both of them.

'Are you in, Terry?' Bob asked without looking at his colleague.

Terry gulped nervously.

Jo smiled at him and winked knowingly. She balanced the coin on her thumb and raised her eyebrows. 'Well, Terry?' she asked mischievously. 'Are you in?' She could see the bulging erection at the front of Terry's uniform. She did not doubt that whatever his head was telling him, his body would elect for him to join the fun.

Terry nodded. The unhappy frown on his face showed he still had some reservations.

Jo grinned and tossed the coin. 'What a surprise!' Jo exclaimed. 'It's heads! Congratulations, boys. You two win the prize.'

'Keep watch, Terry,' Bob said, moving closer to Jo as he spoke. He took her in his arms and lifted her from the top of the doctor's desk in one swift motion. 'You're the prize, are you?' he asked.

She was pleasantly surprised by his unexpected show of strength. She was even more surprised by the hard bulge that shoved against the coarse fabric of his uniform trousers. 'I'm the prize,' she agreed. 'Aren't you lucky?'

'I'm about to find out,' Bob said with a wicked grin.

She rubbed herself against him. 'It didn't take you long to work up an appetite,' she noted wryly.

Bob planted his mouth over hers. It was a passionate kiss, made more thrilling by the urgency of his desire. His tongue entered her mouth and she allowed him to explore her freely. Jo felt flattered by his eagerness to possess her and she shivered beneath his touch. His hands crudely caressed her body, his callused palms dragging roughly over the flimsy fabric of her blouse and skirt.

Jo moved her mouth away from his and pushed his

head down, so he could pay attention to her breasts. Happily, Bob obliged.

'Come and join us, Terry,' Jo called. Her words were ragged with arousal. 'Although it doesn't have to be in that order,' she added with a devilish grin.

Terry glanced nervously at her, then looked away. 'I'm keeping watch,' he replied shyly.

Jo frowned theatrically. Bob's head had moved to her chest and he was sucking her breasts through the fabric of her blouse. His mouth had managed to find her nipples and he ran his tongue over the silky material, creating a scintillating frisson.

'Let him keep watch if that's what he wants,' Bob said. 'I'm sure I won't disappoint you.'

'But I want both of you,' Jo explained patiently. She fixed Terry with a meaningful look. A knowing smile curled the corners of her lips. 'I want both of you together.'

The invitation was enough for Terry to finally get the message. Abandoning his position as look-out, he turned to face Jo and began to ease his arms from the tunic of his uniform.

She smiled indulgently as he quickly tore off his tie, then pulled the shirt from his torso. Her first impressions about his physique had not been misleading. His broad chest was muscular and sun-bronzed. As he hurriedly removed his boots and trousers, she stared at the huge length straining against the fabric of his boxer shorts. She grinned appreciatively.

'This place really is secure at night, isn't it?' she said. 'It seems like you two are always ready for action.'

Bob moved his head from her breasts to between her legs.

Jo stifled a gasp of surprise as she felt his fingers massage the insides of her thighs. Then his tongue was lapping gently against the exposed lips of her vagina and she quivered helplessly.

177

Terry stepped out of his boxers to reveal himself naked. He had a long, thick cock, as sun-kissed as the rest of his body. She hungered for it as soon as she saw it. She placed her right hand on Bob's head and caressed the hairs at the back of his neck whilst he deftly tongued her labia. With her left hand, she pointed a meaningful finger at Terry. When she had his attention, she curled the finger around and slowly gestured for him to join them.

This is the way life should be, Jo thought happily as Terry placed his mouth over hers. There were two male tongues entering her and exploring her. Two men, desperate to have her and longing to please her. She squirmed into a position that would allow Bob to please her more easily. He was working her pussy into a raging whirl of sensation and she did not want to hamper his action in any way. Without even realising she had done it, Jo put her hand on the back of Terry's head and pulled him harder against her mouth. His sporty good-looks and naive impatience made him a good kisser, if not a great one.

Jo could feel her excitement mount quickly as the pair eagerly touched, stroked and caressed her. Terry placed his hands on the front of her blouse and slowly unbuttoned the garment. As soon as he had unfastened the last button, he pulled it open to reveal her bared breasts. Her nipples stood hard and erect. The areolas were flushed to a dark crimson that revealed her intense arousal. Jo felt so close to the brink of orgasm she doubted it would take much more than a finger against her breasts to push her past the point. If her hands had not already been occupied holding the two men in their respective positions, Jo would have stroked her nipples herself and instigated her own climax.

Jo knew that both of these men wanted to please. She so rarely got the chance for such fun she decided to let them try. They both seemed more than capable and they were obviously willing. She could satisfy herself anytime she wanted. Enjoying the attention of two eager able-bodied men was such a rare occurrence that Jo thought better than to try and rush things. It had always been her belief that pleasure was far more satisfying when someone else administered it.

Continuing to kiss her mouth, Terry took a breast in each hand and began to gently knead her wanton flesh. His hands cupped her orbs at first, pressing the flesh firmly, yet gently, with the heels of his thumbs. As she gasped with growing excitement, he moved his hands down so they were rudely teasing her nipples. His strong fingers tweaked the hard erectile nubs, then slowly rolled them between his thumb and forefinger.

Bob continued working his tongue into her hole. She raised her behind on to the doctor's desk and squirmed eagerly against his mouth. Now he was able to lick greedily along the full length of her outer lips, teasing the sensitive folds of her inner flesh with a degree of skill that was surprising. Occasionally his tongue would slide into the slick darkness of her hole.

Jo groaned happily.

She had not wanted to make such a loud sound but the pleasure went beyond her anticipation. She reached one hand down to touch Terry's length and her fingers encircled his huge girth. The urgency of his kissing increased as she slowly rolled his foreskin back over the bulging head of his glans. A pant escaped him as she tugged the skin back with a languid roll of her wrist.

'Take your clothes off, Bob,' she whispered, moving her mouth away from Terry's. 'I want to have your cock inside me.'

Bob needed no more encouragement. As Bob moved away from her, Terry pushed his groin between Jo's legs and rubbed himself against her.

Jo began to kiss the muscular guard once again. She gasped happily as she felt his prick rubbing between her legs and with one hand she teased the lips of her sodden pussy wide apart. With her other hand she guided Terry's thick cock towards her hole and rubbed the huge tip against herself. She could feel Terry trying to force his cock inside but Jo was in control. She smiled at his impatience and continued to tease, allowing him to press his dick against her without actually entering. His hands were still fondling her breasts and his thumbs were rubbing perfectly over her erect nipples. Every pore in Jo's body wanted him to plunge into her but she was determined to stretch the moment out for as long as she could. She repeatedly teased his swollen head against her sex, marvelling at the thrill of delight this intimacy brought. She rubbed his glans against the hood of skin enveloping her clitoris. The friction inspired a shiver of pleasure.

Her pleasure intensified when she felt a second pair of hands begin to caress her. She moved her mouth away from Terry's and took a moment to study Bob's naked body. He was not the same formidable build as his muscle-bound colleague, but he could not be called unattractive either. She guessed he was ten years Terry's senior. His body was in good physical shape, and although his cock was a lot shorter it was considerably thicker. Jo noticed that it was also furiously hard and desperate to be inside her.

She pressed her mouth against Bob's as she reached out for his cock. She had to stretch her fingers so that she had sufficient grip on his length to tease the foreskin back and forth. Slowly, relishing the sensation, Jo wanked both men as they kissed and caressed her. Her hands moved up and down to an unhurried rhythm. She squeezed each alternately, then released the tension of her grip. Her dextrous finger-play had both men urgently gasping for more.

'More?' Jo enquired innocently.

It was an unreal situation, made more exciting by the

fact that it was actually happening. To have a cock in each hand was a tremendous sensation and she felt her body thrilling with excitement as she turned this thought over in her mind. She distantly remembered this had all started out as a bribe for safe egress from the doctor's surgery. Now the situation was turning into the most thrilling evening she had enjoyed for a long time.

She knew the thought was unfair to Nick. He had increased his skills as a lover tremendously since they had ceased their relationship. The night she had spent with him, when he had taken her in his bath and pleased her so totally, had been an overwhelming experience. However, after talking on the phone with him earlier, Jo did not care to be fair to Nick. He had annoyed her and he had upset Stephanie and she felt justified in dismissing him from her thoughts.

She slid easily from the doctor's desk and allowed her skirt to spill to the floor. Shrugging the unfastened blouse from her shoulders, Jo released her hold on the two cocks for a moment before kneeling down on the floor. Her grin widened as she took hold of them again. She smiled coyly up at the two men who towered above her.

Gently wanking the pair, Jo rubbed the two stiff dicks carefully against her tits. Terry was in her left hand, and she traced the tip of his cock around the sensitive flesh of her left areola. Bob was in her right. She pressed the tip of his dick against her right nipple. As she did this she continued to roll her fingers up and down the short length of his thick shaft. He had a large, wide eye in the end of his penis and she tried half-heartedly to slide her nipple inside it. It was an impossible task, she realised, but that did not stop her from extracting as much pleasure as she could from the moment.

She stroked Bob's cock with her right hand and moved Terry's away from her breast. With a broad smile on her face she pulled it towards her mouth.

She heard him moan with excitement even before she had done anything else. Her fingers stroked his balls playfully, then she encircled his length and brought the tip close to her bottom lip.

'This is a lovely cock, Terry,' she told him earnestly. 'I wonder if it tastes as good as it looks?' Without waiting for his response, Jo flicked the tip of her tongue over the head of his erection.

Terry gasped with delight.

She allowed her tongue to rub slowly over the glans as she stared at him.

'You lucky bastard,' Bob breathed gruffly.

Jo turned to face him, a deceptively innocent smile twisting her lips. She moved Terry's cock back to her breast, where she rubbed it in slow circles around the nipple. 'Why is he lucky, Bob?' she asked innocently. 'Because I did this?' As she had with Terry, Jo ran her tongue over Bob's short, fat length. A shiny pearl of his excitement glistened on the tip of his length and she lapped at it greedily.

Bob groaned.

'Do you think he was lucky because I did that?' Jo asked softly. 'You'd have thought he was luckier if I'd done this.' Without any hesitation, she moved her mouth around the wide girth of Bob's dick and took it into her mouth.

Bob released a pent-up sigh of elation.

Jo sucked hungrily on his cock, moving her head backwards and forwards at the same time. It was so thick she felt her jaw beginning to ache as she stretched her mouth to accommodate him. The thought of how it would feel when she had it between her legs made Jo's inner muscles tingle with furious anticipation. She continued to take him into her mouth, sucking hard, and teasing his balls with her fingers. She could sense that he was near to the brink of climax and she only relented her eager pace when she sensed he was getting too close.

She moved her mouth away and wiped her lips dry on the back of her hand. A mischievous twinkle glinted in her eyes when she glanced up again. 'I bet you wish I'd do that for you, Terry, don't you?' Jo asked.

Terry nodded eagerly.

Jo smiled. She guided his cock slowly towards her lips. With her other hand, she continued to play carelessly with Bob's dick, careful not to push him beyond the point of no return. When she had Terry's cock close enough, she moved her tongue out and licked the swollen tip lovingly. Her tongue caressed the vast purple dome, and she savoured the salty taste of his arousal. Then she pressed the tip of her tongue against his glans and deliberately licked beneath the sensitive rim of his helmet. Jo allowed her tongue to work its way around Terry's rigid dick, savouring every moment. When his cock was sodden with her saliva, she turned away from it and began to use her mouth once again on Bob.

She prolonged their agony for as long as she dared. All the time she was slowly pushing and pulling their foreskins backward and forward. Careful not to show one more favours than the other, she shifted her mouth from cock to cock until each man was on the point of coming.

They reached down to her and stroked her hair as she worked them into a heated frenzy. Occasionally, Terry would try and hold her head against his cock as she tongued him but this was not done with any force and she enjoyed the sensation of mild restraint. Still kneeling on the floor, she pressed her thighs together and rubbed them hard. The action provided little in the way of satisfaction but it did give some stimulation to the tingling lips of her pussy. She could feel the wetness of her arousal pouring from her. As she pushed her thighs furiously together, she realised the tops were drenched with the creamy slickness of her own juices. She had not yet orgasmed and the need for that sensation was overwhelming. She ground her thighs together again, in one last desperate attempt to extricate some pleasure by herself, then stopped aware that it was not helping.

'Enough,' she gasped eventually, moving her mouth from the two cocks. 'I want this in my pussy,' she told Terry, squeezing his length meaningfully.

Jo knelt on all fours, shoving her arse high into the air for him.

Terry took a moment to caress the cheeks of her arse. There was a tender smile on his lips as he nuzzled his cock against her sodden hole.

Jo groaned in anticipation. She was facing Bob's thick length and held it steady with one hand as she tried to take it all in her mouth. It really was a huge organ, she thought, as she stretched her mouth wide to accommodate him. She wondered idly how such a thick cock would feel ejaculating inside her mouth. That idea alone would have been enough to make her orgasm. Coupled with the feeling of Terry's cock sliding inside her wet, velvety depths, Jo found she could fight the inevitable no longer.

A sigh of delight drifted from her as the waves of pleasure rushed through her body. Her thoughts were clouded by a hazy mist of exhilaration as a dozen explosions of joy erupted inside her body.

Terry's magnificent cock continued to ride her as she came again and again. He did not hurry his pace. More likely, she thought, he was probably slowing it down. Her inner muscles were clamping hungrily on to him, squeezing him ever closer to his own climax. His hands held tightly on to her thighs as he continued to ride her with a measured, almost leisurely pace.

If her mouth had not been so full, Jo would have screamed with elation.

Taking her mouth away from Bob's cock, then shifting her pussy away from Terry's, she smiled

184

indulgently at the pair. 'Let's try it this way,' she suggested, lying down on the cool, tiled floor. This time she offered her pussy to Bob, placing her head just beneath Terry's long, stiff member. Neither of the men said a word in protest and within a minute she was enjoying the satisfying delights of two cocks again.

In her mouth she savoured the honey-sweet taste of her own juices. Terry's cock was dripping with pussy cream and Jo licked it clean before sucking the throbbing member furiously hard.

Between her legs, she was experiencing a wealth of new delights. She had enjoyed sex with two men before but it had never been like this. Normally she found it easier to accommodate the second man after the first had satisfied her. Because Bob's dick was so wide she could feel the lips of her vagina straining to welcome him. It was an uncomfortable feeling that bordered on being painful. However, it stopped just short of discomfort. Instead of hurting, as she had anticipated, Bob's stocky little cock made her quiver with delight. She knew this was partly due to her own arousal, and partly because of the excitement of the situation. The inner walls of her quim struggled hungrily to accept him and they were rewarded with the breathtaking satisfaction of his entry.

Jo sighed delightedly. She felt the waves of pleasure wash over her body like a torrent. The scent of her own pussy juice on Terry's cock was intoxicating, as was the feel of his gorgeous cock filling her mouth. These sensations were coupled with the intense fever that Bob was igniting inside her. Jo bit back a shriek of heartfelt gratitude. He rode her slowly, and she relished the experience. His tremendous girth was more than she could have wished for.

However, the feeling was not so debilitating that she lay idle. Once her pussy was used to his size, Jo bucked her hips back and forth along his length at her own careful tempo. The heated friction in the lips of her labia felt divine. She thrilled to the myriad sensations it inspired.

'I'm coming,' Bob gasped, breathlessly. 'Slow down, won't you. I'm coming.' There was a desperate plea in his voice that Jo was tempted to heed. She squeezed her inner muscles tightly around him for a moment, amazed that her over-stretched pussy could still manage that feat.

Then she released him.

Bob staggered away from her. He held his swollen cock in one hand and watched as it twitched furiously. Jo moved her mouth from Terry's cock and went towards Bob's. She pressed her lips over the head of his penis and sucked hard on him.

It was too much for Bob to fight against. He groaned happily. His cock jerked maniacally against Jo's lips and his seed shot into her mouth. Jo lapped eagerly at the tip of his swollen prick, determined to taste as much of his semen as she could. She felt rivulets spraying her cheeks and dousing her lips. The heady scent of his ejaculation filled her nostrils.

Glancing at Terry, Jo realised she still held his rigid cock in her hand. She could feel the hardness of his arousal and she knew that he too was close to coming. She suspected the sight of Bob's climax was a contributory factor. Because of this, she wiped Terry's hard cock against her semen-drenched cheek.

When she took him in her mouth, she was able to lick Bob's seed from Terry's long length. Not that she was able to savour that flavour for long. Within five seconds of entering her mouth, Jo felt the impatient pulse of Terry's orgasm as his red-hot seed sprayed the back of her mouth. She swallowed greedily, wishing she had the chance to savour the taste of him. When he eventually withdrew from her mouth, she traced the tip of her tongue around his failing member and kissed the end of his cock tenderly.

Smiling from one guard to the other, she said quietly, 'I suppose this means that I can go back to my room without being reported.'

'I doubt that very much,' a woman's voice answered.

They all turned and stared at the unexpected source. They had been so involved with each other that none of them had heard the surgery door open.

Mistress Stacey surveyed the scene. A dark frown furrowed her brow as she glared at Jo.

No one knew how long she had been standing there, or how much she had seen. However, they were all aware that this post-coital scene was sufficient for her to guess what they had been doing.

'I won't be so stupid as to ask what's been going on in here,' Mistress Stacey said slowly.

Terry reached for his clothes whilst Bob began to babble an apology.

Jo watched them distantly, still high on the euphoria of all the pleasure she had just experienced. She realised Mistress Stacey was staring angrily at her and she tried to think of something appropriate to say. She was on the point of saying something facile and crude when Mistress Stacey spoke softly to her.

'So, you're Jo Valentine.' The words were spoken with a note of sour contempt.

Jo frowned. The woman was not supposed to know her identity. She was Jenny Vaughan in here: submissive Jenny Vaughan; ideal fodder for the agency's inner-pentagon training programme. Aware that the situation could not be salvaged, Jo decided it would probably be best if she stayed silent. Defiantly, she met Stacey's gaze as the two men dressed.

Casting her dour frown on Bob and Terry, Stacey snapped angrily at them, 'You. If you want to have the slightest hope in hell of keeping your jobs, take her to the black room, now.'

The black room.

Jo knew she should have been scared. Even on her short acquaintance with the Pentagon Agency she knew this was a last resort.

A defiant streak inside her was determined not to show fear in front of the brutal Mistress Stacey. Her determination was made resolute by the fact that Stacey knew who she was.

Silently, although they both looked as though they regretted having to do it, Bob and Terry did as Stacey had told them.

Without a word of protest, Jo allowed the two men to lead her to the black room.

Nine

She stopped outside the apartment, the tip of her key resting on the lip of the Yale lock. 'You've been enjoying the Pentagon Agency's training for a week now,' Vanessa said quietly. 'Do you think you've learnt anything?'

Kelly found she could not meet the woman's eyes. 'My training has been very thorough,' she replied humbly. There was an awkward silence and Kelly realised something more was expected. Trying not to think about her feelings of loathing for Vanessa Byrne, she searched her mind for an appropriate comment. Kelly's hatred cast a dark cloud over her thoughts and eventually she gave up, unable to think of anything she could add.

Vanessa slapped the back of her hand across Kelly's face. It was a short sharp blow, intended more as a shock than a punishment.

Kelly put a frightened hand to her face and stared miserably at the woman. She felt a moment's revulsion for herself as she realised the blow had ignited a spark of dark sexual excitement.

'Don't mumble. Look at me when you speak, and answer my questions properly in future,' Vanessa barked. 'Do you understand?'

Kelly bit back the automatic response she was about to give, aware that it did not satisfy the criteria Vanessa had just outlined. She stared meekly into the woman's face, hoping her expression did not look defiant or antagonistic. 'Yes, Mistress Byrne,' she replied, forcing her voice to sound firm and confident.

Vanessa stared warily at her for a moment. Her piercing gaze seemed to take in every aspect of Kelly's appearance. A scowl curled her lips, as though she was unhappy with what she was looking at.

Kelly held her breath and hoped she had not incurred the mistress's wrath.

'That's better,' Vanessa remarked coolly. 'You're learning.'

Kelly felt a wave of relief sweep over her body. The storm had passed, she thought. She was sensible enough to know that Vanessa's black mood could recur at any moment and she cautioned herself against disobedience in the future.

Vanessa unlocked the door to her apartment and allowed Kelly to walk in ahead of her. She closed the door behind them before turning the light on. The illumination revealed the modest splendour of her home.

'You and I are going to talk tonight,' Vanessa told her calmly. 'I have some questions for you and I want answers. Lies and dumb insolence will be punished severely. Do you understand?' She glared at Kelly with a malevolent frown that was a constant reminder of her lack of tolerance.

Kelly swallowed nervously. She wished she did not find this woman's intimidation so arousing. A dull, heady tingle had begun to sparkle in the pit of her stomach. She could feel the flush of colour that burnt her cheeks. She was still determined to keep her true feelings from Vanessa if that was at all possible, but somehow she doubted it would be.

Vanessa slapped her hand across Kelly's cheek again. This time there was more force to the blow and Kelly gasped with surprise. She could feel the reddening sting of a hand mark against her face. 'I asked if you understand?' Vanessa said. In spite of her authoritative posture, her tone was still calm and unruffled.

'Yes, mistress,' Kelly replied quickly. She met the mistress's gaze, miserably aware that her own eyes were shining with excitement.

Vanessa's smile was predatory. 'Good,' she replied shortly. 'I think you and I should get along famously tonight. The kitchen's through there. Go and prepare a salad for me. I'm going to shower and change.' With her instruction given, Vanessa set off towards one of the other rooms.

Kelly did not bother to watch her go, she was busy doing as she had been told.

She entered the kitchen and quickly accustomed herself to the room. It was quite spacious for an apartment kitchen. Within a few minutes she was busy preparing Vanessa's salad. She knew better than to organise a meal for herself. Vanessa had made no mention of Kelly eating and she knew better than to misinterpret a mistress's instructions. She quickly prepared the vegetables. It was such a mundane task that she found it impossible to keep her mind on the chore.

Her hatred of Vanessa Byrne, and the cause of that emotion, kept recurring to her. She loathed the woman vehemently and felt physically sick at the thought of having to do everything the depraved bitch commanded.

Worse than her hatred for Vanessa was Kelly's dark feeling of self-loathing. The fact that she was doing Vanessa's bidding reminded her of how weak and ineffectual she really was. Even more unsettling was the thrill of pleasure she received from debasing herself in such a way.

These thoughts tumbled haphazardly through her mind as she prepared the meal. She was lost in her own world of unpleasant memories and dark recriminations.

191

She only escaped from this sullen reverie when a hand fell on her shoulder.

'That's good,' Vanessa's voice came from behind her. 'You've started doing as you're told.'

Kelly continued rinsing a lettuce in the sink. She had not been instructed to turn around and she knew better than to try and second-guess a superior.

'Fetch the honey from the pantry,' Vanessa barked. 'And bring me a couple of bananas.'

Kelly put the rinsed lettuce leaves down and fetched the items Vanessa had requested. She retrieved them without looking at the mistress. She was only a trainee and she knew it was not her place to look at a mistress unless she had been ordered to.

It then came as something of a shock when she happened to glance at Vanessa. She stopped herself from releasing a cry of surprise and set her face in a stoic mask that concealed her emotions. Kelly's training at the Pentagon Agency had taught her two things about her own emotions: they were unimportant and they should never be made known to a mistress.

Vanessa stood proudly in the kitchen, dressed in a red-satin basque. In one hand she held a long riding crop with a battered leather tassel on its tip. Her other hand was carefully caressing the strap-on phallus she wore.

Of all the cruel instruments of torture Vanessa could have used on her, Kelly thought the phallus had to be the worst. It was difficult to maintain an expression of quiet acceptance in these circumstances, but Kelly managed it.

'Undress and spread the honey on your tits,' Vanessa snapped. A wistful smile played across her lips, as though she was extracting a good deal of pleasure from simply fondling the strap-on cock. She did not repeat her instructions. She did not have to. Kelly responded instantly.

As soon as she was naked, Kelly opened the jar of honey and dipped her fingers into the thick, golden syrup. She cast a hesitant glance in Vanessa's direction and realised the mistress was watching her intently. Unperturbed, Kelly smeared a handful of honey across her own bared breasts.

It was a bizarre sensation. The liquid was so viscous it was almost sickening. Globules of the thick sticky fluid stuck to her body and trickled slowly down her chest, towards her stomach. The cloying sweet scent of the honey reached Kelly's nostrils and she inhaled deeply.

'That's it,' Vanessa said. 'Rub it in.'

Kelly obeyed. She rubbed the honey into her breasts, concentrating on the stiffening nubs of her taut nipples. Her excitement was intense and she had already begun to forget about Vanessa's hated strap-on. Lubricated with the sticky fluid, her nipples slid coyly from her fingertips.

'Rub some between your legs,' Vanessa said sharply.

Kelly scooped another fistful of the honey and placed it against the cleft between her legs. Some of the nectar spilt through her fingers and she wondered if she would be forced to lick it from the floor. It did not matter to her. She was prepared to do whatever Mistress Vanessa commanded. All that mattered right now was doing as she had been told. Being able to do that gave Kelly as much pleasure as the unfamiliar sensation of lubricating her pussy with honey.

She pressed the palm of her hand against the heated nub of her desire. The lips of her labia were thick with the glutinous fluid and, regardless of how hard she pressed against herself, she could feel her skin sliding easily away. Her fingers dripped honey in long golden strings. They were so thickly coated she had no problem inserting first two, then three easily into herself. The sensation was electric. Her labia parted effortlessly to accommodate the entry of her fingers. She quickly realised she could fit a fourth finger inside herself. Without any hesitation, she did it.

'Having fun?' Vanessa asked quietly.

Startled, Kelly opened her eyes. She had been lost on her own plateau of exhilaration and had almost forgotten that Vanessa was there. Smiling, Kelly nodded and said softly, 'Yes, it feels incredible.' She did not know if this was the truth but it was close enough. The honey on her chest already felt sticky and uncomfortable. Between her legs, she could feel swatches of her pubic bush matting together with the viscous liquid. However, the oily lubrication it offered was such an unprecedented stimulus she could not honestly call the experience unpleasant.

'Now,' Vanessa said. 'I want you to stroke some on my cock.'

Kelly paused, wishing the woman had not reminded her about the strap-on she was wearing. There was no thought of disobeying. She had been given an instruction and it was her duty to obey. Nevertheless, she hesitated for an instant.

The riding crop whistled through the air and bit wickedly at her thigh.

Kelly released a shocked cry of surprise. At the same time, her inner muscles squeezed excitedly against the tips of her four fingers. Morosely, she realised that the experiences of pleasure and pain were now inextricably linked. The crack of a whip against her leg brought with it a sexual response. If she was being totally honest with herself, it had heightened her arousal immensely.

Vanessa sliced the riding crop through the air a second time. This time the battered leather tassel snatched cruelly at Kelly's left nipple.

She muted the natural response to exclaim and reached quickly for the honey, as she had been told to do. Smearing the fluid over the full length of Vanessa's strap-on phallus, Kelly risked a nervous glance at the mistress's face.

'That's better. You'll either learn to do as you're told when you're told, or you'll taste this whip on your arse for the rest of the night. Do you understand?'

'Yes, mistress,' Kelly replied meekly. She glanced down as her hand encircled the cock-shaped length of plastic. Her earlier revulsion for the strap-on had now gone. She was too busy concentrating on the needs of her mistress to consider her own thoughts. She took a second fistful of honey and smothered the cock's length with it.

Vanessa placed her hand on Kelly's honey-soaked breast. Her fingers found the nipple she had struck with the crop and she squeezed it between her forefinger and thumb. It was a passionless exchange, done purely to inflict more pain on Kelly. Both women knew this, but Kelly stifled a gasp of delight. A shiver of excitement coursed through her body. She was reaching for more honey when Vanessa twisted the nipple hard, then tugged it downwards.

Trying vainly to ignore the flurry of excited responses this treatment caused, Kelly glanced warily at her, wondering if she had inadvertently upset the mistress.

'That's enough honey, honey,' Vanessa joked, a winsome smile on her face. 'Now you may lick my cock.'

It was an unusual request but Kelly was not surprised by it. She knelt down in front of the mistress and stared timidly up at her. She had never had a cock in her mouth before, neither plastic nor real. She wondered if she should tell the mistress this much, then realised it was not something the woman would want to know. Without any further hesitancy Kelly moved her mouth over Vanessa's cock and began to lick the honey from it.

She stroked her tongue over the hard plastic, filling her mouth with the thick yellow honey, and swallowing it greedily. The taste was sickeningly sweet. The fragrance filled her nostrils with a cloying aroma that was almost unbearable. Regardless of this, Kelly continued to lap honey from the plastic dick until the mistress told her to stop.

'Take this banana and use it on yourself,' Vanessa barked.

Kelly took the banana Vanessa was offering. Without moving from her kneeling position in front of the mistress, she stripped the skin from it then slid it easily into the honey-wet hole between her legs. The sensation of the cool fruit sliding into her honey-drenched depths was disturbingly arousing. She relished the feeling. As she slid it in and out, fucking herself with the hard yellow fruit, Kelly felt the thrill of an orgasm building deep inside her. Every muscle in her body seemed tense with anticipation. She moved the length in and out of herself with a greater urgency. At the back of her mind she wondered if the mistress would punish her for this obvious self-gratification. The thought was unsettling but even the fear brought a sharp flavour to her excitement.

A low groan of bliss escaped Kelly's lips as she pushed the banana deep inside herself. A majestic symphony was playing between her legs and she found herself wishing that this happiness would never end.

Vanessa looked down on her. A cynical frown creased her brow. She reached between her own legs, behind the strap-on dildo she wore, and spread the lips of her labia wide apart. 'Now use it on me, you little slut,' she commanded sharply.

Vanessa's cold tone and cruel words added impetus to Kelly's impending orgasm. She felt the inner muscles of her pussy grip tighter against the length of yellow fruit. Although she was reluctant to take the fruit from inside herself, Kelly knew better than to disobey. The honey-smothered banana slid easily from between her legs. Her pussy muscles clenched tightly around its egress.

196

Kelly used one hand to spread the mistress's lips and with the other she stroked the tip of the fruit against Vanessa's hole.

Vanessa sighed. 'That's nice,' she encouraged softly. 'Go on.'

Kelly pushed the banana slowly inside the mistress, moving her face closer so that she could see exactly what was going on. She considered flicking her tongue across Vanessa's clitoris. It was not something she had been instructed to do but the temptation was there. As she forced the yellow length inside, then withdrew it slowly, the desire to push her own tongue against Vanessa's pussy increased. Repeatedly she reminded herself that she had not been told to. Trainees did not do things on impulse, she told herself. They did things they were told to do. In spite of these thoughts, Kelly realised the temptation would not go away.

Vanessa's cries increased in volume. She growled words of encouragement down to Kelly. Occasionally she would bark an angry rebuke at the submissive when she did not seem to be using the banana properly.

Kelly could sense Vanessa was close to climax. She smiled happily as she realised she had given her mistress this pleasure. She once again resisted the urge to lick at her clit.

It was difficult to believe she had held Vanessa Byrne as a figure of loathing and contempt earlier in the evening. Kelly knew that nothing had really happened to make her change her mind about the woman. She had simply come to accept Vanessa's dominance and her own servility. As Vanessa had physically forced her to humiliate herself, Kelly had come to realise she was not worthy of hating Mistress Vanessa.

Unable to resist the temptation any longer, Kelly pressed her nose forward and inhaled the musky scent of Vanessa's sex. She stroked her tongue across the woman's clitoris and was gratified by a scream of unparalleled pleasure.

When Vanessa climaxed a spray of creamy liquid squirted from her tightly packed hole.

Kelly felt the banana being pushed out, into her hand. She quickly licked up the mistress's juices from the woman's tingling labia. She still had her face buried between Vanessa's legs when she felt a hand pulling her hair backward.

'Did I ask you to do that?' Vanessa asked. Her face was glowing with the warmth of her orgasm but a cold, menacing light glinted in her eyes. She dragged Kelly up from the floor, her hand holding firmly on to a fistful of Kelly's flame-coloured tresses.

Kelly felt her face being pulled towards the mistress's. Their noses were so close they almost touched. With a huge effort of willpower, Kelly forced her eyes open and stared unhappily at Mistress Vanessa.

'Well?' Vanessa demanded angrily. 'Did I ask you to do that?'

Kelly shook her head, unable to bring the words to her mouth.

Vanessa shook her angrily. 'Answer me, you little slut!' she exploded.

'I'm sorry, mistress,' Kelly wailed. 'I mean ... You didn't ask me. No. I'm sorry.'

A frown of contempt darkened Vanessa's face. She pushed Kelly down and away from her, releasing her hold on the submissive's long red hair at the last possible moment. 'Bend over, on all fours,' she barked. 'I won't tolerate this sort of behaviour. I don't expect you to think for yourself. When you're with a mistress you should only do what you've been told. Nothing else.'

Kelly adopted the position as she had been instructed, thrusting her buttocks high in the air. She knew what was about to come and she was prepared for it. She had acted for her own satisfaction and that went against everything the Pentagon Agency had taught her.

The first blow of the riding crop struck smartly across both buttocks. It was all that Kelly could do to stop herself from screaming. She had been anticipating the blow but she had never believed it could be so forceful. Bravely she suppressed the cry of despair, warmed instead by the response the punishment inspired.

Vanessa delivered a lengthy series of blows to Kelly's arse. She used the crop first on one cheek, then the other, then finally across both cheeks. Her aim was unerringly accurate and each blow felt as though it were landing on top of the last one.

As well as the stinging discomfort they inflicted, Kelly realised the blows were also fuelling her treacherous libido. She hated herself for getting pleasure from torture like this but she did nothing to stop Vanessa from administering the punishment. Instead, she simply revelled in the delight of having her backside properly beaten.

When Vanessa eventually threw the riding crop down, Kelly sighed with regret. She stared sadly at the instrument that had been used against her. She almost wished the punishment had not ended so soon. Her buttocks were a flaming red welt of burning flesh. She wondered if the heat of her striped backside had any relationship to the heat of the arousal inside her. As she slowly came to terms with her enjoyment of servility, Kelly suspected there might be a link.

She did not have time to give the matter any great thought. She felt Vanessa moving behind her. Then she felt a hand on her backside. It was a hand that was wet and sticky with honey. Her burning cheeks were daubed with the thick fluid and Vanessa rubbed it in with a cruel hand.

Kelly gasped back sobs of pained embarrassment, determined not to break down in front of Mistress Vanessa. When a honey-soaked finger slid into her anus, she could not stop a cry from escaping her lips.

'It feels good, doesn't it?' Vanessa asked coolly.

Kelly could not think of a reply at first. Then the fear of being punished for not answering encouraged her to respond. 'Yes, Mistress Vanessa,' she said quickly. She was not sure if the answer was the truth. She had already guessed what was coming next. This exploratory finger was simply a precursor to Vanessa's inevitable goal.

The idea of what was about to happen chilled her. It was cruel and obscene but, no matter how much Kelly detested it, she could not deny that the feeling of the woman's finger up her arsehole was disturbingly pleasurable.

For a moment, Kelly was caught off guard.

Vanessa still had her fingers up the submissive's arse but Kelly felt something prodding against her pussy lips. She expected it would be the dildo; she could mentally picture it sliding inside when she closed her eyes. Because the phallus did not feel as solid as she had anticipated, Kelly glanced awkwardly between her legs. It came as no surprise when she saw the banana was being pushed into the dark depths of her deep wet hole.

Kelly groaned, a wave of elation sweeping over her as the fruit filled her wanton hole. Her arms and legs began to tremble in an involuntary spasm. The thrill of an orgasm threatened to erupt yet again inside her. Vanessa only slid the banana in and out twice but it was enough to make Kelly scream with delight.

'Here,' Vanessa barked.

Kelly heard the voice as though it were far away. She half turned to face the mistress and saw the woman was offering her the banana. Not sure what she was expected to do with it, Kelly took the offered fruit and breathed a soft thank you.

'Eat it,' Vanessa told her coldly.

Kelly swallowed nervously.

'Eat it right now,' Vanessa repeated.

Kelly sniffed the fruit warily. The scent of the banana was still there but it was mingled with so many other aromas. Knowing better than to incur Vanessa's wrath, Kelly pushed the banana into her mouth and began to chew. She could taste the flesh of the fruit but this was just a subtle flavouring. The taste of the honey filled her mouth, sickeningly sweet and a poignant reminder of all that had transpired so far. There was also the subtle musky taste of her own and Mistress Vanessa's juices. The two flavours were beautifully intermingled and Kelly felt her arousal being rekindled as she enjoyed the fruit.

She would have loved to savour the flavour. Kelly could not believe it was possible to enjoy such a strong arousal from a taste but this was exactly what she was experiencing.

Vanessa did not allow her any time to savour the pleasure.

As Kelly took her second bite from the banana, Vanessa removed her fingers from the girl's anus. She pressed the tip of the strap-on dildo against the rim of Kelly's arsehole and bucked her hips forward. In one slow movement, the dildo entered Kelly's backside.

She sighed with a mixture of shock and euphoria. She had barely had a chance to catch her breath when Vanessa started to slide the strap-on out of her. The muscles of her sphincter were clamping tightly down around the intrusive length of plastic. A tingling rush of pleasure filled her entire body.

Then Vanessa plunged the dildo back into her.

Kelly shrieked happily.

'Eat your banana,' Vanessa said.

This was all being done for a purpose, Kelly realised suddenly. She knew exactly why Vanessa had her in this position. It was not merely an act of sexual humiliation; this was far more personal than that.

It should have been upsetting, she thought. She was

suffering total humiliation on so many levels she could not begin to calculate them all. Her face was crimson with shame and the cheeks of her arse burnt furiously from the beating she had received. She could picture the scenario Vanessa was replaying for her and the memory stung far worse than the marks on her backside. And yet, the embarrassment and mental discomfort were just as sexually arousing as the languid strokes of the plastic cock that filled her arse.

As she swallowed another mouthful of the pussy-juice-scented banana, Kelly fought against the rising threat of an orgasm. It was a futile struggle but Kelly thought it was probably her last hope. This was the ultimate she could envisage in humiliation. If she did not try and fight against it now, she would spend the rest of her life as a submissive. She did not know if this was a good or a bad thing but she wanted time to consider all her options before committing herself to just one of them.

Unfortunately for Kelly, the decision was out of her hands.

Vanessa struck her hand against Kelly's backside. Her fingers landed hard and accurate on the stinging red marks that striped the trainee's arse. At the same time she plunged the strap-on dildo deep inside the submissive's anus.

Kelly lost her battle against the impending rush of pleasure. A cry of bewildered joy burst from her lips. She felt her limbs trembling with uncontrolled ecstasy. Her knees buckled first, then her elbows. The tingling wave of delight continued to sweep over her. Helplessly, Kelly collapsed on to the kitchen's linoleum floor.

Vanessa stared down at her, an inscrutable expression on her face.

Kelly looked into the mistress's eyes, wondering what the woman was thinking. She did not know whether to apologise for collapsing, or thank her for the pleasurable punishment she had given. Eventually she remembered it was not her place to speak until she was spoken to. Her tremors of delight were quickly replaced by a nervous shiver as she lay beneath Vanessa's icy-cold stare.

'Get washed, finish my salad, then join me in the lounge,' Vanessa said. 'I think that you and I have a lot to talk about.'

With this said, she turned her back on Kelly and walked away.

Alone in the kitchen, Kelly hugged herself on the floor. She wondered what else it was possible for Vanessa to do to her. Whatever the woman had in mind, Kelly knew it was not something she should look forward to. She quickly went about the business of cleaning herself up, then dressed and finished the mistress's salad. Hurried on by nervous anticipation of what was to come, Kelly had the meal prepared within five minutes. She took it into the lounge, as the mistress had commanded, then sat on the floor and watched the woman eat.

Vanessa remained silent throughout the meal. It was only when she had finished the last of the salad that she turned a knowing eye on Kelly.

'I know who you are, don't I?'

Kelly shrugged uncertainly. 'I'm your slave, Mistress Byrne,' she said quietly. 'I don't need to be anything other than that, do I?'

Vanessa shook her head, a wry smile curling her lips. 'Of course you're my slave. Your name is Rogers, isn't it?'

Kelly swallowed dryly. 'Yes, Mistress Vanessa,' she replied meekly.

'I know your husband, don't I?' Vanessa persisted.

'I don't have a husband,' Kelly said quietly.

Vanessa slapped her hand across Kelly's face. It was not the hardest blow she could have delivered but it was sufficient to sting Kelly's cheek. It was also enough to remind Kelly of her position. She could be stubborn and uncommunicative with trainees like Helen but Mistress Byrne would not tolerate such behaviour.

'Don't lie to me, slave,' she growled. 'I don't have to accept that.'

Suppressing a nervous shiver, Kelly nodded and stared down at the carpet. She mumbled an apology and admitted, 'Yes. I think you do know my husband. He was one of your slaves.'

Vanessa smiled, her suspicions confirmed.

It was not something Kelly wanted to think about. The memory was still as painful as the reality had been. Distressingly, the recollection forced itself into her mind.

She and her husband had never enjoyed a particularly torrid relationship. Even at the beginning of their marriage the sex had not been spectacular. After three years of matrimony Kelly had come to think of the whole act as some sort of chore or obligation. It was not that she did not enjoy sex. On the contrary, she loved it and in the early months of her marriage she had been delighted to discover she was an adept lover. However, her husband lacked interest. Before their wedding photographs were one year old, he had stopped visiting the matrimonial bed whilst she was awake.

For a second anniversary present, he treated them to separate beds.

Kelly could have lived with this subtle rejection. She had battery-powered toys and her fingers. She also had her imagination. Each time the urge had fallen upon her, she had employed all of these substitutes.

She had been brought up to believe that sex was not the most important thing in a marriage. Eventually she came to believe it had very little to do with marriage. If things had progressed differently, Kelly could have happily continued her life as the sexless Mrs Rogers.

But then her husband met Vanessa Byrne.

It was an encounter with repercussions that Kelly was still experiencing.

She did not know when, or where, the pair met. Her husband had a number of lucrative businesses and Kelly supposed he had met her through some connection with his work. Kelly only saw Vanessa once, but it was sufficient.

It was the night that changed her entire life.

That night, she was roused from her sleep by a muted cry of pain. It was a soft sound but she was a light sleeper and easily woken. She glanced at her husband's single bed on the other side of the room. Unhappily, she realised it was empty.

Unnerved by the sound and her husband's absence, she reached for a dressing gown and walked out of the bedroom. On the landing she froze with nerves.

She would not have dared to make the journey down the stairs if she had not heard a woman's musical laughter. Like the groan that had stirred Kelly from her sleep, it was a muted sound but she heard it distinctly. She climbed cautiously down the steps to the hallway, aware that the voices were emanating from the dining room. She supposed it was just possible that her husband was entertaining a business colleague.

Cautiously, she crept to the door of the dining room. She did not want to embarrass her husband by bursting in on him and his colleagues. She was only dressed in her dowdy night clothes and she knew such an intrusion would be an embarrassment. The door was closed firmly but she bravely pressed the handle down and pushed it slowly, forcing it slightly ajar.

For an instant she was surprised by the brilliant white explosion of light. The explosion occurred a second and then a third time before she realised it was simply someone taking photographs. Hoping that the flash bulb was enough of a distraction to allow her to open the door, she pushed it slightly more ajar. She could only see a small part of the room but what she saw was enough.

Save for a blindfold across his eyes, her husband was naked. He was on the floor, kneeling on all fours with his buttocks thrust high up in the air. As Kelly had suspected, he was entertaining a business colleague. But not at all in the way she had expected.

Vanessa Byrne stood over him, completely naked except for a strap-on phallus. She was just putting down the instamatic camera she had been using, and did not seem to be looking at the door.

Kelly watched as the woman picked up a short, severe riding crop. Vanessa's attention was focused on Mr Rogers. She stood behind him and, as she pushed her makeshift cock into his backside, she brought the crop down on to his bare thighs.

Kelly's husband stifled a groan, a smile of delight showing his true feelings about the game. His tiny cock, an organ she had so rarely seen or used, stood proudly beneath him. 'I'm sorry, Mistress Vanessa,' he mumbled. His voice was a choked whisper of delight. 'Please don't beat me again.'

Ignoring his request, Vanessa sliced the crop down sharply three times in swift succession. It bit the air with a fearsome whistle and striped his flesh like red paint.

It was obviously the punishment he wanted, Kelly thought. She watched her husband's cock pulse furiously and shoot tiny dollops of semen on to the carpet. A grin of broad delight split his masked face in two. Even though he wore a blindfold, Kelly knew his eyes would be closed with dreamy elation as his orgasm pushed the seed from his body.

A tear trickled from the corner of her eye as she studied the scene. She could not define her emotions. She did not know why she was crying and she could not be bothered to try and work it out. Idiotically, she stared at the scene, wondering what was going to happen to her marriage now.

'Lick it up,' Vanessa barked. 'Lick it up now,' she hissed. 'And if there's a drop left when you've finished, I'll make you drink my piss, do you understand?'

Kelly heard her husband groan excitedly. He hurriedly whispered his agreement. She watched as he moved his head down to the floor and began to blindly lap up his own cream.

Mistress Vanessa still had him impaled on her strap-on phallus and Kelly noticed she was sliding in and out of him as she barked her commands. She fixed her attention on the woman, wondering what she possessed that her husband had found missing in his wife.

Before she had the chance to draw any conclusions, Kelly realised Vanessa was staring at her. Their eyes met and Kelly saw an encouraging sparkle in the woman's eyes. Vanessa tossed her long golden curls away from her face and smiled softly. With one neatly manicured fingernail, she beckoned Kelly to join her.

Kelly stared at her, unable to believe the woman's audacity. She watched her husband licking his own seed from the carpet as this other woman fucked him with the plastic cock she wore. Her welcoming smile and obvious enjoyment seemed so wholly sincere that Kelly felt as though she was being awkward for not accepting the invitation.

Horrified by the thought of participating, Kelly fled the room.

Sitting in Mistress Vanessa's lounge, Kelly was fervently trying not to think about the scene she had witnessed. Stubbornly, it would not leave her mind's eye. The whole scenario explained so much about her husband she felt stupid for not having anticipated it.

In the early days of their marriage she had coyly suggested that they should experiment with role-playing games. His reaction had been derisory, and now she knew why.

He was as sexually submissive as she was but he was scared to tell her. That fact alone would not have bothered her. She would have been happy to try any game or activity that brought them closer together. In spite of their sexless marriage, she was not a prude.

The thing that bothered her was that he had shared his fantasies with another woman. Not only had he shared his fantasies with another woman. Kelly had watched as he turned them into a reality.

'It's not uncommon,' Vanessa explained.

Kelly was surprised by the note of tenderness in her voice. She found herself studying the mistress warily.

'I'm no philosopher,' Vanessa went on, 'but there's a Yin and Yang to most people's nature. It makes them want to experience both sides of life. I know a heavy-metal guitar player who spends his free time listening to ballet music and opera. It's the same thing with your husband. Like a lot of aggressive business-men, he needs a release for the submissive side of his nature. It's not uncommon. It's the same with me.'

Kelly stared at the mistress uncertainly. 'But, mistress,' she said carefully, 'you're ...' She paused, aware of the damning indictment she had been about to make against a mistress. Swallowing nervously, aware that Vanessa was studying her closely, Kelly quickly reconstructed the sentence in her mind. 'You enjoy an aggressive, dominant role in your social life.'

'Yin and Yang,' Vanessa explained glibly. 'At work I'm a real pussycat.'

'But ...' Again she stopped herself, aware that she was on the point of causing offence.

'You were going to say that I acted like a real bitch today, weren't you?' Vanessa asked slowly.

208

Unable to meet her eyes when she responded, Kelly nodded.

'I was a real bitch to *you*,' she said. 'I was also a real bitch to Helen and Russel. With everyday clients and customers, trust me, I'm a real pussycat.'

Kelly could not picture the image in her own mind. Her thoughts and emotions concerning Mistress Vanessa were still too personal and one-sided. However, she did not doubt the woman was sincere and she nodded her understanding.

'Yes, mistress,' she said quietly. 'And you're probably right about Mr Rogers' nature.' After a moment's thought, Kelly added, 'I bare the man no ill will, but you are wrong about one thing.'

Vanessa frowned at Kelly, reminding the redhead exactly where her place was.

Bravely, Kelly continued, 'Since the day I left his house, I have stopped thinking of him as my husband.'

The stern frown vanished. Vanessa leant forward and stroked her curled fingers down Kelly's cheek.

'His loss,' she breathed softly, 'is the Pentagon Agency's gain.'

She pressed her mouth against Kelly's lips and kissed the redhead passionately.

Ten

Jo walked quietly with the two security guards, uncomfortable in the stony silence. She was still naked and the scent of their lovemaking still filled her nostrils. Under other circumstances she would have enjoyed the reminder.

'I hope I haven't screwed up your jobs here,' she said, addressing them both.

Bob smiled at her. 'I was getting fed up with the work anyway,' he said comfortingly. 'Besides, Terry and I have been thinking of going into business together. So I suppose you've just hurried the process along.'

'Yeah,' Terry agreed, his voice an embarrassed mumble. 'It's no big deal.' A broad smile split his face and his cheeks turned crimson. 'And, anyway, you were worth it.'

Jo stopped and looked at the two men hesitantly. 'You're not just saying that are you? Not the bit about me being worth it. I know that's bound to be true. Were you really fed up with the work here?'

Bob's smile tightened and he gently encouraged her to start walking again. 'It's not us you have to worry about now,' he said carefully. 'You've got to look out for yourself in this place. I've heard terrible things about this black room.'

Not knowing why, Jo shivered. She too had heard many things about the black room. She had not heard anything specific. None of those she had spoken to had

210

actually been taken there. They were only repeating hearsay and third-hand accounts.

In spite of that, Jo had heard enough about the place to dread being taken there. She wondered if she should make a break for it. She knew she would not need to put up much of a fight. It was even possible Bob or Terry might lead her to the front door of the building and let her go. She would need to find some clothes first but, again, she could see a way around that.

Jo discounted the idea before it was fully formed. The two guards were in enough trouble already. If they allowed Jo to escape they could face far worse punishment. Jo knew she could not ask them to take that risk. Bravely, she turned into the final corridor that led to the black room.

The door was open and she bit back a cry of alarm. The thought that she was so close to being a prisoner in the black room chilled her. Unconsciously, she slowed her pace down to a crawl.

A figure appeared in the doorway. It was a tall man, dressed in pale jeans and an open shirt. Jo recognised Mr Smith instantly and she swallowed nervously. Her arse still stung from the spanking he had administered at her interview. At the time she had realised he was holding back. Now she wondered just how far he was likely to go.

Behind him she saw a smaller figure, meek and cowering. Jo guessed the woman was one of the Pentagon Agency's trainees. More specifically, she realised the woman was the latest victim of the black room.

Tears stained the woman's face. Her entire body trembled beneath the baggy folds of the towelling dressing gown she wore. She stared at the floor. As Jo neared her, she realised the girl's teeth were chattering.

Mr Smith was addressing the blonde in a kind, almost avuncular manner.

'You see, Helen, we weren't lying about how bad the black room is?'

Helen shook her head, still staring at the carpet.

'I trust you'll remember everything that's happened in here,' Mr Smith went on. 'It should help you to realise that we don't tolerate insubordination here at the Pentagon Agency.'

Helen nodded quickly. She had still not dared to look at the man who was talking to her. Jo noticed that everything about the woman's posture and body-language indicated she was terrified of Mr Smith. If he had reached out to touch her cheek, Jo guessed the blonde would have screamed in horror.

'Now you can go back to your training and become the best temp we have on our books,' he told her reassuringly. 'I've never known a trainee yet who's needed to endure a second visit to the black room, although . . .' His kind smile disappeared for a moment. A dark malevolent frown crossed his brow and his tone of voice was drained of all its former warmth. 'It has been agreed by the directors that a second visit to the black room will be a lot more memorable.'

Helen sighed miserably. Her shivering intensified and the chattering of her teeth was now clearly audible.

For the first time she seemed to notice Jo and her escort. She glanced nervously at the three of them then turned away. After a moment she cast her frightened glance at Jo again. Jo stared into the girl's eyes and was shocked by what she saw there. Despite her terror and discomfort, the blonde was staring at Jo with an expression of anguished pity.

God only knows what she's been through, Jo thought, panic rising in her chest. Whatever it was, it was sufficient to make her sorry for the room's next unfortunate victim.

Mr Smith turned his attention to Jo and studied her calmly. 'Two visitors to the black room in one night.

There's one for the record books.' His smile broadened. 'Do I call you Jenny Vaughan?' he asked. 'Or do you prefer to be addressed as Jo Valentine? I really do have difficulty knowing how to address a spy properly.'

Jo considered replying with a smart 'fuck off!' but she stopped herself before the words were properly formed. Whatever Mr Smith had lined up for her, Jo knew it was not going to be a pleasant experience. He was already upset by her presence in the hostel and she realised that it would not be sensible to antagonise the man any further.

'Call me Jenny,' Jo responded evenly. 'I don't know who Jo Valentine is.'

'If that's the way you want to play it, Jenny,' Mr Smith replied tonelessly. He turned his attention to the two guards. 'Take her for a shower, guard the door whilst she's in there, then bring her back here. The room will need to be prepared again.'

Helplessly, Jo allowed the two guards to lead her down the corridor to the shower room. A feeling of relief washed over her as she realised that her visit to the black room had been postponed. Admittedly, it was only a temporary reprieve. The short trip to the shower room was only delaying the inevitable. However, she found the prospect of the black room so utterly terrifying that any reprieve, no matter how small, was a consolation.

Helen was led back to her room by a fellow trainee. She was so lost in her own thoughts that she did not even know if it was a man or a woman leading her. All she was aware of was the hand on her dressing gown and the silent figure escorting her through the hostel's corridors. The trainee took her back to her room and sat her down on the bed. Without a word, the unseen figure turned off the light and closed the door, leaving Helen alone.

Helen collapsed on the bed and gripped her thighs tightly. They still ached and she relaxed her grip so she did not have to endure any more pain. She had already experienced enough of that for one night. Trying not to think about the last three hours, Helen closed her eyes and tried to shut the memories out. Her fingers moved up the sore flesh of her inner thighs and she quivered as a tingling ache rekindled the memory of her suffering. Her hands moved slowly upward and she found her fingers were hovering dangerously close to the lips of her vagina. She was scared to touch herself, fearful she would still be in pain and unsure if self-pleasuring was permissible. She did not dare to consider touching her own breasts. The rough fabric of the towelling robe she wore was already irritating the tender flesh of her nipples. To actually touch them was unthinkable.

She remembered Mr Smith's parting words as she had left the black room. He had told her that she would spend the next day confined to her room. She would be brought her meals and supplied with whatever books she required. He had also told her she could come to terms with her punishment in whatever way she thought best.

Helen licked the tip of her index finger and tentatively moved it towards her pussy.

The ache in her loins was tremendous and unsatisfied. She yearned to feel the thrill of pleasure she had previously taken for granted. Her finger moved towards the hood of her clitoris and she shivered feverishly. Her eyes were still closed and in the darkness she hoped that any pleasure she could give herself would start to wash away her memories of the black room.

As her finger touched the soft pearl of exposed flesh, Helen was split by conflicting feelings. She could have screamed loudly as the tip of her finger met the flesh: she was still sore and the last thing her clitoris needed was such intimate contact. She was also in a state of

214

unnaturally high arousal. Eagerness smouldered inside her like a fever. The need to satisfy herself was stronger than she would have believed and, because of this, Helen continued to play with herself.

The pain acted as an aphrodisiac, she noticed. The more she pressed against her clitoris, the more it hurt. The more it hurt, the greater her enjoyment. Within a moment of her fingers beginning to explore, Helen realised she was on the brink of an orgasm.

Her shivering had subsided slightly. When she licked a second finger and allowed that one to stroke the tender folds of her pink pussy lips, the tremors returned.

Although it felt uncomfortable, Helen believed her moistened fingertips were acting like a soothing balm. As she rubbed herself lightly she knew it would not be long before she experienced the blessed relief of an orgasm. She had convinced herself that such a wave of pleasure would release her body from the misery she was currently enduring. The thought was an appetising one and she held on to it with a zealot's faith.

It was true, she had been in the black room. From now on, Helen realised she would always be a different woman. She would do as she was told. She would obey instructions and never break the rules. She had experienced the black room and she had no intention of returning there.

The orgasm swept through her and she cried softly. Desperately tired, she felt unable to find the energy to give proper voice to the strength of her climax. A chaotic jumble of thoughts and emotions filled her mind. Even though she had not touched them her nipples throbbed with a delightful aching pleasure. Her clitoris screamed with the furious burning of delight.

Exhausted and spent, Helen turned her face into her pillow and took comfort from the moment's reprieve her orgasm had given. As the waves of pleasure had flooded over her, the pain of her aching body had briefly

215

subsided. The sensitivity of her nipples, the burning fire between her legs, the throbbing ache of her backside: they had all paled into insignificance. In that moment of pleasure, Helen had been able to forget her misery and revel in the euphoria of pure elation.

Before the pain had a chance to return, Helen took a moment to think about the brunette she had seen at the door of the black room. She had never seen Jo Valentine before and did not know who she was. All that Helen knew about the woman was how strongly she pitied her. It was unsettling to think of someone else enduring the same things she had just experienced. Quickly, Helen tried to close these thoughts from her mind. The relief of her climax was already beginning to ebb away. As it did, the aches and pains of her suffering returned. They were still poignant enough to remind her of all she had been through.

Helen pushed her tear-stained face into the pillow and prayed for sleep. I'm a changed woman now, she told herself, unable to believe the transition had finally been made. I'm a changed woman.

It was a comforting thought and she supposed she ought to have been grateful to Mistress Stacey and Mr Smith for their lesson. However, the lesson had been severe and she could not summon up the magnitude to be grateful.

As sleep enveloped her, Helen's last waking thought was for the woman they had been taking into the black room.

You poor bitch, Helen thought. You poor, unfortunate bitch.

In spite of the room's warmth, Jo shivered nervously. Her hands were manacled above her head and she knew there was no escape.

You shouldn't be here, Valentine, she thought unhappily. This room is for submissives and you don't fall into that category.

She swallowed nervously as the truth struck home.

She was a prisoner in the black room.

Jo took a moment to study her surroundings. One wall was lined with mirrors from ceiling to floor. The others, as she had half-expected, were lined with copious drapes of luxuriant black velvet. Aside from a closed cupboard in one corner, the rest of the room was bare.

It was not the torture chamber she had been anticipating. There were no severed heads impaled on spikes protruding from the walls. There was no discreet rack in one corner with a choice of cat-o'-nine-tails hanging from it. Most surprisingly, the walls were not carved from stone and daubed with the blood of previous victims.

Like everywhere else in the Pentagon Agency's hostel, the black room was nothing more than a subtly converted room from a detached suburban residence. Jo suspected that the only thing that made this place any different was the people who inhabited it.

Muted lighting increased the air of hushed anticipation and Jo began to suspect the room was sound-proofed. The silence was so profound she thought it was deafening. Admittedly, she did not expect to hear many sounds at one o'clock in the morning but would have anticipated something. She strained her ears to hear any sound other than that of her own nervous heartbeat. There was nothing.

Studying her naked reflection in the full-length mirror, Jo wondered what they had in store for her. She had been left in the middle of the room. Her hands were manacled above her head. The manacles were secured to a chain suspended from the ceiling. She was having to stand on tiptoe to keep in contact with the rich pile of the carpet. Her legs and arms were already beginning to ache.

She wondered what else she would be subjected to before the night was over. It was a thought she did not dare to contemplate too deeply. She could still recall the expression of mournful pity Helen had graced her with. That expression, and its myriad implications, had been deeply unsettling.

She watched the door open behind her. It came as no great surprise when Mistress Stacey and Mr Smith entered. They were both dressed in their normal day-clothes. Each carried a menacing-looking cane. Jo swallowed nervously.

She was determined to keep her fears to herself. 'Great,' she said, with brash self-confidence. 'I'm pleased you two could make it. Now, I hope you both realise, I summoned you here for a very serious purpose.' Her heart was pounding fiercely in her chest and she could see that her reflection had paled significantly. Bravely, she tried to continue with her confident façade.

Mistress Stacey walked over to Jo and stood directly in front of her. She held the cane loosely in her hand, as though she had forgotten she was carrying it. Placing her mouth over Jo's, she kissed the investigator passionately on the lips.

It was an unexpected gesture and Jo was surprised by the instantaneous response her body supplied. Her nipples hardened against the swell of Stacey's chest as the woman pressed close. The dull pulse between Jo's legs began to throb and she inhaled the soft, subtle fragrance of the mistress's perfume.

When Stacey stepped away she stared into Jo's face with a broad smile on her lips. A sly expression of enjoyment lit her eyes. Almost casually, Stacey reached out and stroked one of Jo's rock-hard nipples.

Jo shivered, not having anticipated such intimacy.

Behind her, she felt a hand caressing her buttocks. A quick glance in the mirror confirmed it was Mr Smith. His rough palms brushed over the bare flesh of her arse and he kneaded the skin with a careless disregard.

It was a peculiar situation, Jo thought. She could have tolerated his unsolicited attention a lot more easily if she had not found herself responding to it. Stacey's kiss and Mr Smith's touch were unsettlingly exciting. The pair were good, she conceded. They were very good. It would have been easier to deal with the black room if it had not begun like this, she thought. The hint of forbidden pleasure was something she had not anticipated. She could feel her control of the situation slipping away. It was a sensation she was not used to.

'What are you doing here?' Mr Smith asked, his lips pressed close to her ear as he whispered the question.

Jo glanced up at her manacled hands, suspended from the ceiling. 'Would it sound trite if I said I was just hanging around?' she asked glibly.

Mr Smith's smile disappeared. Jo watched his reflection in the mirror as he raised his cane and brought it smartly across her buttocks. She stifled a gasp of surprise. The sting of the rod bit cruelly into her. It was a powerful blow, stronger than she had been expecting.

Stacey placed a kiss on Jo's mouth. She cupped the swell of her breast with one cool hand. Their tongues entwined. It was the fluid motion of warm desire. Again, Jo was not expecting it and she was surprised by the way her body reacted. The combination of pleasure and pain inspired her arousal to a degree she would not have thought possible.

'Your name is Jo Valentine,' Mr Smith said stiffly. 'You are a private investigator by profession and we'd like to know what you are doing here at the hostel.'

It was a shocking statement for him to make. At first Jo could not accept that Mr Smith knew so much about her. It was possible that a member of staff or a trainee had recognised her but Jo did not think it was likely. Trying not to dwell on the matter, in case he saw the consternation on her face, she tried to salvage her assumed identity. 'My name is Jenny Vaughan,' Jo replied defiantly. 'And I am here because I'm training to be one of your temps.'

This time the cane stroked her arse three times. Once for each buttock, then once across the pair of them. The force he used was intolerable. Jo could feel the muscles in her legs wanting to give up. The pain was so excruciating it took a concentrated effort to stop herself from falling. Not that she would have been able to fall, Jo realised. The manacles would stop that from happening. Tears stung her eyes but she blinked them back, determined not to start crying. Her backside was a fire of flaming coals and she doubted she could endure much more of this punishment.

There was only one saving grace in all of this, she realised. She was reluctant to admit it, even to herself, but the pain was not just causing discomfort. She had never anticipated that she was the sort of person who could get pleasure from being submissive. The notion had always been alien to her. Now, as she endured Mr Smith's caning, she began to wonder if there was a masochistic streak lurking somewhere inside her own make-up. It was a disturbing thought and she did not want to dwell on it for too long.

'Jenny Vaughan signed her agreement to all punishments here at the agency,' Mr Smith said quickly. His voice was ragged and Jo wondered about the cause. He could be angry, or breathless with exertion after beating her with the cane. There was a third option, she realised, but it was not one she wanted to contemplate.

It was unnerving to think Mr Smith was aroused by the punishment he had administered. Whilst she suspected this was the cause, Jo tried not to let her mind dwell on the matter.

'If your name isn't Jenny Vaughan, if you're not one of our trainees, then we could release you from this room.'

Stacey pressed her face into Jo's neck and nuzzled her

gently. The palm of her hand moved down over the flat of Jo's stomach. Slowly, it went further. She trailed her fingers lazily through the dark curls of Jo's pubic bush. 'That's right,' Stacey whispered. 'If you're not Jenny Vaughan, then we have no right to keep you here.'

'All we want to know, Jo, is why you're here,' Mr Smith told her. From behind, he reached around her body and caressed one breast. His fingers found the stiff bud of her nipple and he squeezed it roughly. His body was pressed against her back. Even though he was still fully clothed, Jo could feel the swell of his erection pressing through the fabric of his trousers. The urgent hardness pushed uncomfortably against her bare backside.

Unwittingly, Jo responded with a sigh of delight. She realised this was just a beginning and wondered if there was an easy way out. They already seemed to know too much about her. Considering this, she knew lying would accomplish nothing.

'OK,' she agreed heavily. 'You're right. I am a private investigator and my name is Jo Valentine.'

'Very good,' Mr Smith said encouragingly. As his right hand continued to play with her breasts, his left went between her legs.

Jo felt his fingers stroking clumsily against the swell of her sex. Almost unconsciously, she shifted position so he could touch her more easily.

'You seem like a fast learner, Jo,' he told her. His mouth was close to her ear and he whispered the words softly.

Stacey pressed her mouth against Jo's other nipple. She flicked her tongue against the taut bud of flesh. The stimulation was incredible and Jo shivered excitedly as she enjoyed the man and the woman attending to her like this.

Mr Smith pressed his lips close to her and blew against the sensitive flesh of her neck. When he spoke his words were soft and almost loving. 'So, your name is Jo Valentine. You're a private investigator by occupation, and you're here because . . .'

'I'm on a case. I can't say any more than that. You know, client confidentiality and all that,' she added glibly.

Mr Smith's fingers were still on her nipple. He squeezed the bud hard and twisted it roughly. The effect was dynamic.

Jo heard herself scream but could not decide whether the sound was caused by pain or pleasure. The two sensations, which had once seemed to be at opposite extremes, were becoming inextricably linked inside her mind.

'I'd rather hear the truth,' Mr Smith said with disdain. 'But if you want us to play rough, Jo, then that is what will happen.'

Jo barely had a chance to take his words in before she realised the pair had moved away. Mr Smith left the room. Stacey was moving towards the cupboard in the corner. From her position, Jo could not see what she was getting, but all became apparent when the woman turned around. In her hands, the mistress held a shaving mug, a brush and a cutthroat razor. She smiled sadly at Jo as she moved towards her.

If she had not been manacled to the spot, Jo would have backed away from the woman. 'What are you going to do?' she asked nervously.

Stacey ignored the question. 'You really should have told us the truth,' she said softly. 'It would have been a lot easier for you.'

'I am telling the truth,' Jo told her desperately. She stared at the razor in Stacey's hand. 'What are you going to do with that?'

Stacey shrugged, a disarming smile on her lips. 'I'm just going to shave you,' she said innocently. 'That won't be so bad, will it?'

Jo doubted her explanation was as full as it could be but she nodded reluctant acceptance of the situation. She watched as the mistress knelt down in front of her and began to create a lather with the soap and brush.

If I was James Bond, Jo thought desperately, I could kick her unconscious from this position, reach my legs up, pick the lock on the manacles with my toenails and make my escape. It was a ludicrous thought and she smiled at the farcical image it presented. Even if she had the ability to pick locks with her toenails, Jo knew that there was no way in hell she could lift her legs up that high. Sourly, she wished she had kept up her new year's resolution about the exercise video.

Jo watched as Stacey placed the first creamy dollop of lather into her pubic bush. She had been excited whilst Mr Smith and Stacey had been touching and caressing her. It did not take much for the strange feeling of the lather to reawaken her arousal.

Stacey teased the foaming brush through Jo's pubic mound. She eased lather into the neatly trimmed triangle of hairs and then moved downwards. Without a word to Jo, she slid the brush between her legs and lathered the lips of Jo's vagina.

Jo felt her breath deepening as she enjoyed the stimulation. She was uncomfortable. Her arse still burnt from the caning she had received and her arms were a dull constant ache. However, she could not deny this whole experience was having a powerful effect. She wished her hands had been free so she could either caress herself or touch Mistress Stacey.

Stacey moved the cool blade through Jo's pubes with a well-practised ease. She handled the razor with skill and had shaved her bare within two minutes. Her fingers slid against Jo's soapy flesh and held her steady as she used the razor. Without employing any intimacy, she shaved each dark, wiry tendril from the lips of Jo's pussy, leaving a smooth, pink expanse of flesh.

It was an unnerving experience. Jo knew she could not trust Stacey. Whilst she doubted the woman was going to use the razor as a weapon, the fear was still there. She held her breath as the blade scratched the hairs from her skin. She was aware that her entire concentration was focused on the area Stacey was shaving.

When Stacey finally folded the blade into its handle, Jo breathed a heartfelt sigh of relief. She took a moment to collect her thoughts then stared at her bare reflection in the mirror. Almost absently, she tried to decide if she liked the look.

It seemed unreal to be considering such a thing. The danger of her situation had not escaped her. The enormity of the predicament still weighed heavily on her mind. But Jo knew there was also her vanity to consider.

The shaved look was not something she had ever contemplated before. She had always been rather fond of the curly thatch of pubes that covered her sex. Since they had first appeared during the early years of her adolescence she had considered the hairs to be an essential part of her femininity. She wondered idly what Stephanie would make of the bald pussy she now sported. Pragmatically, she reminded herself that she and Stephanie were not yet on such intimate terms.

Stacey took the shaving equipment back to the cupboard and reached for something else. Jo was trying to see what the woman was getting when she heard the door open.

She swallowed a nervous mouthful of fear when she saw Mr Smith had returned. He was wearing a pair of sturdy gardening gloves and in each hand he carried a prolific bouquet of lush, verdant foliage. Her heart began to beat nervously.

Jo knew very little about flowers and plants. In a florist's shop she could just about tell the difference between the yellow roses and the red ones. However, even she knew what these plants were.

'Nettles,' she gasped. She was horrified by the thought of why he might be carrying them.

Mr Smith graced her with a tight smile. He was obviously enjoying her discomfort. 'Yes,' he agreed. 'Nettles. Perhaps these will encourage you to tell the truth.'

Jo closed her eyes and considered her predicament. They were offering her a simple choice, she realised. She could either tell them all about Mr Rogers and his missing wife, or she could endure a nettling, along with whatever else they had in store for her. To Jo's practical mind there should have been no contest between the two choices. She had always adhered to the rule of client confidentiality before, but she had never had to pick from two such options.

'I've been trying to locate a missing person,' she said carefully. 'I trailed her to this address and saw that the only way in was to disguise myself as a new recruit.'

Mr Smith and Stacey exchanged a glance.

'Go on,' Mr Smith encouraged her.

Jo considered telling him about Kelly and Mr Rogers but she could not find the words. The fact that she had never betrayed a client had not seemed important before. Now it seemed paramount.

'That's it,' Jo assured him.

'Can you supply us with any names?' he asked.

'I'd rather not,' Jo replied evenly.

Mr Smith turned to Stacey and nodded meaningfully.

Jo watched the woman approach and kneel down again in front of her. She had a tube of fluid in one hand and she squirted some on to her fingers. Without a moment's hesitation she smeared the ice cold liquid over the lips of Jo's newly shaved pussy.

'Is that some sort of soothing balm?' Jo asked nervously.

Stacey shook her head solemnly.

'It's an electrolyte,' Mr Smith explained calmly.

In this context, Jo thought, electrolyte was quite a frightening word. 'An electrolyte,' she repeated numbly. Whatever else the pair had planned for her, Jo doubted she was going to find it a pleasant experience.

'Yes,' Mr Smith explained patiently. 'An electrolyte. It helps to conduct the electricity more efficiently. I believe it's some sort of saline solution, although I'm not very technical with these things.' He graced her reflection with a wry smile. 'Mistress Stacey is the expert. That's why she operates the controls.'

Jo stiffened, aware that her heart was now pounding furiously inside her chest. She stared unhappily at Mistress Stacey, then at Mr Smith. Her hands strained against the manacles that held her but she knew there was no way out of the situation. She would have to endure whatever they had planned for her.

It was a chilling thought.

Mr Smith walked calmly behind her. He was carrying one of the bouquets of weeds in his thickly gloved hand. As he passed Jo, he brushed the nettles lightly over her back and buttocks.

The touch of the nettles was not as bad as she had anticipated. She stiffened herself against the million pinpricks scratching at her flesh but the pain was minimal. However, the stinging that flared inside her flesh afterwards was the real agony. The gentle brush of the nettles was almost a caress in comparison. The red-hot burning of their aftermath was the real cause of suffering.

Mr Smith walked around to Jo's front. His cruel smile was despicable yet, when he leant towards her and kissed her, she responded eagerly. He pushed his tongue into her mouth, exciting and thrilling her with his intimacy. Jo felt her arousal being rekindled and she writhed her legs together with urgency.

Instead of holding her or caressing her, Mr Smith drew the nettles over Jo's flat stomach. With slow deliberation he moved the greenery up towards her breasts.

Jo groaned. It seemed incredible that this sort of torture could feel so exciting. Her body was responding so eagerly she had difficulty believing it. Her inner muscles were throbbing with a hungry desire that demanded to be satisfied. At the same time, her tits were stinging furiously and her buttocks felt as though they were on fire. Neither the humiliation nor the physical pain seemed to dampen her arousal. Contrarily, it seemed both of these factors were stimulating her.

She watched as he rubbed the nettles roughly against her breasts. He tapped the leaves and stems almost playfully against her nipples. A cry of unbridled anguish welled inside her but she stopped herself from releasing it. Her breasts felt as though they were on fire. Her nipples burnt, as though they had suffered a thousand bee stings. In spite of this, or because of it, she felt dangerously close to orgasm. Her breathing deepened and she began to pant with obvious arousal.

Mr Smith stepped away from her and allowed Mistress Stacey to move in. She was holding a small black box in her hands. Thin wires trailed from the back of it and they swung lightly in the air as the mistress approached.

'Who is this missing person, Jo?' Mr Smith asked kindly. His tone was so friendly and genial she found it difficult to believe he had just been inflicting so much suffering on her. 'Who are you looking for? If you tell us now, it will be a lot easier for you.'

Stacey nodded her agreement. 'That's right,' she agreed. 'If you don't give us any names, then we have to consider that you might be investigating the agency.' She ran her finger over Jo's breasts as she spoke.

The nipples were painfully sore but they hardened at Stacey's touch. Jo shivered with delight as the woman squeezed one agonised bud between her fingers.

The discomfort was greater than anything she had ever tolerated. At the same time, the pleasure it inspired was magnificent.

'I can't say,' she whispered softly. 'I wish I could, but I can't tell you.'

Mr Smith patted her warmly on the shoulder. His smile was warm and reassuring. 'Don't worry, Jo,' he told her confidently. 'You will tell us.' He snapped his fingers in Stacey's direction.

At his command, the mistress began to work. She had been extracting the wires from her electrical box with careful deliberation. At Mr Smith's signal she moved closer to Jo and began to attach the leads to her body.

She had four wires in her hand and she attached them to Jo with scrupulous care. Each of her inner labia was clamped with a tweezer-like connector, and the third connector was placed on the hood of Jo's clitoris.

The feeling was excruciatingly uncomfortable but Jo tolerated it without a frown. She watched as Mistress Stacey took the fourth electrode and applied the electrolyte solution to it. It was a long, slender length of metal, and Jo was not surprised when she felt it being pushed up between her legs.

She noticed that Stacey's finger lingered a long time over the lips of her pussy. The woman seemed to extract a good deal of pleasure from teasing the lips of Jo's labia with her long fingers. The electrolyte gel was cool against her sensitive flesh but Jo realised it was also an ideal lubricant. Stacey rubbed her fingers over Jo's pussy until the stirrings of her arousal were a strong, urgent heat.

When Jo had begun to pant excitedly, Stacey stepped away from her. She carried the little black box in her hands. She graced Jo with a sad look then glanced at Mr Smith. When he nodded, Mistress Stacey pressed a button on the box's console.

Jo gasped. Her body was struck by an unprecedented

wave of shock. The lips of her labia thrilled to the sensation of a shrill, bristling charge, as a low-voltage current brushed against them. Deep inside the velvety depths of her hole, Jo felt her muscles clamping furiously in response to the tingling electrode. The strength of her orgasm was phenomenal.

She stared from Mr Smith to Mistress Stacey, her expression somewhere between dull fury and eternal gratitude.

'You're our second guest in this room tonight,' Mr Smith said conversationally. 'Helen, the girl who was in here before you, had to be taught a little discipline.' He smiled tightly, oblivious to the whirling emotions Jo was experiencing. 'She was fitted with those same electrodes you're wearing. And I used a similar bunch of nettles on her body too.'

'Are you trying to tell me that this is what you do with all the girls?' Jo asked dryly.

Mr Smith's smile faltered. His good mood evaporated instantly and Jo knew she had made a mistake. The thought was terrifying. A cold sweat erupted over her entire body and she shivered. When she thought of all the things Mr Smith had done to her whilst he was in a good mood, she did not dare think how he might respond in anger.

'I'm trying to tell you what Helen went through,' he explained tersely. 'She had to hold the nettles between the cheeks of her arse. If she dropped them, she got lashed with them. If she managed to hold on to them, she got a reward.'

Jo shivered at the thought of what Helen had been through. 'Why would she have dropped them?' Jo asked.

Mr Smith nodded at Stacey again. Before Jo could say a word in protest, her body exploded again with a furious, electrically charged orgasm. The tingling began in the pit of her stomach and reached out to every erogenous zone in her body. She felt herself shivering and trembling. Even when she saw Stacey was no longer pressing the button, Jo could still feel tremors causing spasms in her body. The pleasure of the orgasm was euphoric. It was an intense explosion of pleasure that filled her every pore. Her clitoris was sparkling with the most intense delight she had ever experienced. Not just one orgasm struck her but wave after wave rode through her. The thrill of so much pleasure left her breathless and frightened. She had always loved good sex and had been proud of her ability to enjoy it. Even so, she had never experienced anything of this magnitude.

'I'm sure I don't have to tell you,' Mr Smith said conversationally. 'That a press of the buzzer was the reward she received.'

Shivering, Jo fixed him with the sternest look she could manage. 'Why are you telling me all this?' she asked quietly.

He smiled. 'I'm trying to set up a comparison for you,' he replied thoughtfully. 'Helen was a problem we have to deal with here on a fairly regular basis. As you saw, she was properly subjugated when she left. You, on the other hand, are a far more serious problem. We intend to deal with you. I just want you to know that it might take quite a lot of effort on our part.'

Jo was terrified by the prospect of what he might be planning. His sadistic enjoyment of her plight was so obvious it was almost tangible.

A knock at the door of the black room disturbed the moment.

Mr Smith and Mistress Stacey exchanged a puzzled frown.

It was clear to Jo they were not used to being disturbed like this. She found herself wondering who had dared to risk interrupting the pair in such a way.

Mr Smith opened the door and left the room quickly.

Jo tried to see who was there but the figure outside was draped in shadows. Alone with Mistress Stacey, she smiled uncertainly at the other woman.

'I've told you everything I can about my case,' Jo explained. 'Do we really have to carry on with this?'

Stacey graced her with a questioning look. 'As Mr Smith said, I'm sure you'll be able to tell us more.'

Jo was about to add something, a desperate plea for solidarity or sisterhood, she had not decided which. Before she could speak, the door opened again.

'Change of plan,' Mr Smith said dourly. He glared at Stacey as he spoke. Jerking his thumb back at the door, he said, 'He wants her blindfold.'

Stacey responded quickly.

Jo turned from the mistress to Mr Smith, unable to keep the panic from her face. She wanted to ask who Mr Smith was referring to. She also wanted to know why she needed a blindfold. She was willing to tolerate just so much but a blindfold was stretching it. She did not bother asking the questions because she knew they would not be answered. A moment later she felt a large rubber mask being placed over her face. The black hood covered her eyes tightly and blocked out all light. There were holes beneath her nostrils and around her mouth but they were the only openings in the mask. Now she was aware of nothing but a rich, all enveloping blackness.

'Secure?' Jo heard Mr Smith ask.

'Secure.' Mistress Stacey repeated the word flatly.

Jo heard the door open. She strained her ears to hear what was happening. A cool draught blew from the door across her back and she suppressed a shiver of nervous anticipation.

'I trust I will see you later, Jo Valentine,' Mr Smith told her.

'Who said that?' Jo asked, for no other reason than to hear her own voice. She knew things would be easier if she acted with servility but the rebellious streak inside her did not seem to care.

She heard Mr Smith's impatient growl and realised he was addressing someone else when he next spoke. 'She's been full of smart-arse crap like that since she was brought in here,' he exploded. 'I do hope you won't be lenient with her.'

Jo felt a chill as she heard his words. With her vision cut off, she could not see who he was talking to but she knew it was the room's new occupant. The newcomer made no reply to Mr Smith. The next sound she heard was the door slamming.

'Would you like me to leave?' It was Stacey's voice. Jo realised the question was not directed at her. She listened for a response but only heard Stacey's reply.

'Very well, sir.'

It was a man, Jo thought. She would have guessed this much anyway when a pair of masculine hands began stroking her body. The fingers moved over her sore arse, cupped her bare breasts and then moved down to explore the heated cleft between her legs.

'If you want *me* to leave, I will do,' Jo said quickly. It was a slim chance, she thought. The line would be more likely to antagonise the newcomer than make him set her free but she couldn't stop the words from coming out.

She felt a second pair of hands, Stacey's she thought, removing the clamps from her labia. The tapered electrode that had been resting in her vagina was gently pulled out.

All the time, the man was touching her. His fingers played with her breasts and stroked her body with a care that was almost loving. Although she felt aroused by his touch, Jo was simultaneously chilled. This man had acted like Mr Smith's superior and to Jo's mind that meant he had to be far more dangerous.

It did not take long before her worst fears were

confirmed. A hand, broad, masculine and hard, struck the left cheek of her arse. Jo flinched, surprised by the blow. She suppressed a cry of surprise, determined that this unknown newcomer should not know how easy it was to hurt her.

He followed up his first blow with a second one. The hand smacked so hard against her nettled cheeks that Jo sucked in her breath noisily. She briefly congratulated herself on the fact that she had not exclaimed, but it was small consolation. If it had not been for the arousal she felt, Jo would have been frightened.

'That one.'

His voice was disturbingly familiar. She tried to place it. There had to be a reason why she thought she knew this man. It niggled at the back of her mind like the title of a forgotten song. She would have dwelt on the thought longer but Mistress Stacey's words brought her attention back to the black room with a resounding jolt.

'The sauna whip?' It was a question.

Jo guessed that because the woman had not been contradicted she had selected the right implement. Her fears were proved correct a moment later.

The stinging pain that bit at her aching nipples could only have been caused by a flexible sauna whip. Jo had seen one of the trainees being punished with one earlier that day. She could mentally picture the short leather strands at the tip of the cruel whip.

First he flogged her left breast, then the right. He repeated the action again and again until she lost count of the number of times he struck her. Relentlessly, he administered blow after blow. Each crack of the whip landed with cruel accuracy, inflaming her nipples with a wealth of pain so debilitating it was exquisite.

Unable to stand the pain any longer, Jo let out a soft groan of pleasure. She did not want to beg her captor for anything but it seemed she had no choice. The words spilt from her mouth without her realising she had spoken them.

233

'Please. No more,' she begged softly. 'No more.'

Her nipples stung with a biting raw pain that was blissful. If she accepted any more of this pain, Jo believed she would explode. It was like music to her ears when she heard the heavy thud of something falling to the floor. He's thrown down the whip, Jo thought, relief sweeping over her. He's thrown it on the floor. She would have extracted more pleasure from the thought if her mind had not rushed ahead: what's he going to do now? she asked herself.

Stacey's hands returned to Jo's body. She could feel the woman's fingers stroking her legs, caressing their entire length as she moved slowly upward. The man's hand reached down and brushed against the heated swell of Jo's pussy lips. His fingers stroked the length of her labia, then gently rubbed at the nub of her swollen clitoris.

Hating herself for enjoying it, Jo moaned excitedly.

Her cries increased when she felt his fingers gently toying around the rim of her anus. He pressed carefully against the yielding muscles and Jo gasped as she felt a finger slide into her arse.

The pressure of warm breath fell against her shaved pussy. Jo was not surprised when she felt Mistress Stacey's mouth against the lips of her vagina. The woman lapped at Jo's sex, guiding her tongue skilfully over the bald inner lips.

Jo moaned happily. She tried shifting her position so Stacey could guide her tongue fully inside. Her manacled hands made the movement awkward but her need for Stacey's mouth forced her to try.

Then she felt the man's cock. Naked and hard, it pressed against her back for a moment. He continued to slide his finger in and out of her arsehole. Jo felt a moment's panic as she wondered what the man was preparing her for. He slid his finger slowly from her forbidden depths and then she felt his hands on her hips.

There was something familiar about the pressure of his fingers. It was a disturbing thought but Jo did not have time to consider the matter. She heard herself gasping happily as the cock pressed against her and she vainly tried to wriggle herself closer to him.

The tip of his cock pressed gently against the rim of her anus and Jo moaned, a low guttural sound. She expected him to push down on her and enter her there. She braced herself willingly for the penetration.

Then his cock moved away. It slid over her arse a final time before moving further between her legs. Slowly it entered the cleft of her sex. He pushed himself easily into her warm velvety depths and Jo shuddered with pleasure. Mistress Stacey continued licking at the pearl of Jo's clitoris. Her able tongue occasionally flicked against the rigid cock that filled Jo's hole.

As Jo was bracing herself for the impact of orgasm, she felt the man's hands reaching down. Careful of her nettle-sore buttocks, he, once again, slid his finger inside her anus.

Jo screamed with delight.

She lost track of how long she was there. The dull ache in her arms was forgotten. The torture she had suffered was quickly becoming a distant memory. The man's able dick rode in and out of her with long, measured strokes. Jo was breathless with pleasure. Deep in her anus, his finger seemed to know exactly where to touch. He knew exactly how much pressure to apply.

In front of her, Mistress Stacey continued her gentle lapping, occasionally reaching a finger upwards to tease one or the other of Jo's nipples. Unable to see any of this, Jo revelled in the tactile delight of the moment.

She was puzzled by a niggling memory. There was something disturbingly familiar about the man behind her. It was so indistinct a feeling she easily ignored it. There were other, more relevant, things for her to concentrate on.

When her orgasm finally came she shrieked happily. The inner muscles of her pulsing sex clamped tighter and tighter on the cock inside. Jo could feel that the man screwing her was close to climax himself. She was not surprised when she felt his cock shudder deep inside her. It felt as though the tip was pressing against the neck of her womb. The sensation inspired another climax.

As he slid his cock from her warmth, Jo realised the man was kissing her gently on the neck and shoulders. Again, she remembered her earlier feeling of familiarity. This intimacy, and those other thoughts, now seemed of vital importance.

'Should I release the manacles?'

It was Mistress Stacey's voice and Jo did not bother to answer the question. Her mind was still racing with this unexpected turn of events. She valiantly backtracked through her memory, trying to recall what had felt familiar about the man and why.

When he spoke, she stopped trying to remember. His voice was enough for her to know who he was.

'Yes. Take off the manacles and the hood,' he said quietly. He kissed Jo once again on the shoulder. His hand carefully cupped her breast.

She pulled away from him, suddenly furious. When her hands were freed from the manacles she felt a wave of relief but it did not calm her anger. If anything, she blamed him for the pain she had received. And not just the physical pain he had administered with his hands and the sauna whip.

Jo held him responsible for everything that had happened this evening and she knew she had every right. He was the one who had blown her cover. He was the one who had told Mr Smith and Mistress Stacey to take her to the black room.

When the hood was pulled from her head she blinked awkwardly against the room's dim lighting. Eventually her gaze settled on Nick's face.

236

'You lousy bastard,' she spat.

He considered her words for a moment and then smiled at her fury. 'Yes,' he agreed amiably. 'I suppose I am.'

Eleven

Jo sat sullenly in Mr Smith's office trying to get her arse comfortable on the chair. She would still have been naked if Stephanie had not chivalrously volunteered her trench coat. Wrapped inside the warm folds of her friend's clothing, Jo wished she could stop herself from feeling cold.

'Why are you here?' Jo asked quietly.

'Nick said he was coming down here to sort things out,' Stephanie replied quietly. 'I insisted he bring me along.' She paused and studied Jo's face. Concern was etched into every feature. 'Are you OK?'

Jo considered the question for a moment. 'I'm fine,' she said, staring at Mr Smith. 'Never better.' There was a cold, hurt tone to her voice that seemed to ridicule her words.

Stephanie noted the look she had given the man, then fell into silence. There were times when it was best not trying to talk to Jo. She realised that this was one of them.

Jo stared angrily at the four people behind the desk. Dr McMahon seemed absorbed with her fingernails whilst Mr Smith and Mistress Stacey were locked in a furious, whispered debate. Nick, sitting between Mr Smith and Dr McMahon, stared fixedly at Jo.

She returned his gaze defiantly.

'Where the hell is Vanessa anyway?' Mr Smith demanded angrily. He was studying his watch as he spoke. After asking the question he glared angrily at anyone whom he thought might have the answer.

'More to the point,' Nick replied stiffly, 'what the hell is she doing with a trainee off the premises?'

'I don't think answering that would take a lot of imagination,' Stacey said quietly.

Nick glared at her.

He turned the expression on Jo. 'You've put us in a very awkward position,' he said quietly.

'How ironic,' Jo replied tautly. 'You just had me in a very awkward position.'

Nick had the good grace to blush.

Stacey and Dr McMahon both turned their faces away to conceal broad grins.

'Where the hell is Vanessa, anyway?' Nick demanded impatiently.

'She called to say she was on her way,' Stacey told him. 'She's bringing the trainee with her.'

Nick rolled his eyes and shook his head in desperation. 'How incredibly security conscious,' he said sarcastically. He glared at the top of Mr Smith's desk with an expression of dark contempt. 'This isn't good enough,' he said to no one in particular.

Before his mood could darken any further, the office door pushed open and Vanessa Byrne entered the room. Kelly Rogers followed her at a respectful pace. She closed the door softly behind them.

'Dear God!' Vanessa exclaimed theatrically. 'My worst nightmare has come true. It's a 3.00 a.m. board meeting and we're all fully dressed.'

'Well spotted,' Nick said, speaking between clenched teeth. 'But it was convened as a 2.00 a.m. board meeting. We've been waiting for you.'

Vanessa shrugged off Nick's anger with a grin. She glanced at Stacey and asked, 'Who pissed on his Cornflakes?'

Without replying, Stacey pointed at Jo.

Vanessa blushed slightly when her gaze fell on the private investigator. 'Jo?' she said incredulously. 'Jo Valentine? What the hell are you doing here?'

Jo glared miserably at the woman. 'It's a long story but stick around, Vanessa, and I'm sure you'll hear it. Then you can tell me your story. It might help to explain why you've come to this board meeting. I'm only curious because this is an organisation that you know nothing about. Isn't that what you told me when I asked about the Pentagon Agency?'

'What the hell is she doing here?' Vanessa demanded. This time she threw the question at Nick.

He rubbed splayed fingers through his hair and shook his head. 'Sit down Vanessa,' he said quietly. 'Now we're all here, we can begin.'

Mr Smith put a restraining hand on Nick's shoulder. 'I can understand Valentine being present for this,' he whispered. 'But what about the other two?'

'Stephanie stays with me,' Jo said softly. There was no obvious threat in her voice but her instructions were heeded.

Gratefully, Stephanie slid her arm through Jo's.

Under other circumstances Jo would have revelled in the nearness of her colleague but tonight things were different. This evening she felt cold, miserable and deeply unhappy. She only wanted to get this stupid meeting out of they way so she could go home. There she could try to forget she had ever heard of the Pentagon Agency and its damnable black room.

Mr Smith pointed at Kelly. 'What about her?'

Jo glanced at the redhead, recognising her features instantly.

'She can go,' Nick said quietly.

'She better stay,' Jo told him. She turned to the redhead. 'Your name is Kelly Rogers, isn't it?' she asked.

Kelly nodded. Her face remained blank and she showed no emotion at being recognised.

240

'This concerns you as much as it does the rest of us.'

Mr Smith sat heavily back in his chair. 'Why not call in the rest of the trainees?' he asked pompously. 'I suppose we could go out on the streets and drag in a couple of passers-by to make up the numbers. The more the merrier.'

Prick, Jo thought contemptuously. She did not give voice to the thought. Standing awkwardly, she wrapped the trench coat tight around her naked body and tried to address the entire room at once.

Seven faces stared back at her expectantly.

'I think Kelly should stay in the room because this case is all about her. She's the reason why I'm here. It was her husband who asked me to locate her.' She glared angrily at Mr Smith. 'Now, perhaps you'll realise that I'm telling the truth. I didn't come here to expose you and your sadostic friends. I have no interest in upsetting your perverted little apple cart.'

For a moment Mr Smith seemed lost for words. It did not take long for him to find his voice. 'We have a reputation to maintain here,' he began quickly. 'A scandal could cost us everything that we've worked for.'

Jo pulled a face. It was a childish, juvenile expression but she could not stop herself. 'Tell it to someone who cares,' she snapped churlishly. She turned her back on Mr Smith and walked over to Vanessa.

'Thank you for all the help you gave me with this case,' she began icily.

Vanessa frowned. 'Like he just said,' she replied, 'we have a reputation to maintain. What was I supposed to think when you called me? You're a private investigator, Jo. I was bound to think the worst.'

'A couple of honest answers at the beginning, and you could have saved me an awful lot of trouble,' Jo said stiffly. 'I believe you owe me.'

Vanessa nodded. 'You're right, Jo,' she agreed. Her lips creased into an apologetic smile. 'I'm sorry.'

241

'Not as sorry as I am,' Jo said. She looked at Kelly. 'Do you want to go back to your husband?'

'I no longer have a husband,' Kelly said boldly.

Jo nodded as though she had expected this much. 'I'll take that as a definite no,' she said calmly. She gestured for Stephanie to join her side. Her legs were still aching and she needed the support of her friend just to stay on her feet.

'You can send my things on to me,' she told the room. 'I won't be returning.'

'Hold on a second,' Nick said firmly.

Jo paused, her hand on the office's door handle.

'There's a couple of points to be addressed here,' he said quietly. 'You've shown us that our security and our cover here are piss poor,' he remarked. 'You've also shown us that you have tremendous integrity. Because of that, I'd like to make a proposition.'

Jo shook her head. 'Don't bother, Nick,' she told him quietly.

'You haven't heard my proposition yet,' he pointed out.

'And I haven't told you to stick it up your arse yet,' Jo said impatiently. 'But I will.' She opened the door and walked out of the room with Stephanie at her side, closing the door softly behind them.

Nick stared around the room. 'Well,' he said with an unhappy frown. 'I suppose that's it then.'

Vanessa shook her head. She turned to Kelly and said quickly, 'Stay here. I'll be back in a minute.'

As she rushed out of the door they all heard her calling after Jo.

Jo collapsed on the bed, exhausted.

'You look like you've been through the wars,' Stephanie said sympathetically.

Jo grinned tiredly at her. 'One day, you'll have to get me drunk and I'll tell you all about it.' She turned over on the bed and nestled her head into the pillow.

When she next opened her eyes, the lighting in the room had changed. Jo guessed Stephanie had turned off the main light and replaced it with the bedside lamp. She wondered what had woken her, then realised Stephanie was trying to ease the trench coat from her body. Amazed she had fallen asleep so effortlessly, Jo shrugged her arms out of the garment and passed it to the blonde.

'Jesus!' Stephanie exclaimed. 'Look at the marks on your body!'

Jo glanced down at her bare breasts. She was not surprised to see the rash of nettle stings that spotted her flesh. The burning spots were interspersed with darkening bruises where the sauna whip had bitten her. She turned over and glanced down curiously at her backside. She was still marked with the red lines where Mr Smith had caned her. The crimson stripes merged together in places. In other areas they were lost beneath a million prickly nettle stings.

Jo sucked in her breath unhappily.

'What the hell did they do to you?' Stephanie asked. She was staring at Jo's body with a look of horror on her face.

'Don't ask,' Jo replied.

Stephanie frowned. 'Have you got any calamine lotion?'

Jo shrugged. 'I don't know. Is it alcohol based?'

Stephanie could not stop herself from snorting laughter. 'No,' she replied, grinning.

'Then I doubt I ever bought the stuff,' Jo told her. 'Try the bathroom cabinet,' she suggested. 'If I have any, that's where it'll be.' She lay back on the bed and placed her head on the pillow. When her eyes closed, she was asleep.

This time the rest seemed to last longer before it was disturbed. Jo did not know how long she had been sleeping. When she opened her eyes and saw what was

243

happening, she was not even sure she had really woken. This looked like a scene from her favourite dream.

Stephanie was rubbing creamy layers of calamine lotion into Jo's body. The bottle sat in a cup of warm water by the side of the bed. Once she had kneaded the lukewarm liquid into one part of Jo's body, Stephanie poured some more into her hand and began to work on another part.

Jo felt the blonde's hands encircle her thighs. She rubbed the emulsion softly into her legs. The warm liquid was a soothing balm and Stephanie's dextrous manipulation hinted at an innate talent for massage. As her fingers moved up Jo's body, Stephanie seemed to hesitate near her bare vagina. Jo could not recall the nettles being brushed there. She still felt sore from where the electrodes had been attached but she did not feel unduly uncomfortable.

She breathed a heavy sigh of relief when Stephanie's fingers moved away from her sex. Jo could feel the pulse beating in her loins and she wondered if it was safe to let Stephanie carry on. The young woman was oblivious to Jo's feelings. She did not know about the strong passion she was inflaming. Her hands moved over the flat of Jo's stomach and she stroked the calamine lotion slowly over her nettle-stung body.

Jo reached out a hand to try to stop her. She was weary and her arms still ached from the time she had spent in the black room. Her fingers fell clumsily against Stephanie's arm, then rubbed accidentally against the woman's breast.

Stephanie smiled knowingly down at her. 'Lie still. You'll feel better after this.' She poured a handful of calamine lotion into one hand and then massaged it into Jo's breasts.

The cream was not so thick as to be unpleasant. In fact, it was just the right consistency to stimulate her. Jo was not surprised to feel her nipples harden beneath Stephanie's touch. It was both soothing and exciting to have the lotion rubbed into her sore and aching breasts. She blushed slightly as Stephanie drew her fingers accidentally over the taut nubs of her arousal.

It seemed unfair to let Stephanie see her like this. Jo felt it was only right to warn her what she was doing. She had yearned for Stephanie for months now. There had been times when she would have sold her soul to have the woman massaging her like this. However, a sense of decency told Jo that this was not right. She was lying here, getting sexual pleasure from her colleague simply because the woman was trying to treat her injuries. She knew that things would have been different if she had confessed her feelings before. Jo believed that Stephanie would not have dared come near her now if she had previously told her how she felt. As a mark of respect, Jo decided that, regardless of the consequences, now was the right time to tell Stephanie how she felt.

After that, the blonde could make up her own mind as to whether she stayed or left.

Before she could think of the right words to use, Stephanie kissed her. Her sweet young mouth was placed over Jo's. Within a moment, their tongues were intertwined. Her hand continued to massage calamine lotion into Jo's body, concentrating on her breasts and upper body. Then she moved on to the bed and straddled Jo. The hem of her short skirt lifted slightly and Jo was treated to a tantalising glimpse of the skimpy panties she wore.

'I'm sorry,' Stephanie breathed softly. 'I shouldn't have kissed you like that, but I couldn't help myself.' She was blushing deeply. 'I guess I was taking advantage of your vulnerability.'

Jo wondered if she was dreaming. This was something Stephanie would have been likely to say in a dream. The idea of it actually happening in real life was a notion Jo had not dared to entertain. 'If you hadn't done it to me,' she said quietly, 'I would have done it to you.'

She tried to change positions on the bed. She wanted to sit up so she could look into Stephanie's face as she spoke.

Stephanie pushed her back down. 'You need calamine first,' she said primly.

That's not what I need, Jo thought as she stared happily into Stephanie's eyes. She reached out for the buttons on the blonde's blouse and slowly began to tease them open. After three, she could see a glimpse of the lacy black bra Stephanie was wearing. It was an enticing sight and she could have marvelled at it for hours.

Stephanie moved Jo's fingers away. 'Later,' she promised firmly. 'Turn over and let me get the rest of this lotion on to you.'

Obligingly, Jo rolled over and buried her face in the pillow. She felt Stephanie shift position. Then her hands were kneading at the sensitive flesh of Jo's arse. Using her palms as roughly as she dared, Stephanie rubbed the lotion firmly into Jo's skin. Her splayed fingers pressed hard against the naked flesh, tracing lines and circles that followed the perfect contours of Jo's body. She rubbed the calamine firmly into the scratched cheeks, only pausing when Jo flinched uncomfortably.

'Don't worry,' Stephanie whispered quietly. 'I'll kiss it all better when I'm done.'

Jo felt herself aching with desire. The whole experience was so relaxing she could feel the memory of the black room paling into insignificance.

Stephanie's fingers stroked tenderly between the cleft of Jo's buttocks, sending a thrill of excitement through the private investigator's body. Delving deeper, they touched the bare flesh of her newly shaved pussy.

Jo shivered beneath her.

'Did they shave you like this?' Stephanie asked quietly.

Jo nodded into the pillow. She raised her head and turned over. 'Yes. I know how stupid it looks.'

'I don't think it looks stupid.' There was a smile in her voice as she said, 'I think it looks good enough to eat.' Without another word she pressed her mouth against the heat of Jo's sex. She delivered a series of soft, gentle kisses to the aching lips of Jo's hole. Her tongue gently teased the lips, cooling them with moisture, before she kissed them dry. Her retroussé nose tickled against the hood of Jo's clitoris. When she realised she was doing this, Stephanie nuzzled the organ playfully.

Jo gasped for breath, bewildered by the enjoyment she was receiving. Her breath was coming in ragged bursts. She longed to touch Stephanie and please her in return. However, she was too weary to even lift the girl from her body. It was all that she could do to just lie there and endure Stephanie's kisses.

'What are these marks on your pussy lips?' Stephanie asked curiously. 'Did they use the nettles on you down here?'

Jo shook her head. 'That's probably where the electrodes were clamped,' she explained. It seemed unreal to say something so shocking in such a banal voice.

Stephanie almost shrieked with horror. 'What the hell were they doing to you?' she demanded.

Jo grinned. She used every aching muscle in her body and managed to sit up. Draping a weary arm around the girl's shoulders, Jo smiled into her face. Her affection and admiration were blatantly apparent. 'I can't remember what they were doing to me,' she said. She placed a soft kiss on the corner of Stephanie's mouth. 'You were just in the process of making me forget.'

Stephanie returned her smile. 'I'll carry on then, shall I?'

Jo lay back down on the bed and allowed her to.

Two hours later, when they finally curled up to sleep together, the black room was just a memory.

* * *

'Come in,' Vanessa said cheerfully. 'The pair of you, please, come in.' She was in the process of closing the Venetian blinds in her office as she spoke.

Jo held the door open and allowed Stephanie to walk ahead. She closed the door behind herself and sat down in front of Vanessa's desk. 'You said last night you could help us,' Jo said. 'Was that for real, or just more bullshit?'

Vanessa bit her lip, trying to disguise how unhappy she was with Jo's rudeness. 'It was for real,' she said. 'You should have stayed to hear Nick's proposition. You might have been interested.'

'Did it involve Nick castrating himself?' Jo asked dryly.

Stephanie put a steadying hand on her arm and Jo nodded silent agreement.

They were here on business, she reminded herself. There was no place in the business world for pettiness. She had to rise above her natural instincts.

'Sally. Ask Russel to come in here will you?' Vanessa barked into her desktop intercom.

The three women sat together in an uneasy silence.

'May I ask why you're holding Nick responsible for all that happened?' Vanessa asked stiffly.

'I'm not,' Jo replied evenly. 'I hold you partly to blame as well.' She spoke over Vanessa's outraged rebuttals and protests, determined to make her point. 'Nick takes a greater portion of the blame though. He could have told me where Kelly Rogers was and I could have dealt with the case without having my arse nettled and my fanny lips singed by your home-made cattle-prod.'

Stephanie tightened her hand on Jo's arm.

'Mr Smith was just looking after our interests at the Pentagon Agency,' Vanessa said carefully.

'I hold him partly responsible too,' Jo said conversationally. 'And his friend Stacey.'

Vanessa grunted dry laughter. 'At least Dr McMahon has something to be grateful for,' she commented.

Jo frowned at Vanessa. She was unhappy that the woman saw fit to find humour in her predicament. She did not bother making the cutting remark that occurred to her because a knock at the office door interrupted them.

'Come in, Russel,' Vanessa called sharply.

Jo studied the man who entered the office. He had the look of a well-built office-boy. There was an expression of corruptible innocence etched on his features. Under one arm he carried a large black-bound ledger.

'Thank you for looking after it,' Vanessa said, holding her hand out for the book.

Hurriedly, as though he expected to incur her anger if he did not pass it to her immediately, Russel pushed the book into Vanessa's hands.

She smiled, pleased with the trainee's behaviour. 'This is where I keep pictures of all my slaves,' Vanessa explained. 'I have a couple of nice photographs of Russel in here. Here,' she said, pointing to a page where the volume had fallen open.

Jo and Stephanie leant forward to study the instamatic pictures. They exchanged a broad grin and settled back in their chairs.

Stephanie glanced up at Russel and saw that his cheeks were burning a shameful crimson. She also noted that his pants now hung awkwardly because of the huge erection he was sporting. She was closer to him than Jo. Before she realised she was doing it, Stephanie reached her hand out. She stroked the swell of his manhood through the fabric of his pants.

'I see the camera doesn't lie,' she observed. She traced her fingers along the full length of his cock.

Jo watched Stephanie, amazed by her behaviour. She glanced at the trainee's face and saw he was struggling to contain his joy.

Vanessa grinned. 'He was trained by the Pentagon Agency,' she said proudly. 'I'm thinking of taking this one permanently into my employ but they have plenty like him if you need an amenable body in the office.'

Stephanie continued to stroke her hand up and down Russel's length. 'He seems like he could handle most things,' she agreed.

Jo watched her friend caressing the office-boy's cock through his pants. It was behaviour she never would have expected from Stephanie. Last night her appetite for sex had seemed insatiable but Jo would still never have expected it. Intrigued, she felt torn, wondering which of the pair to watch.

Stephanie turned to Jo and smiled. 'Do you know what I want to do?' she asked eagerly.

'I can guess,' Jo replied.

Stephanie stifled a giggle and turned back to Russel. Slowly she unzipped his fly. Her hand disappeared inside his pants, only to come out a moment later holding Russel's huge length. She stroked the foreskin slowly backward and forward, her light touch stimulating the sensitive flesh of his cock.

'I don't think we have time for that,' Jo reminded her.

Stephanie stared wistfully at the cock in her hand. She glanced at Vanessa. 'Will you take care of him after we've left?' she asked.

Vanessa smiled. 'Don't worry,' she said. 'I'll take real good care of him.'

Russel beamed fondly at his mistress when she said the words.

Jo noted his expression and smiled to herself sourly. 'Do you have the items you mentioned last night?' she asked.

Vanessa nodded. She produced a plain, white envelope from her desk drawer and placed it on her desk. After leafing through the ledger for a moment, she fell on the page she had been looking for. She removed three of the photographs stored there and then stuffed them in the envelope. She sealed it, then passed it to Jo.

'I don't need to tell you to use them carefully,' she said. 'All of us at the agency are agreed. You have quite a lot about you.'

Jo grunted the complement away. 'You can get Mr Smith to organise my fan club,' she said. Wafting the envelope at Vanessa, Jo rose from her chair. Her legs still ached and she held herself stiffly. She was determined not to falter or sway but it was not easy. 'I'll return these, if circumstances allow.' She gestured for Stephanie to join her side. Not wanting to say the words, but feeling obliged to, Jo glanced at the blonde behind the desk. 'Thank you, Vanessa,' she said quietly.

'Nick will be calling in to see you today,' Vanessa said suddenly.

Jo glared at her coldly.

Vanessa continued. 'Hear him out, Jo. You might find that his offer could benefit all of us.'

Jo felt Stephanie's hand on her arm again. The reassuring squeeze was enough to stop her from saying something truly out of place. She nodded and left the room.

'Get out of my bloody way,' Mr Rogers bellowed as he burst through the door. His face was a furious shade of purple and he looked as though he was ready to explode.

Obligingly, Stephanie stepped out of his way. She was just returning to the office with the coffees Jo had requested and she had missed the inevitable confrontation.

She turned an expectant frown on Jo.

The investigator was smiling broadly. In each hand she held a tightly packed envelope. She wafted them against her cheeks.

'How did it go?' Stephanie asked.

Jo shrugged. 'We got paid. That's always a bonus isn't it?'

'He didn't look very happy,' Stephanie observed.

Jo nodded. 'It wasn't really a triumph for customer relations,' she agreed. 'The letter from Kelly saying she never wanted to see him again didn't really satisfy him. If I hadn't had Vanessa's photographs he might have refused to settle his account.' She casually tossed both of the envelopes to Stephanie. 'If you want, you can bank these two for us.'

Stephanie raised a surprised eyebrow. 'Bank them?' she enquired. 'Don't you usually like to take envelopes like this to that Italian restaurant down the road?'

Jo's smile saddened. 'Perhaps we can do that another time. I need to do a little thinking.'

Stephanie walked over to Jo and kissed her softly on the cheek. She put a comforting arm around Jo's waist and squeezed her reassuringly. 'It's bound to take time to get over it, you know.'

Jo nodded. A week ago she would have volunteered to spend a day in hell in return for Stephanie touching her like this. Now, after spending a day in hell, it seemed more difficult to enjoy the pleasure. She reached out to hold Stephanie in return but the blonde pulled away.

'Nick's standing outside,' Stephanie said quietly.

Jo frowned. 'That should lower the property value,' she said dryly.

'He's determined to see you.'

'He's seen enough of me already,' Jo said sharply. She noted the unhappy frown that crossed Stephanie's face and felt a moment's regret at the sharp retort. 'OK,' Jo said, falling heavily into her chair. 'I'll see him. When he's finished, you can take the money to the bank and we'll do the restaurant tonight.'

She smiled confidently into the blonde's uncertain face. 'I'm dealing with it,' she explained in response to the unasked question she saw there. 'It wasn't easy in the black room,' she said quietly. 'I discovered things about myself that I'm still uncomfortable with. My self-confidence has been knocked off balance. A couple of days and I'll be fine. I just need a little time to get things straight in my own mind.'

Stephanie nodded. 'Are you sure you want me to stay in on this conversation with Nick?'

Jo grinned. 'I won't ask you to hold him down whilst I try and kill him, if that's what you mean,' she said. She planted a kiss on Stephanie's mouth. Sitting uncomfortably on the cushioned seat of her chair, she began to toy with her double-headed sovereign.

Stephanie walked over to the door and told Nick he could come in. She walked back to the desk and sat down next to Jo.

Nick stood awkwardly in the middle of the room. 'Hi, Jo,' he said quietly.

Jo watched him walk across the room towards her. They had lived together for two years and even after their break-up she had thought she knew him. Now she realised she had never known him. That notion made her unhappy. She tossed the sovereign idly into the air then caught it.

'Hello, liar,' she said cheerfully. Stephanie squeezed her arm and Jo smiled at her.

Nick frowned. He sat in the chair facing her. 'Why am I a liar?'

She shrugged. 'Just a couple of things. The two years we spent together when you didn't care to mention your penchant for domination. Your involvement with this Pentagon Agency –'

'I wasn't involved with them when we lived together,' he broke in.

Jo ignored him. 'That night a week ago when I asked you for help on this case and you fed me all that bullshit –'

'I didn't lie to you,' he pointed out. 'I just didn't tell

253

you about my involvement with them. It's true, there is a cover-up in the office about the Pentagon Agency. I just didn't say I was responsible for the cover-up.'

Jo shook her head. 'I can't be bothered having an argument about this. OK, you didn't lie to me. You just didn't tell me the truth. Make your proposition, Nick, and then fuck off. You're no longer a priority on my schedule.'

They were bold words and she stared defiantly at him as she said them. She expected Stephanie to squeeze her arm with her now familiar caution. Instead, from the corner of her eye, she saw that the blonde was nodding agreement.

Nick swallowed nervously. His gaze never left Jo's face. 'I admit I blew your cover as soon as Stephanie told me what you were doing. I could have organised that a lot better. If I'd given it a bit more thought I could have got to you before Mr Smith and Stacey.'

'Well,' Jo said angrily, 'that really makes my arse feel better.'

'I did go a little rough on you,' he said slowly.

'A little rough!' Jo was outraged. 'I'm lucky I've still got my nipples where God put them in the first place. You nearly whipped my tits off, Nick.'

Nick flushed. His eyes remained fixed on hers. 'There's something else I'll admit,' he said quietly. 'When I went into the black room and saw you there, I knew I wanted you. I couldn't stop myself. I just had to have you.'

Jo stared at him blankly. 'I wasn't complaining about that,' she said flatly. 'Say what you've come to say.'

He smiled broadly. 'We agreed it last night,' he told her confidently. 'We want to put you on a retainer. Mr Smith, Vanessa and Stacey all have outside business interests that could benefit from your talents. We also have a number of clients who could use the services of a good private investigator with a reputation for integrity.' He shook his head, an unwilling smile of admiration resting on his lips. 'The way you stuck to your beliefs in the black room left us in no doubt about your integrity. We could really benefit one another.'

Stephanie and Jo exchanged a glance.

'How much?' Jo asked.

'That's to be negotiated,' he began carefully. 'My own thoughts were that five thousand a month sounded appropriate. I also thought you could keep your own business going too, if that was what you wanted.'

Jo considered him carefully. She cast a glance at Stephanie and tried to read her thoughts. There was an expectant smile on the blonde's face and Jo guessed her partner was as eager for the stable income as she was. The idea of continuing her own business and being kept on such a lucrative retainer was an attractive one.

She realised that the reason for her loss of confidence was down to one thing. For a moment in the black room, she had lost control. The fact that it was a pleasant experience did nothing to salve her conscience. She had not been in control of the situation and that had never happened to her before. She was determined that it would never happen again. Nick's offer was giving her the chance to be back in control again.

The idea was tempting.

Jo came to a sudden decision. 'Take your clothes off,' she said flatly.

Nick stared at her, an uncertain smile faltering on his lips. 'Excuse me?' he said softly.

Stephanie turned to Jo. There was a broad grin of disbelief on her face. Jo graced her with an arch expression. Stephanie's grin broadened. Jo was beginning to seem like her former self.

Jo glared at Nick. 'Undress. Get naked. Take your clothes off,' Jo snapped. 'I'll consider your proposition when you show me your sincerity.'

Nick studied her doubtfully. 'You want me to undress?'

'See,' Jo told Stephanie, 'there are some bright ones in the police force.'

As the pair of them watched, Nick stood up and began to undress. He removed his clothes and began to fold them neatly on the chair.

Jo stopped him. 'Drop them on the floor,' she said cruelly. Considering Nick's patent dislike of untidiness, Jo found it amusing to tease him in this way.

He obeyed her instructions, dropping the clothes into a crumpled pile on the floor. He paused before removing his boxer shorts, a hesitant frown creasing his brow. 'You want me to take everything off?'

Jo grinned. She nodded slowly.

Stephanie put a hand over her mouth to hide her smile.

Nick stood before the pair, trying not to appear vulnerable. He had broad shoulders and a build that could easily be described as athletic. His cheeks were burning.

'He's got quite a nice body,' Stephanie observed.

'Not bad,' Jo said. Her voice was icy with detachment. She smiled into Nick's face. 'You're not hard.'

'I'm not aroused,' he said stiffly.

Stephanie moved from her seat and walked round the desk to him. She pushed herself against his naked body then drew her long manicured fingernails across his bare chest.

Nick shivered. His cock twitched slightly between his legs.

Jo slid from her chair and went to join them.

'Have you considered my proposal now?' Nick asked.

'Bend over,' she replied sharply. 'I'll consider it when you bend over.'

He stared at her defiantly. 'I'm not bending over. If you're not interested then I'll leave. But I'm not bending over.'

Jo moved her face close to his. Their mouths were so close they could have kissed. Instead, she treated him to an expression of the darkest contempt. 'Leave now and you'll never see me again. Stay, and I'll consider your proposition. It's your decision, Nick. I don't care a damn either way.'

He studied her face. His eyes flitted nervously as he tried to gauge her intentions. After a moment, he bent over.

'Nice arse,' Stephanie said encouragingly. She slapped it playfully with her open palm.

Nick tried forcefully not to move a muscle. He felt a familiar stirring between his legs and glared angrily at his hardening length.

Jo laughed softly. 'I think we've found something you like, Nick,' she observed cheerfully. She raised her hand and slapped his arse with all of her force.

Nick flinched beneath the blow. His cock continued to rise.

Stephanie reached down for his length and began to tug it softly. His cock quickly stiffened as she stroked her fingers along his shaft.

Jo slapped her hand against his backside again. She was not surprised to see his length quiver eagerly with each blow. Aware that her palm was beginning to sting, Jo glanced around the office for a suitable implement. She snatched up the slender, wooden name plaque from her desk and casually tested its weight. Before Nick had a chance to stop her, Jo had paddled his arse with it three times.

'I'm not comfortable with this,' he told her through gritted teeth.

Jo grunted dourly. 'You look like you're enjoying it,' she observed. She brought the plaque across the bare cheeks of his arse a fourth time.

'He feels like he's enjoying it,' Stephanie agreed. She gave Nick's cock a reassuring squeeze.

'Have you considered my proposition yet?' he asked.

Jo glanced at Stephanie and raised her eyebrows in silent question.

Stephanie nodded.

Jo slapped his arse one final time. 'Sit down,' she commanded, 'and then we can talk.' She moved back to her chair and studied him thoughtfully as he settled himself in the facing chair. 'Five thousand?'

He nodded, his lips breaking into a smile. Even though he was naked and had suffered Jo's humiliation, he still felt confident. It was a good offer and he doubted she could refuse.

Jo seemed to be considering it as she rolled the double-headed sovereign between her knuckles. She glanced at Stephanie. 'Does five thousand sound reasonable to you?'

Stephanie smiled. 'It would help to have a guaranteed income,' she said thoughtfully.

Jo grinned. She turned her attention back to Nick. 'Five thousand sounds more than generous,' she said. 'And Stephanie and I are prepared to accept it.' She paused and smiled carefully at him. 'Would you consider tossing for it?'

Nick frowned. 'How do you mean?'

Jo flicked the coin high in the air. 'Five thousand a month retainer,' she said quickly. 'Heads, you double the offer; tails, I work for nothing.' She reached out and snatched the coin from the air, slapping it against the back of her hand. 'Is it a deal?'

Nick grinned at her. 'It's a deal,' he said.

Jo kept her hand over the coin so that he could not see the result. He studied her face expectantly.

'There's one more thing,' Jo said, a broad smile teasing her lips.

'Go on,' Nick said. 'What else do you want?'

Jo's smile was whisper-soft. She glanced slyly at Stephanie, then turned her gaze to Nick. 'I'd like to use the Pentagon Agency's facilities if I'm to be kept on a retainer,' she told him.

Nick frowned. 'The facilities. I'm not sure I understand.'

Keeping her hand over the tossed coin, Jo fixed her gaze on his. 'If this is heads, Stephanie and I get to take you in the black room tonight. Is it a deal?'

Nick considered the gamble for a moment. It's a fifty-fifty chance, he thought. If I win, I'll have Jo working for me with nothing to pay. If I lose, I doubt she could be so terrible in the black room.

'OK,' he told her carefully. 'It's a deal.'

Jo smiled knowingly.